T0115033

God's Naked Children

Selected and New Stories

God's Naked Children
Selected and New Stories

by

Tanure Ojaide

malthouse MP

Malthouse Press Limited

Lagos, Benin, Ibadan, Jos, Port-Harcourt, Zaria

First Published 2018
978-978-58798-0-3

Published by
Malthouse Press Limited
43 Onitana Street, Off Stadium Hotel Road,
Surulere, Lagos, Lagos State
E-mail: malthouselagos@gmail.com
malthouselagos@yahoo.co.uk
Tel: +234 (0)802 600 3203

Distributors:

African Books Collective Ltd
Email: abc@africanbookscollective.com
Website: http://www.africanbookscollective.com

Acknowledgements

Thanks to Malthouse Press, Lagos, Africa World Press, Trenton, NJ, and African Heritage Press, La Rochelle, NY that first published the collections from which the selected poems first appeared.

"Can't Wait!" has appeared in *Per Contra: The International Journal of the Arts*, Literature, and Ideas (Winter 2014, Issue 34).

Preface

Malthouse Press, Lagos, published my first short story collection, *God's Medicine-Men and Other Stories*, in 2004. This was followed by two other collections published in the United States: *The Debt-Collector & Other Stories* (Africa World Press, 2009) and *The Old Man in a State House & Other Stories* (African Heritage Press, 2012). I have selected three stories from each of these three earlier collections to add to this new collection. This book thus provides a platform to project some of my old stories and new ones through a single publication.

I discovered early in my writing career as a writer that there are things, feelings, and ideas that can better be expressed in prose or fiction than in poetry. It is true that, as a minstrel, I tell stories in my poetry but those stories or experiences are of a different nature from the stories in this book. The fictional narratives here have characters acting out their experiences through time and place. These stories could be realistic but are fictional. I will not deny though that many of these stories are not inspired by actual happenings. In these short stories, I say what I feel only short stories (and not a novel or a poem) can do best in communicating to the reader.

So, though different as poetry and fiction are as genres, I call them relatives or cousins in the sense that they are products of the same literary artist like descendants of one progenitor. I write poetry, memoir, and fiction in the forms of short story and novel. I expect some threads to connect whatever I write irrespective of the genre. I find no difficulty writing in whichever genre I choose to write. With me, one genre or type of writing occupies me at a particular time even as I have no problem moving from one to another. I expect all my writings, including creative and scholarly works, to complement one another in their community of letters.

Here is an assembly of selected and new short stories. I used my personal judgment to select from the earlier stories. I wrote the new ones for about five years and have gone back to read, revise, or edit many of them. The subjects of the new stories are diverse and many of them cover areas which my earlier stories did not explore. It is my hope that these stories will not only provide pleasurable reading but also provoke thoughtful discussion. I have titled the collection *God's Naked Children*. With an omniscient eye, the literary artist in his or her imagination *makes* characters behave, feel, talk, and live among themselves in society and reveal their true nature.

Tanure Ojaide
Effurun and Charlotte, February 25, 2018

The Stories

1

Come back when you are ready to die

My mother was not all that old. At sixty-eight or thereabouts she was strong. Therefore her sudden deterioration from what appeared to be a common ailment alarmed all of us, the more so after the doctors at Eku Baptist Hospital, the best hospital in the area, had told us not to worry about her condition. At first the doctors diagnosed fatigue, exacerbated by malaria. Almost everybody once in a while suffered from malaria which incapacitated one for a week or so and then one bounced back.

My mother had asked to be taken to hospital because she did not like the way she felt. She was a hard worker who never complained of fatigue. It was rare for any ailment to weaken her to the extent of preventing her from going to farm or the market. Hence when I was informed that Mother wanted to be taken to the hospital, I knew that she had a premonition about something terrible happening to her. I began to understand the full impact of her remark when of recent I had visited. She told me to always look back, which was her cryptic way of saying that I should not be too far away in case she might need me.

At the hospital, I spent many hours by her sick bed and her voice was as strong and penetrating as ever.

"One doesn't know when the tree will fall," she told me.

I nodded. What else could I say to such words of deep foreboding? She got up on her own to go to the toilet and refused help of the nurses. This encouraged me to think about when she would be discharged, a thought that was further strengthened by the fact that she was unusually cheerful when she started the story that she insisted on telling me that night, the third night of her hospitalization. She, however, interrupted the real story to make what I considered to be unrelated comments.

"When you think the tree is strong, then comes the hurricane to knock it down," she said.

We live in a rain-forest area where hurricanes harass us during most of the raining season. True, branches get torn from trees all the time; and in other cases, the trees themselves fall. I am not used to speaking in proverbs but I found an opportunity to calm her with these wise words:

"Mother, you don't have to worry. You know a tree with many branches will never hit the ground."

"That's true, my son. Who could have thought that I, the only child of my mother and who for long was believed to be barren, would have all of you? Yes, I am now a big tree with many branches; that's why I am happy," she commented.

"You are almost well already, so don't be afraid," I advised.

"I cannot be afraid. I have surprised myself in my life. Whether I become well or not, don't cry when I die," she said.

"But you are not going to die," I told her as if was God.

"Sooner or later the tree will fall," she insisted.

After she completed telling me her story, our story, on that third night, I went home very late. I felt that she had passed the worst stage of her sickness and would soon be out of hospital. Restless as she had always been, I thought she would ask for her discharge even before I arrived the following day.

The following morning when I arrived at the hospital, she had died. The nurses did not even know until some twenty minutes before my arrival. They had wanted to give her the tablets she needed and found her still sleeping, or so they thought. The nurse who approached her screamed in response to the sight of her body, and other nurses soon came. They called a doctor to examine her. In my presence, she was pronounced dead.

* * *

There are orders which are too difficult to obey. I cried at her death, even though I recalled her advice that I should not. In Agbon, it is said that you can borrow money to celebrate a great festival. After the festival in which you have lavishly treated your guests, you work hard to recuperate your expenditure. Fortunately, I did not borrow, but you will know why I went to such length to make her posthumously proud after you hear the story she had told the night before her death.

"I was the only child of my mother and my mother wasn't my father's favourite wife."

This was how she began her story.

"My father was rich, but preferred to marry more wives than to send his children to school. Out of the envy that he had for other men who sent their sons to school and in an effort to ward off scorn from the townspeople, my father reluctantly send his older boys to school. Late or not, the boys went, but not the girls.

"I cried that I wanted to go to school as well, but my father's heart was rock-set on leaving me along with his other daughters at home. A few girls were going to school in the village and I liked their uniform, but ready as I was, I was never myself given the opportunity.

"At home, I was responsible for farm work, fetching water and firewood, washing clothes, and cooking. And, of course, all I had to do was to wait until I was married off.

"Today I cannot read or write. I could not learn that magic. But I swore from the beginning that I would someday make up for this deprivation. Our elders say that if you don't own something and that thing is in your house, it is still yours. You have graduated from the university; Ese and Ejiro are now there, and others will follow. You see, I can say that I can read and write because you, my children, can read and write. You have even gone farther in your studies than the boys my father had sent to school.

"I learnt from my mother the will to succeed without help. If you are handicapped, you have to get to the fruiting tree before the able-bodied. That was my reasoning, because, as the daughter of a woman who was not her husband's favourite wife, I was very handicapped. My mother had to try many trades to feed me, herself, and sometimes even my father. He married the women to serve him. My mother was among the first women in Urhobo to tap rubber. She also had big cassava and yam farms. All my father did was to point at a jungle to the women and tell them, 'That portion is yours, that yours, and that yours' and they knew what to do to fend for themselves. After all, they had children and did not have to wait for a husband to feed them. 'In this world, don't allow anybody to kill your hope,' my mother always told me. 'Don't let anybody feel sorry for you. Work hard and persist and you will succeed,' she advised me.

"At sixteen years of age, I was given in marriage to a man from Agbarha, the town of only kings and queens. I was excited. What young lady would not be happy to be betrothed at that time when there was nothing ahead for girls other than marriage? If you stayed too long before marrying, people began to wonder what type of girl you were that could not get a man to marry her. You could be called names and, after a period of time, it would become more difficult for you to marry. 'If she is a good girl, why has she not married all this while?' men would ask. That was why many young did not wait to choose but jumped at the first available men who approached their parents. 'Marry and settle down,' the older women counselled us. 'Have your children and bring them up to serve you,' others said. 'May you prosper with your husband,' the family elders prayed.

"My man was young and handsome. I was his first and only wife; he had no concubine yet. That was the dream of us young girls at the time. We had seen our fathers with many wives and did not like the way our mothers were treated. We did not like the way our mothers lived, trying to out-rival one another at great costs to please one man who laid claim to all of them. The men were like kings and our mothers were their servers.

"I could not forget that I was the only child of my mother. She drummed it into my ears in different ways. Her encouragement to me was to have one child after until my house was full. So I went into the marriage thinking that I would be pregnant from my first night. I had hitherto not known a man and passed the night in fear and prayers.

"Everything is in God's hand. I have come to believe more strongly in Him than ever. A woman who has only one child always wants him or her when grown-up to make up for the other children she couldn't bring from her own womb. My mother was waiting to see me pregnant. Six months of marriage passed without my becoming pregnant, then eventually two years.

"I had a standing invitation from my mother to come during my first pregnancy to deliver at home. At the time, expectant mothers did not go to maternities or clinics.

"Five years passed. When I visited my mother, I was asked many questions, most of them quite embarrassing. It seemed that my people believed that my husband didn't sleep with me. Can you imagine that? Our Ughievwen neighbours are very blunt: they call marriage 'sex partnership'. How could they ask whether my husband slept with me or not? Was he a eunuch perhaps? They even asked me that question! His own relatives must have said worse things about me. Being the woman expected to be pregnant, if my husband did his job, the rest was left for me. None of his relatives abused me directly. I nevertheless suspected that they blamed me for their son's childlessness.

"Ten years passed. I went to masseurs and herbalists known to crack serious cases of barrenness. Desperation drives one to go to any length.. How could I have submitted myself to the insults of many of those masseurs? They were more interested in sleeping with their patients than making them have babies with their husbands. My father did not show any signs of being worried. His other daughters were as prolific as dogs. My mother was noticeably agitated and grew moody because of me.

"Don't worry about me," I told her.

"Why should I not be worried? A tree standing alone in a landscape is vulnerable in any storm," she said cryptically.

"I know that. It is not our fault," I explained.

"People are laughing. You don't hear what my mates say about you and me; if you did, you will be worried," she revealed to me.

Before now she had never ventured to tell me about what others thought about the two of us.

"I say, don't worry. I will have my children when *Osonobrughwe*[*] wants me to. It's not just the time yet," I said with some confidence.

---

[*]

"Better soon before you begin your menopause. Have you ever heard of a woman getting pregnant after her menopause?" she asked me.

"No, but I am still young. I still have many years to bear ten children if that is what *Osonobrughwe* wants for me," I said.

"How many years in a lifetime that you have to spend ten or twenty years of adulthood in a hut instead of a real home?" she asked.

"Her proverb was loaded. I loved my husband, but there are people not made to live together. We were not blessed with a child and because of this, we knew by the twelfth year that our marriage was doomed. We had tried every possible way to have a child but to no avail.

"I chose a good time to approach him to discuss what we should do, now that we had lost hope in our having a child together.

"Efecha was a good man and even though we would go our different ways, it was painful for both of us.

"My man, let this annoy you. You know a woman's time runs out fast. You know our customs. It's not that I don't want you, but I will want us to try ourselves elsewhere with other partners," I begged him.

"He thought deeply. He must have faced the same dilemma without telling me. Our situation was not unique. There were precedents in Agbon of husband and wife separating for reasons of childlessness simply to re-marry and have children. Irede and Tega, for instance, are now both happy in their marriages.

"'It's neither your fault nor mine, I believe," he told me. "I can understand."

"Don't be annoyed with me. I think our separation will be good for both of us," I told him.

"We have to act before it is too late for either of us. This is like a boil which we have to cut—it will at first be painful, but in the end it will save us future pain," he told me thoughtfully.

"No Agbon man would want to give up his wife to go and sleep with another man. And I knew it pained him. A brave man does not weep in public but instead at night in his bedroom, I believe he must have wept when he was alone.

“We did as our customs demanded for the dissolution of our marriage to make me free again. We informed our families about our decision. Before representatives of the two families, he released me from my oath to be faithful to him. He asked for and got back a token amount of money in place of the bride price he had paid for me to be his wife.

“When I arrived home, my mother wept. I had to console her.

“I am neither sick nor dead, why do you have to mourn?” I asked her.

“Yes, twelve years of marriage and still childless!” she intoned.

“Don’t let that bother you. I will have my children at the right time,” I pleaded with her.

“It is always clumsy for a big woman to live with her parents. Such a situation puts the woman and her mother in an awkward position. A few times when men visited, the mother would feign she had something to do outside and leave her big daughter and her male visitor alone. But her doing so made me uncomfortable. After all, I was a full woman already and did not need to be shy before men. What does a cock skirt round a hen for other than to stir desire? Some men are scared from coming out openly to court a woman. But the brave and those really in love are not deterred by a market of eyes; rather, they are ready to cross seven rivers to meet you.

“A woman divorced, not for quarrelling with her husband or for any fault of hers or his, attracts many men. For reasons I cannot explain, I looked much younger than my age. I could compare favourably with many girls who were very grown-up before they married. My body was fresh, men told me; but I did not need to be told what they felt I would like to hear. I soon had many suitors.

“Freedom provides thrills and vexations. Half-men came, as well as full men. Poor and rich, handsome and ugly also came. My mother at first pretended as if she did not give birth to me from having a man, my father. She later told me that her house was like a market, to which came all kinds of men who sought me.

"You remember I told you of men who fear to come out or to say what they want. There were many of such. Those who will enter the storm to seize what they desire are few.

"Once Charles Itofe visited, I knew he would father my first child. He had gone through Standard Six before he started his own business in Okpara. He was a very neat man and everything he wore fitted him well.

"That's how I came to marry your father. In those days, big and experienced as I was, my bride price had to be paid before I stepped out to go to his house. Your father was not rich but was a very kind man. It is sometimes difficult to be kind and rich at the same time. Giving out what he worked hard for with both hands left no big fortune at home. A strong man, he impregnated me within three months.

"You can imagine my joy at being pregnant! With him what had been so difficult looked so simple. Then it was as if the moon shone continuously every night. I know that the patient fisher with God's help will always make a catch. I thanked God every day as I kept rubbing my swelling belly. I looked at myself in the mirror and danced naked for joy in my room. As if to gain for time lost, my belly was a huge calabash. My mother feared I might have twins, but I knew it was one only one baby. I didn't go to my mother; rather, we arranged for her to come to me after I delivered.

"And you came to brighten my life with your first cry. Who says that motherhood is not enjoyable? It is true that I slept little the first three months of your childhood because you slept during the day and kept me awake at night. Despite that sleeplessness, I so much enjoyed my motherhood. I had been removed from the gossip list of barren women. I was now a mother. Your father and I were really happy and he was triumphant as if he had conquered the invincible. We were like young boys and girls never leaving each other. My mother joked that our love was stronger than *sosorobia*, that perfume that Gambari people sell or give in exchange for coral beads.

"But the twists and turns of my life were just beginning. I have not had the courage to tell you but I have to now. While you were still a suckling, only six months old, your father, that kind man, the man who took me out of childlessness, the man whose life blessed my life, suddenly collapsed and died. All you had been told was that your father died while you were young. I became widowed the first time at thirty.

"Who knows tomorrow? How could I tell that I, once childless in a twelve-year marriage, would suddenly become widowed after my first child? How could I foresee that I would be twice widowed and become a curse to many men? But what happens for the first time does not always start a trend.

"How was I going to mourn my Charles? Everybody told me to be strong to take care of you rather than make you an orphan. I was so distraught that people said I looked worse than a mad woman.

"I was asked to assist in washing his body. I felt it was cruel of his relatives to bring me face to face with the corpse of my dead husband at that time. They said it was the custom for the widow to perform some rites and I did them all, including having to take a sip of the water used in washing the body. One could be misconstrued as not showing love for the deceased, if one refused to carry out what tradition prescribed. And I could be branded a witch if I didn't do the strange things they wanted done. I did my part to show gratitude and respect for your father.

"I worked hard as I mourned. You grew fast. Our people consoled me.

"Everything is in God's hands," they said.

"Only God knows this," others said.

"Kind words poured from family members. Elders softened the blow with proverbs. Soon I, who had almost killed myself by jumping into a well, saw cause to live. You were there for me.

"You have this fine boy to take care of," some counselled.

"The stump will grow back into a tree," others told me.

"Even before I had done a year of mourning, the Itofe family wanted to transfer me to some other man. Fortunately, your father was his father's only child and I refused to re-marry in the extended family. They said I must choose one of many men in the family and when they could not bend or break my resolve to be left alone, they asked me to choose you. I chose you as my husband, but everybody knew it was a meaningless gesture to keep me free as I wanted.

"Who says time does not heal wounds? It heals even the deepest of wounds. As you grew, I saw a plant out of the old stump. The elders are right, the stump of the *eke* tree is still the *eke* tree. You carry your father's birthmarks in two places.

"I remained in your father's compound. I had pressure from his family and mine to leave. Even friends asked why I should bite what I did not want to eat or swallow. Either I married from the Itofe family or left them and continued on with my life. Certain fires take a long time to cool. Such was the relationship between your father and me.

"You started elementary school. I was happy that the magic I was denied would now be exercised in my house. I was able to buy books and uniform for you without any problem. I did not mind that none of your father's relations, even those who wanted me as their wife, one day asked how you were being provided for. As you mature, you learn that everybody cares only for his or her own. Very few want to give out where they would not get back something. Since they could not have me, they abandoned me and mine, you. But the joy of your going to school invigorated me to work hard. My trade prospered. You were my *Obo* god; hence whatever I touched brought enough money for you and me to live on. I could raise my head high because I did not depend on any man who would ask me to do his bidding.

"When you were eight, I felt you needed a father. I also needed a man. I could not pretend that I was not a woman and so live alone the rest of my life. Men came to me again. They swarmed to me for attention. Some helped me clear my farm; others gave other types of assistance. I am a woman and after giving your father due respect, I threw away my rags. I chose Tebu who performed the customary demands of a would-be husband. He had divorced and I didn't really know why he had done so. However, I liked him and married again.

"It was as if a floodgate was opened. In five years I had three children, your two sisters and one brother. I thanked *Osonobrughwe* for the kindness. I went out to look for a worm and found a snake! Three other children surpassed my expectation. I gained weight from happiness and well-being. Tebu was happy, I was happy, you and the other children were happy.

"Then a storm struck from nowhere. That has always been my bane. Death visits when least expected. A healthy man went to bed at night and did not wake up. That was how Tebu died. He was not sick of anything I knew of. He went to bed and the following morning when he did not respond to knocking on his door for so long, we had to break in to find his body already lifeless and stiff. You were already at St. Peter Clavers Grammar School at Aghalokpe then and came after your brother informed you of the bad news.

"Again widowed, I mourned. How could I take care of four children alone? My mother was dying herself, after she suddenly aged and I was alone like a water-lily shaking in the wide waters. I was bent on not getting torn off to drown. I did not need to be told. Men who married me who gave me love and children died suddenly. In Agbon bad things are said behind you. How was I not sure that they did not point fingers at me when I passed by them?

"I am not a witch, but I must be taken as one. I have heard of confessions of witches, I have heard of their flights to coven at night. They visit people with sicknesses or other problems in order to impoverish them. Women have been accused of killing their husbands. I did not make any effort to deny whatever the public chose to call me behind my back. I had no control over their imaginings.

"Again, I performed my rites when Tebu died. He was buried with a dog and I swore, as his parents and close relatives also did, that if anybody was responsible for his death, that person should fall sick, bark like a dog, and die. I was told it was a trap they felt would catch me. My mind is as clean as Orise's white chalk and I had no fears. My fear was for how I would take care of you all.

"I continued my farming and trading. Fortunately, after your early poor performance in college as a result of which I took you to my cousin in Jos, you changed to be so bright. I wanted you to be far from home so as not to be distracted by my mourning mood. You were already big enough to be troubled by my condition. With my mother dead, I had to think of dead husbands and a dead mother!

"With you away with my cousin who was then a major in the army, I set my mind on getting over my adversities. When you passed your examinations very well and got a scholarship for university education, I poured libation on my Obo shrine. That was my way of thanking God on the good things I got despite the deaths surrounding me.

"For three years, I was like the *ogbo* charm tied to a fruiting tree. No man was bold enough to come close to me. No man appeared to want me and I wanted no man either. I was occupied with how to take care of my four children and that thought consumed all my time.

"More years passed. But soon, the fear that had kept men away appeared to be gone. They started to approach me, first indirectly and later directly. I was very surprised that men still wanted me. Men must be fearless or foolish because of women. If not, how could one explain their determination to have a woman like me as their wife or concubine? I would not allow my brother to go to a woman like me.

"Do you want to die?" I asked my suitors.

"After that blunt question, they did not return. They should have felt I was a witch or a crazy woman to ask them such a question. Human beings are fond of hiding their weaknesses or bad side. But I preferred to brandish the danger before those who wanted me. I would not, if at all I carried a jinx over my lovers, want anybody to die. Better warn them to run away.

"Thus, they flirted around me and whenever any came very close and expressed interest in a relationship, I drove them away with 'Do you want to die? Have you not heard that two husbands who gave me children died?" The chickens retreated and I didn't care about them. Those who had appeared very warm turned cold.

Igbudu had lived among our people for so long that young Agbon people did not know he was not Urhobo. He had been accepted by our people as one of them. You know he is really from Awka but speaks Urhobo more fluently than most of our orators. He has been repairing bicycles in Okpara from my youth. He could forge iron into any farm tool. People loved him and he loved the town. I heard long ago that he had married, but the wife died a long time ago.

"Igbudu was the only one not frightened by my question.

"Are you ready to die?" I asked him after he make known to me his proposal for us to be friends.

"Yes," he told me.

"I looked at him from head to toe. He looked down on me because of his height. We gazed at each other for a long moment.

"Are you not afraid of dying?" I asked again.

"Your own people say that if you hear a gunshot, none should be afraid of the tortoise," he told me.

"So you are the tortoise?" I asked.

"Yes, in a way. The hunter goes for grass-cutters, antelopes, porcupines, and other animals but he never shoots at the tortoise," he explained.

"You must be foolish to put yourself in the hunter's way and not fear being shot," I told him.

"I am not afraid," he insisted.

"I looked at him. I wondered whether he understood Urhobo ways enough, despite his long stay with us. He knew I was still worried about his daring proposal.

"Do you know I had lost a wife when I was much younger?" he asked me.

"I believe he felt it was his turn to frighten me out of a close relationship now that he had declared that he cared more for me than for his own life.

"Yes, I know," I answered him.

"I couldn't tell whether it was folly or courage, but there was love in our eyes. I knew he was serious about me.

"Come back to me when you are ready to die," I told him.

"I am not going to think about it anymore. I have told you before and I want to tell you again that if I have to die for you, let it be," he said so eloquently.

"If you are thinking right, why do you have to eat the very food that has killed others?" I asked him.

"I felt if he was not frightened stiff with this, then he should be a rare man. True to Igbudu, he did not waver.

"I am ready to die for marrying you. Nobody is going to live forever and whatever time I spend with you will be enough for me," he said.

"My mind was made up. I would not give up the man who was ready to die for me.

"If I too have to die for you, I will," I told him.

"He was greatly moved and sang one Urhobo song and Igbo one for me. I cannot forget either of them. I had heard him before singing as he blew the bellows of his forge. Then he sang in a low tone as if coaxing the fire and his tools to do his bidding. Now his *Ubiebi fude, ubiebi fowe* made me young and excited again. I could only embrace him and we became husband and wife in everything but name. We were seen as concubines because we did not live under the same roof—he lived in his house and I lived in mine. I must say that marriage cannot be more delightful than what I have experienced with him. Igbudu gave me my last-born, Tietie. We have been together these past fifteen years. When he went to visit his people who were driven from the North, he was caught up with the war. I have not seen him for the past six months but I know he will cross the front-line of war to come back to me.

"I can tell you my son who will bury me that I have lived quite a life. Whether I recover or not, I have tasted the sweet and bitter draughts of life. There couldn't be more of life that I was denied."

That was how my mother, the great mother, my own Ayayughe, concluded her story. True to her prophecy, Igbudu came back, only too late. He arrived on the day the burial ceremony started. A man is not supposed to cry openly and profusely, but he did. Later he put the loss behind him and helped us in the burial, which I made as lavish and memorable as was possible. My mother would be proud of him as of us wherever she is now.

Death is such a depth that when I call, she cannot answer. Death is so severe that it cares not about those left behind. If death has not put such deaf distance between us, I would have liked to show her my gratitude for her love, care, and thoughtfulness. I remember when I failed my West African School Certificate examination and she took me to my cousin Major Akoro in Jos. There they put me in a prep school and I had eight A's. I who had been dismissed as a dunce for failing every subject I wrote had become a wizard! All my brothers and sisters have been doing well at school and that has gladdened my mother's heart. She more than deserves the lavish burial we have given her.

2

God's medicine-men

They lived in Igbi Street and we lived in Ginuwa Road. Igbi Street runs into Ginuwa Road where my father's house still stands. My friend's home was less than five minutes' walk from ours. From childhood, we played in the same churchyard, the Anglican mission. We children did not know any difference between the Catholic and Anglican churches as our parents did. Endurance's father was a pastor, an Anglican reverend. My father was a churchman of the Catholic faith and he went daily to Mass in the cathedral a half-mile away. After school, the open Anglican school was ours for play till we were tired. We girls played together, so we established a common bond.

Even though we went to different elementary schools, we ended up in the same Government Teachers' College at Bomadi for our Grade II Teacher's Certificate. Government was neither Anglican nor Catholic, so those of us who went to different denominational elementary schools converged in a government-run teachers' college. We girls in the college were not many and so knew ourselves very well. For me and Endurance who came from the same town and had known each other and played together for years, it appeared we were from the same family.

That's how we became even closer and I got to know not only Endurance's father but also Odele, two of God's medicine-men. That's how I also came to see Endurance's disappointing marriage as partly caused by me even though in the end people should make their own choices. I thought I was helping my friend but I could have been playing the matchmaker without knowing.

Whenever Endurance was going to bed, she always double-checked to ensure that the doors were properly secured. Although it was unusual to padlock the door from inside, she did so anyway. Her parents noticed it and believed their daughter was paranoid and hoped her fears would subside with more years. It was not that she was afraid that burglars would break in, but she could not identify the source of what was happening to her. She was determined to stop a burglary of another kind.

It was vacation time when her two other sisters and her brother were around. She shared one room with her sisters and so she did not sleep alone. She slept in one bed, but there were two other beds in the room. Even when she changed beds with her junior sisters, there was no reprieve from the strange intruder. And yet she was always on her guard.

Her mind travelled in all directions. Where could this stranger come from to be able to enter into her at will? She knew that for all the quarrels they had in daytime and which were tightly hidden from outsiders, her father and mother slept together. After all, what would the congregation think of a pastor who quarrelled with his wife? What kind of example the church's First Couple would be giving if their exchange of insults was heard outside their home? But they fired abuses at each other in low tones and their voices were never raised to reach the street.

Endurance marvelled at her parents' self-control in bottling up their fracas. While she hated their squabbles, she admired the limits they placed upon themselves. Quarrel, but let no outsider hear of it. Quarrel, but put on a cheerful face for the world to see. Sleep in the same room and the same bed but ignore the other as much as possible for the children not to know that they did not really sleep together. They had to give a good example not only as a good and happy couple but also as good and happy parents.

There were two men in the house at night: her father and her sibling brother. She could not imagine the impossible, that her father or brother could be the one. There were certain things she did not want to think about and suspecting her own father or brother was ruled out. Endurance was at a loss on what to do.

She was twenty-one and had made love several times before. She knew as a pastor's daughter she had to hide to have her fill in this respect. Her mother and father might think she was still a virgin, but she could not afford to let them know any better. Being a pastor's daughter, she had little chance of going out at will outside the mission compound, and no young man had the courage to come to see her in her father's house.

Their five-bedroom mansion stood at one corner of the massive grounds which also held an elementary school and a big church. Painted brown like the school and church buildings, their house was impressive in size. Endurance and her sisters and brother felt fortunate about their home because they could tell from their friends' homes that theirs was indeed a very big house. They saw their friends live with their parents in one or two-room apartments.

She made sure that she wore tight underwear to bed, but that did not stop the intruder from entering into her at will. She wore trousers to bed, and yet she woke with a feeling of sticky wetness between her legs.

As a beautiful young woman of twenty-one, she was attracted to some men, but none of them made any serious effort to win her love. Her fear and frustration had been this secret stealing into her and waking without remembering anything but only to see the wet and sticky mess between her legs. She has had faint recollections of her ecstasy, but there was no face to place on the man who came into her in her dream. She would not mind sleeping with somebody who loved her and whose face and name she recognized. But she hated this robber who secretly took away from her, her most private possession.

She was scared for her life. Somebody or spirit was in control of her life and she could become what she had not planned for herself. If some man or spirit made love with her successfully, would she not be pregnant? Will her parents, especially her father, believe her innocence, or will they blow out for being scandalized by their supposedly wayward daughter? After all, he always preached against young girls and boys not following the ways of Christ and knowing what they should not know before they got married. Will they understand the strange phenomenon? But why not, since they knew of the Virgin Mary's type of pregnancy? Endurance acknowledged that though she was a pastor's daughter, she did not have the spirituality of the Holy Mother. Strange things could always happen. But she was not a virgin—she lost that in, of all places, the village where she and her sisters had gone to spend a vacation. There she had been as free as air and her grandfather and grandmother had treated them so specially that they would like to live with them all the time. But she was already a grown-up girl who must go back to school at the end of the holidays.

Recently, when her mother and father travelled out of town, she sat in the sitting room and since she was the eldest child and in control, nobody told her to go to bed. She fell asleep on the couch and woke after another orgasm. Her thighs as usual were sticky with thick wetness.

She thought seriously of buying contraceptives from one of the many pharmacies in the town. She had to protect herself, and she knew all she had to do was to ask for a packet of contraceptive pills and hand over the money to the pharmacist. After all, nobody would recognize her since the pharmacists had the habit of not looking their customers in the face. They avoided visual contacts because all they cared for was their money. They did not want to have to do anyone any favour on the basis of facial recognition. So they avoided it.

But Endurance was not a stranger to strange experiences. She had come home from school to solve a problem, only to face a more intractable one. At school, she had been helpless before a succubus. That was what they called the invisible person who came to press her while she slept at night. Again, this person was not barred by sealed school doors. Even though she shared a room with four other girls, she was the only one who experienced the incubus or succubus, whatever that oppressive spirit was called.

At first she was quiet over the experience which came at long intervals. Later the frequency increased and she could no longer bear the burden without crying out. She told me as her bosom friend about it but I did not have much to say then. What does the daughter of a Catholic Head Christian know about spirits pressing people down at night in their sleep? That was before I spent one of the long holidays with my aunt in Benin. Children of Christian parents, we had been discouraged from believing in the supernatural. We grew up to believe that there were satanic forces, evil spirits that could be overwhelmed by constant prayers to God.

"In the name of Christ, I stop you. With the blood if Jesus, I overtake you," Endurance had chanted many times.

However, like the new evil spirit, the incubus persisted and refused to be annihilated by either the name or blood of Christ or Jesus. She lit candles but the evil spirit still stole in to press her. She placed a Bible beneath her pillow, but the incubus was not scared by the Holy Book; it still pressed her while asleep in bed.

"Why me, God?" Endurance had asked many times.

"Continue to pray for help!" I told her.

I knew that my friend must be going through a very difficult situation, but I did not know of any solution. Endurance was getting more distracted than usual and the former bubbling Black Princess, Warri Queen, as she was popularly called, was losing much of her lustre. It has been because of Endurance's case that I know that worries could hurt more than physical sickness. If she had suffered from malaria or something else, the doctor who visited our college twice a week would have cured her. But this was not a case she could bring to the young doctor who chased many female students who visited him to cook and do other things for him.

It was these strange experiences that drove the pastor's daughter, my good friend, to seek help from her friends.

This was her final year in the two-year program. She decided to go home and tell her parents what was happening to her. She had to tell the matron and the principal why she needed to go home early. The teachers' college encouraged discipline and the principal did not want students to leave for home individually. During vacations, they went home in groups and that was safer than being alone. Of course, while I and mutual friends knew about her condition, she also needed to explain to her other friends what was driving her home so early.

We had always cherished our camaraderie—gossiping about other female students and their teachers and male students, recollecting common adventures, and other things that bound us together as young girls.

But Endurance realized that she did not really need to explain her problems to the whole world. She thought that when she was back at home the aura of prayers would drive away the evil spirit that tormented her. So she had to manufacture a reason to the Principal and she got her permission to leave.

The boat journey home on the Warri River always frightened her. She did not know how to swim, but she spent ten hours on the wide river that was notorious for crocodiles, sharks, and big fishes that wrecked small boats. A few students have been victims of the vast and deep river, which yearly had its casualties. The current was violent in the salt side of the river. The boat was not as packed full as when she travelled with her fellow students. Then the boatmen filled the boats like the slave ships they read about in history books to make the maximum profit and did not care if the boat sank from overweight. By the time they had come to the fresh water side of the river, she knew she was close to home. The river was narrower, less angry, and had more villages on the banks. Endurance's breath became more relaxed and she started planning how she would tell her mother and father about her problem.

At home she could not immediately tell them about it. She was in a dilemma. On one level, her father railed against evil spirits, witches, and demons in his sermons. In other words, these wicked forces existed to be fought and defeated. On the other hand, she as a Christian was supposed to believe that none of the wicked forces could have power over her as long as she believed in the power of Christ. She believed in God and Jesus who came to the world to save humankind, but that belief had not driven away the incubus that tormented her nightly. She was not sure of how her father in particular would respond to her talking about being pressed at night and she was afraid of being accused of believing in the power of demons rather than of Christ whose blood could wash away all evils. For these uncertainties she told her parents that she was sick, always dizzy and feeling like fainting.

My friendship with Endurance made me to know the Anglican pastor very well. I saw him frequently and as children of the same street, we heard stories about him. People say he had gone to Jerusalem a long time ago. I believe this because Endurance confirmed it and even showed me one of the silver or imitative silver cups he brought from the Holy Land. Some photographs of Christ on the walls of their sitting room were quite unique and could have come only from the Holy Land.

Pastor Efe in many ways had lived up to the expectations of his wealthy name. How could anyone have predicted that the first son of a traditional healer that the white missionaries had condemned to hell before his death would become the pastor of a big church? Pastor Jeremiah Efe had confounded village pundits. Even his own father who had hoped that his son would take over the healing trade from him just as he had taken it over from his own father, no longer felt betrayed. He did not visit his son on Sundays but he saw the big church at the other end of the field in the big compound that his son virtually owned in the name of God. Of course, his pastor son had not visited him on *edewor*, the traditional day of worship, when his home was full of patients needing assistance.

Pastor Jeremiah Efe had gone to school and distinguished himself in the old Standard Six, and a series of missionary schools for would-be pastors had made him very learned. From his preaching, one could tell that he knew the Bible very well. He quoted effortlessly from the Old and the New Testaments. He not only knew the verses but also the very page numbers of his quotes from the King James Version that his church used. He told his congregation that despite being a busy pastor, he read the entire Bible every year, which meant he had read the Bible twenty times or more since he answered the pastoral call.

His congregation loved him, mainly because he was seen as a happily married man of a good family. And he preached very well. He railed against witches, evil-doers, and wicked spirits in the strongest of terms. He could move people to tears and laughter with his words. He got possessed once the sermon began and the Holy Spirit spoke through his tongue. He spoke simple Urhobo-laced English, which worked well with most of his congregation, illiterate, semi-literate and highly literate alike. Men and women, young and old, all were solidly attached to his church, and this meant the Sunday worship at St. Matthew's was a fulfilling experience to the pastor and his congregation.

The white Bishop in Benin must have heard many good things about Pastor Jeremiah Efe, apart from his own favourable impression of the fine young man, so that when the Archbishop of Canterbury created an opportunity for his "Nigerian brothers" to visit the Holy Land, he was easily picked as one of the native pastors in the contingent.

Pastor Jeremiah Efe visited Jerusalem in 1971. Jerusalem, the Holy Land, the Stone City, the City of Golden Sunset, and the Home of Jesus! The experience remained fresh in his mind. The son of an Urhobo traditional healer in the Land of Miracles! He has not forgotten the Wailing Wall, where he put on a Jewish skullcap and scribbled prayers which he tucked into the cracks of the old wall. He wanted to rise to be Bishop. He wanted peace in his home. He wanted his church to grow big, and overflow with worshippers. At the Church of the Holy Sepulchre, he visited different chapels and saw the unity of all churches. He even went to Asqua Mosque and was overwhelmed by the grandeur of this other religion. He wondered why Christians and Muslims in Nigeria frequently clashed violently when, in fact, they were worshipping the same God. He saw the make-up tomb of Christ. He followed the Stations of the Cross. He wished he were in Roman times to help Christ with the Cross as Thaddeus did. Imagine if his wife, Rebecca, had like Veronica wiped tears, sweat, or blood from Jesus's body. Everything had a certain aura of sacredness.

But years later, it was the Arab market that gave him the memento of his life. He bought five silver-looking cups. In fact, the Arab trader had told him they were silver goblets. He had an obsession for these silver goblets, which he always wanted to display before his visitors.

"Drink with the cup of Christ," he told his guests once he offered drinks to them.

Later, his familiar visitors got so used to being served with the cup of Christ that they asked for it, a request that became a code for drinks.

"Let me drink with one of those cups of Christ," they would request, smiling.

Of course, his visitors became many and he spent far more than his congregation and mission paid him. Out of modesty and spiritual concerns, he was reluctant to discuss money even though he needed much more than the little he was paid. He employed innuendoes to inform members of his congregation who paid visits that his pay was not enough, but this never sank into their heads. How could anybody leaving the pastor's wealthy-looking house feel he was close to the proverbial church rat?

"The Anglican Church is not like the Roman Catholic Church that is a state of its own and has gold reserves," he told his congregation. "We need to give to strengthen our church and ourselves," he would also add.

He was not sure whether plain talk about raising his salary would go on well with his adoring congregation. But as a pastor, Jeremiah Efe continued to entertain his church members who frequently came to visit him. It was not that he was obliged to entertain, but those cups of Christ he so much loved exhibiting made him give out drinks with both right and left hands. This was the main cause of the quiet quarrel with his wife.

"What will we use both to clothe and feed the children and also send them to school?" she frequently asked.

"God that sent me to Jerusalem will provide for them," he would tell her.

A pastor's wife, Rebecca remained down-to-earth. She had lost her Ibo name, Ifi, to this Rebecca. Much as she told people she was Ifi, nobody was ready to call her that name. At first she felt the Urhobo did not want her to retain her real name. However, she also noticed that even the few Igbo women around also called her Rebecca or Becky. Rebecca or Ifi Efe, she was Mrs. Efe, Pastor's wife.

I travelled to spend part of my holidays with my senior sister living with her family in Benin and during that period, through my friend

Esther, I first heard of and later met Odele. I saw Pastor Odele and knew immediately he was a strange man, but I also felt that he might be able to help my other friend Endurance to get out of her problems.

Since our parents knew we were friends, it was easy for Endurance to obtain permission from her parents to visit me and spend some time with me and my senior sister, once I sent word that I wanted her to come as soon as possible.

"Pastor Odele," as he introduced himself, projected himself as a man of piety, a man of God. He always wore a special black hat which he had never changed since the many years I knew him. The hat covered his whole head and left a little of the forehead. So, though he was short, you never saw his exposed head or hair. The head might be bald or the hair shaved, but I could not tell. It seemed part of his spirituality had to do with his gentlemanly and fatherly look and covering his hair. There was some power in his head covered by the hat which did not appear to wear out with time.

Pastor Odele held a small pocket Bible almost all the time. The letters were very tiny and he must be very familiar with its content to read it without glasses. He told Esther and me that the words of the Bible were the words of God with which one could cure the worst of diseases and cast out most wicked spirits. The combination of the special hat and the small Bible gave a certain mystique to Pastor Odele's personality. When we first came to him, we were scared but soon got used to his strangeness.

Pastor Odele was not young, somebody in his forties, I guess. Still he lived with his mother and did not appear to be married. He had a big room in his mother's house. He told me that he had his own house but since we were never taken there, we felt he might be trying to avoid embarrassment for living with his mother at his age. Or he might be trying to be consciously innocuous to us, he being a man of God and we being single girls. Though he called himself a pastor, he would not take us to his church to pray as we initially thought he would do. He pointed at a distant direction where his church was, but for the months and years we would know him, none of us would ever see or enter that church.

The pastor who looked every way like a medicine-man ministered to us and other visitors who trickled into his mother's home. If the pastor's appearance frightened us at first, the inside of his mother's house gave us even a bigger fright. We looked at each other, held the other's hand and knew we could not run anywhere. There was no way, we felt, that Pastor Odele would hurt all three of us together in broad daylight in his mother's house.

Pastor Odele's mother's home was a big shrine decked with mirrors, sculptures of god-like figures, animal skulls, and white and red feathers. He knew we would be too scared to ask him any questions, so he tried to assure us of our safety.

"Everything on earth is made by God," he said.

We were so engrossed in the different items in the big shrine of a parlour that none of us responded to him.

"We have to fight battles with whatever arms we can muster," he told us as if he were leading the many figures of ancestors or gods to a battle that needed extraordinary weaponry.

The pastor led three of us into his vast room which was comfortably furnished. The floor was rugged, and there were two three-seaters and a sofa, all dark blue and matching the interior painting. On the walls were pictures of Christ, Mamiwata, and Ukuakpolokpolo, the ruling Oba of Benin. There was a closet at one end of the room.

Pastor Odele asked us to sit down and feel comfortable. After Endurance told him her problems, Pastor Odele said he would take her to Sakpoba River to wash away whatever evil affected her and pray for her so that her problems would be banished forever.

We followed Pastor Odele out after he had taken whatever he went for in that closet. We went about a mile on Sakpoba Road and turned left where the river crossed the road. We walked about five poles inside from the main road to the river which narrows before entering Benin. At this brush-covered side of the river, Pastor Odele opened one of the books of Moses, chanted in English and Edo incomprehensible lines that were meant to exorcise Endurance of evil spirits. He then asked three of us to undress, except for our underwear; enter the water, and bathe. Meanwhile he left us alone for ten minutes or thereabouts before returning to say more prayers.

He came back when we were still in the water and did not feel embarrassed looking at our exposed breasts or body. We also felt no embarrassment since there was a purpose for our nakedness.

"Endurance, I have chased out the evil spirits pressing you or sleeping with you at night," he told a visibly relieved Endurance.

"Are you finished with me?" she asked him.

"I say in the names of Olokun and Jesus, you have been freed from bondage to evil angels," he assured her.

He then prophesied to me that my first child would be a girl and that Esther would not marry her current boyfriend. Esther and I knew that he wanted to appear fair to all three of us by giving each of us something to be happy about. We were very happy that Endurance had been promised success and would be freed from both the incubus and the secret lover.

Endurance must have told her mother who told Pastor Efe about the man of God in Benin, Pastor Odele, who prayed and chased off evil spirits. As Endurance told us later, her father admitted he had feelings of a past life in which he was a medicine-man. He could smell burnt herbs, he hallucinated on seeing himself shaking rattles and invoking gods and ancestors. He was meant to take over from his father but it was too late. He could not resign from his pastoral flock to go to the village to be a full-time medicine-man.

What Endurance and her mother thought would be a difficult task persuading Pastor Efe to go to Benin so that Pastor Odele could pray for them thus became so easy.

"Sometimes, the medicine-man cannot heal himself," he told Rebecca and Endurance.

"Maybe the Benin pastor can help both of us," Rebecca told him.

"I believe in miracles," he said.

"Amen," his wife and daughter replied in unison.

"When do we go then?" he asked.

"Next Friday," he suggested.

And so Pastor Efe, his wife, and daughter went to see Pastor Odele to pray for them. The pastor warmly received his guests in his room in his mother's house. Pastor Efe did not wear his pastoral collar so that he did not cut the strange figure in his gown in a native shrine.

As if he were a diviner, Pastor Odele told Pastor Efe his problems before he mentioned them. And to gain his confidence more, he told Pastor Efe that he prayed and made things for preachers so that they could overwhelm their congregations. Pastor Efe wanted this. He took the Anglican pastor to a corner and told him he would also solve his problems with his wife.

They prayed together noisily, and as was common with Pastor Odele, he invoked Olokun and Jesus Christ to inspire Pastor Efe to preach to move people's hearts. Pastor Odele in his heart was a medicine-man rather than a pastor. He gave Pastor Efe two wrapped things to rub and lick before going to bed and before going to preach. He was to do these things without fail if he really wanted to avoid squabbles with his wife, if he wanted his congregation to lavishly make huge monetary offerings, and if he wished to get promoted in his pastoral mission.

Endurance told me that her parents became closer and had few incidents of quarrels after their trip to Benin. The quarrels had disappeared before Pastor Odele's visit to Warri, as he put it, for a courtesy call on Pastor Efe, a fellow man of God. He had come with his mother in his new pickup van. You could not tell one was a medicine –woman and the other was not a pastor.

Pastor Efe, of course, wanted to be very hospitable and as usual brought out his silver goblets from Jerusalem to entertain his guests from Benin. He reported to his medicine-man, Pastor Odele, that his monthly salary was recently raised without his asking for it. He also reported about his congregation increasing, almost overflowing into the street. In addition, they were now possessed at the time of worship and gave offerings and gifts with open hands. Things could not be better than they were with him, he reported. He thanked Pastor Odele for his prayers and everything, as he put it.

"Thank my mother," Pastor Odele told him.

"Thank you two for your prayers," Pastor Efe told his guests.

"Better things are coming into this house," Pastor Odele assured him.

"Amen," chanted Endurance's father and mother.

By the time his guests were gone, three of his silver goblets had disappeared from the cupboard where they were kept. Pastor Efe had promised his wife that he could hold back on his entertainment in order not to dissipate the new blessings of salary increase and huge offerings. So when the cups could not be found, Pastor Efe made only a feeble attempt to look for them. Then he put the remaining two into a box in his bedroom so as not to lose all of them. These will be his lifelong mementoes of the pilgrimage to Jerusalem. If someday anybody doubted whether he was a JP, Jerusalem Pilgrim, he would bring them out and show the silver goblets to certify his experience.

Visitors who came with the hope of being entertained with the cups of Christ were disappointed. They were asked to join in prayers, because prayers are the greatest food of a Christian because they nourished the soul, the pastor told them. The stream of visitors that depleted their savings dried to a mere trickle and that was good for the man and woman who lived in the mission compound. That did not affect the record of congregation at Sunday services.

Soon Endurance would need Pastor Odele's services and this time they would become part of each other's life for good or bad. If she was no longer being pressed by the succubus or being raped in a dream, what else could Endurance have gone to Pastor Odele to ask for? I can only string together the pieces that my friend told me, but I knew that friends as we were, she told me the crux but not the details of what transpired between them. Sometimes we could hold back particularly embarrassing parts of a story and would expect the other to figure out the true situation. How could we at any stage have foreseen that Endurance, that Warri Queen as she was called at the Teachers' College, would make a choice that most of us were to laugh at? As Endurance told me, she developed a certain body odour which made people to avoid coming close to her. At this time, we were waiting for the results of our Teachers' Grade II Certificate examination and I was again spending the free time with my senior sister in Benin. There was nothing to do till after the results when the successful ones among us would be posted to teach in elementary schools. Some of us might go straight to the university or do the National Certificate of Education program.

I don't know the number of people who convinced Endurance that she had a very bad odour. But she said after many people had told her, she started to smell it herself. She thought it was gas and bought some medications to purge her of the bad smell. That did not stop it. She went to a pharmacist who sold her antibiotics, Terramycin and Tetracyclin, but the smell did not go. She felt it came in her breath too and she found it difficult to leave home. Then she thought of Pastor Odele who had helped her before to perform more difficult tasks.

Endurance did not even come to me or Esther before going to Pastor Odele, unlike in all previous occasions when she had seen him either in our company or that of her parents. The next thing we knew was that she had informed her parents of her intention to marry somebody of her choice now that she had finished school. The person she chose to marry was Pastor Odele.

Pastor Odele had assured her that he would drive away the wicked spirits that tormented her with the repulsive body odour. He asked her to spend the night in his room in his mother's house. He would pray and also perform some sacrifices at midnight in a nearby crossroads. Before that night, Endurance told me, she had placed so much trust in Pastor Odele's power. That very night, she found herself in the experience which Pastor Odele was supposed to have cured her from. The only difference was that this time it was real. When it was over, it appeared Pastor Odele was the one who used to steal into her because it happened in the same manner. She stayed with him in Benin for three weeks without her coming to see me or Esther and while her parents thought she was with me and my sister. Imagine if something worse had happened to her in a city where ritual murderers were many! But we were lucky that bad as things appeared to me and Esther and perhaps her parents, they could have been worse.

Endurance returned to Warri but soon discovered that she was pregnant. That was how Pastor Odele came to marry Endurance, my own friend and daughter of Pastor, rather, Bishop, Efe. Pastor Odele still has no church; he still wears his special hat that covers his head, lives with Endurance and their only child in his big room in his mother's house that is partly Olokun shrine. Endurance found the three silver goblets that were missing from her father's house in Warri, but now owed allegiance to her husband than to her father and so did not report. Her father might have been surprised if told the use to which they were put at Pastor Odele's. they became part of the tools in this God's medicine –man's healing business.

But this, like many other things, did not matter now. Her father was now appointed Bishop of Benin-Delta Provinces of the Anglican Mission in Nigeria. The letter came from and was co-signed by both the Archbishop of Canterbury and the Queen and Head of the Church of England, the spiritual and political heads of the Anglican Church.

Bishop Efe moved to Benin and lived in the same town where his eldest daughter was married. They were really not married in church or in the traditional way, but had become partners in attending to those who came to Pastor Odele or his mother for help. Endurance had become like her mother a pastor's wife, though the mother was now a bishop's wife. The Efes did not resist Endurance's choice since they believed within that Pastor Odele had done them a good turn that deserved reciprocity.

Pastor Odele's prophecies have been fulfilled. Esther broke from her boyfriend and then travelled to marry a man studying in London. We have not heard from her ever since. I have just got my first child, a girl that my husband and I have named Oghenetega. When next I travel to Benin I will visit my old friend and, maybe, both of us would visit her parents at the Bishop's Court.

3

The Wake-keeping

It is only those who lack experience about life who argue that certain things can not happen. Anything is possible. Once something, however strange happens, it becomes an experience. Precedents are set by strange occurrences. I now know that every story is true or capable of being true. This was what I came to learn from what took place in my own Okpara. The big family wanted to do their best to bury their own, but the man's own children ruined the whole thing.

All sons-in-law and their friends assembled for the wake-keeping and burial of Odova. His house was small by Okpara standards for a man with many children. He did not live all his life in shame. He would have been the only man with grown-up children living in a thatched house in his quarter of Okpara but had been saved from shame fifteen years earlier by one of his sons-in-law who paid for the roofing of the house with corrugated iron sheets. The mud walls were plastered with cement and given the appearance of a house built with cement blocks. The roof had now rusted from the frequent rains of the area. He was going to be buried in a house of corrugated iron sheets rather than in a hut, what the people called a home roofed with thatches. He was saved from one shame by his son-in-law's kind gesture.

The sheds outside were made of palm fronds. Odova was a poor man and his several children were not doing well. The crowd was small. The townspeople who hungered for wake-keeping in order to drink, eat, dance, and flirt their fill did not expect much from this one. There were no invitation cards distributed. Everything was by word of mouth. Relations had not come from afar. It is doubtful if the family found it necessary to send one of theirs to Yoruba land of Hausa land, where some of their people lived. The family knew they had double standards in their practices—one for the rich and the other for the poor. None of Odova's children complained because there was no money to send one of them to invite their distant relatives, who would not leave their works anyway because of Odova's death.

Preparations were made for the wake-keeping and burial as in the days before newspapers, radio, and television. There is a proverb which says that one can measure with one's eye the pounded yam that can fill one's stomach. Most Okpara people measured Odova's wake-keeping with their eyes and saw nothing to leave home for.

The people who gathered were sombre rather than celebratory as was common on such occasions in Okpara. After all, Odova was old, about seventy. He had several wives, but had lived with one as far as many Okpara people could tell. The women who were expected to sing dirges were quiet like the men. No-one expected a motorcade as in other burials. None of his male children had left the town; they had all remained scratching a living. An only son, Odova had only half-brothers and half-sisters, none of whom had a car or car-owning friends. His first daughter sold tomatoes in Igbudu Market in Warri. Her husband who had been doing well had had a stroke and was left emaciated and weak. The other daughter was married to a greaser, who sold engine oil in gallons and quarts and greased cars for a pittance. The third daughter who had run from home lived with a messenger in a secondary school in Sapele. All three daughters were there with their husbands and friends. A few motorcycles and many bicycles were parked around.

When Odova died in Ufuoma Clinic in Warri, the senior daughter felt the easiest way for her then was to ask the body to be kept in the clinic's morgue until she had informed the family and decided on what to do about the burial. She did not think of the daily fee for keeping the body there, a fee that was more than any of the deceased's children's monthly earnings. The children had expected the death because of the rare nature of his sickness.

The family held a meeting after the senior daughter cried home to report the news. She had told her brothers and sisters who were all summoned home about their father's body in a mortuary in Warri. None of them took into consideration the fee for keeping the body there when they agreed to tell the larger family that their father should be buried in a month's time.

The family meeting was controlled by the elders and not Odova's children. Orise, the family elder, supported by other elders, fixed three thousand naira as the total amount to be contributed. Every adult knows that a man's children, not his relations, village or town, bury their parent.

"You don't age for the village or family but for your own children," Orise reminded the assembled family.

Others concurred. The children kept quiet when the family split the three thousand naira, which would not even be enough to buy fish to prepare palm oil soup, not to mention the drinks and the other items of entertainment. In the children's thinking, one did not need to flaunt poverty before the extended family. They wanted to maintain some sense of pride and honour. On their part, the elders could not ask the family they knew to be poor to contribute more.

The contribution was like a struggle to squeeze juice from a dry fruit. Very little of the shared money was contributed. When asked for their share of two hundred naira, the Okite branch of the family complained of hard times, sick ones in the hospital, and other responsibilities. The family was able to find only one hundred and twenty naira.

"What's important is contributing something. Here's my share, this amount," another said.

He did not mention the mere ten naira he contributed. Everyone knew that with that type of pittance, nothing could be bought. Things had become so expensive that hundreds of ten naira could not make a dent on whatever they wanted to buy.

As the sun set, more people trickled in. Not the big crowd that characterized expensive burials. The scanty crowd exchanged pleasantries as was customary and no one expected any lavish ceremony, or the turn of events they would remember for the rest of their lives.

"The dead are dead, and the living must deal with the problems of life. Let us drink," the town-crier said.

He attended every wake-keeping in town. He took as compensation for his role of alerting the town of news participating in every public ceremony that provided free drinks and food.

"Bring the drinks," an elder shouted, as if he had cartons of beer or soft drinks in stock somewhere.

The family drinks were not many and had been kept under lock until late in the night. The children had calculated that the sons-in-law and their friends would bring out their drinks and that should carry the gathered folks on for some time. They, children of Odova, would formally entertain people after the corpse had been brought.

It was cool. The sun had set. Night was falling. People were looking out for the pickup can that was to bring the corpse from Ufuoma Clinic. The senior son had left for Warri since three o'clock. He had chartered a pickup van from an Okpara driver living in Warri and had also made arrangements for a coffin in Warri, the extended family had been told.

In the half light of early nightfall, a pickup appeared. Once the van's lights appeared, there were sighs of relief as the waiting had become too long. At last, the body has come, they felt. The van came to a stop. In the dark, one could not see what was inside. But instead of the senior son to unload the pickup van of its coffin, he strolled to where the elders sat.

"They have refused to release my father's corpse," he told them.

The elders listened with bewilderment. How could a morgue refuse to release a corpse to the family claimant? The senior son did not wait to be asked why. He could see on their faces that they wanted to know why the impossible had happened.

"The money I took there wasn't enough to pay the charge," he told them.

There was a murmur among the elders, so loud that it drew the attention of the scanty crowd.

"Every day the strangest thing happens," the oldest man said to the hearing of those sitting around him.

The word soon went round. Odova's children could not pay the hospital bill to recover their father's body. After the initial consternation, sons-in-law well-wishers, and the extended family swallowed the news quietly and behaved as if nothing unusual had happened. They knew that wretchedness made one to do shameful things. They continued the wake-keeping, but without the corpse for the women to dance round.

Still they drank. The sons-in-law brought out their cartons of drinks. The children brought out their drinks. No musician was brought, but the sons-in-law had brought boom boxes and played Urhobo dance music. The young and old danced. The flirtations that usually took place at such nights took place but on a very low scale.

Most of those who came from outside stayed through the night because of rampant armed robbery. They were stuck with the wake-keeping till dawn. By the second cock-crow, it was dawn enough to slip out. Nobody went to the deceased's children or family, as was the custom, to say words of comfort. The sons-in-law took their wives and their own children with them when they left. By the early morning there was no corpse to bury.

Meanwhile the mortuary fee was escalating and nobody knew when Odova's body would be recovered.

"If that body is ever recovered, I won't come to another burial ceremony. I will give one excuse or another," the frail husband of the tomato-selling daughter of Odova said.

"What will happen if the children, extended family, or townspeople are unable to recover the body?" one woman asked.

"Let the clinic burn the corpse!"

The few people around the speaker seemed to have agreed to this solution. Nobody felt offended.

4

The Debt-Collector

When Daniel and Martha came from Warri to their hometown to marry in the local church, the Okpara community saw an opportunity not just to eat and drink to their hearts' content but also to rejoice that their children did not go far away to seek their spouses. Daniel and Martha had broken what the elders had thought was a dangerous trend of their sons taking wives from outside the town or clan and their daughters also doing the same in their choice of husbands.

Okpara people had seen their children marry from neighbouring ethnic groups that they were familiar with. They saw nothing strange in that; after all, they had always known their Isoko, Izon, Itsekiri, and Ukwani neighbours, amongst whom they had married. They had a long history of intermarriage and even boasted about such. However, recently, their children were marrying spouses from faraway groups such as the Hausa, Kanuri, Igala, and Tiv. They now had sons-in-law and daughters-in-law from ethnic groups they had never heard about: Kuteb, Chamba, Bura, and others. But to make matters worse, in the Okpara people's thinking, Igho's son had brought a white woman as his wife from London.

"Where did he see this woman to pick as wife?" they asked.

The woman was bland and looked every bit older than the young man. She could not talk to anybody except through an interpreter, her own husband. Children followed her wherever she went in town. She did not eat the food her mother-in-law prepared for her and her husband.

"Too much pepper," she had complained.

The children sang "Oyibo pepper" after her, and soon ran her and her husband out of town.

Two of Okpara's daughters were married to white Americans. Their mothers loved money so much that they had encouraged their daughters to marry for wealth, the people gossiped. Any American, and for that matter a white male, they believed, was rich. They saw no love in that relationship. The world was changing too fast, they feared. However, the current marriage of their own son and daughter brought a deep sigh of relief and great joy to them. At last their god and ancestors were listening to their prayers, they believed.

"*Orhirhi ruru*!" they chanted in praise of their tutelary god.

The sacrifices to their ancestors and the yearly festival dedicated to Orhirhi, their guardian god, had not been in vain. Those they prayed to were listening to their prayers and responding positively to their needs, they suddenly realized.

The marriage took place on Friday and Saturday, as had become the new custom. The traditional marriage, in which a token bride price was paid to Martha's family, took place on Friday, while the church wedding was held the following day in the Catholic Church. The climax of the two-day ceremony was the wedding reception on Saturday afternoon, when the two extended families danced and chatted in a convivial manner, happy that their newly-wed son and daughter would increase Okpara's number in the outside world. The townspeople believed that the newlywed's offspring would be true Okpara-born. To them, every human being naturally had two hands. And with father and mother Okpara-born, one had the enviable status of being a full-blooded Okpara person with two strong hands.

Daniel Shegbe and Martha Ituru came from old Okpara families. Neither of the two knew about that. It was in fact by chance that they knew they were both from Okpara; they were already attracted to each other before they learnt about their Okpara origin. They had seen themselves as Warri residents and had coincidentally attended the same secondary school, United College of Commerce, in the Igbudu quarter of town. The knowledge that they were from Okpara, though coming late, also gladdened their hearts.

The only person who would have raised an eyebrow or objection to their wedding in the Catholic Church was too weak to attend. Adogbeji was bedridden. He had become too feeble with age to leave home. Even a strong walking stick could no longer support him outside. Age had at last disabled the once energetic man. Though stuck at home, he learnt early, as soon as arrangements were made for the wedding of Daniel and Martha, and got news of the marriage celebrations.

Much as he wanted to laugh at fate for these two young ones marrying, by seeing for himself the wedding of an Ituru and a Shegbe, he could not make it to any of the ceremonies. He now realized that his body no longer obeyed his mind as it used to do for so many years. He knew he had to stay at home now rather than go to battle. This was really not a battle in the true sense, but he would have mocked the two families either at the occasion or afterwards. Now he had to be silent at home, like a dumb parrot, and only reflect on the passage of time and its healing power.

Adogbeji was so old that nobody else alive in Okpara knew his actual age. He was born in the olden days, was all his townspeople could say of his age. Many younger elders maligned him that he was a wizard and used diabolic means to keep himself alive. Some went as far as comparing him to a tree whose lower branches die off as it grows taller and stronger. The accusations intensified after he lost several of his children, two to accidents and one to malaria that was described as a mere fever. A son should live to bury his father and only an evil father survived his children, the people believed.

Adogbeji was tired of protesting his innocence before people who did not listen to him. In a town in which people barely lived beyond sixty, there he was over a hundred years old. He must have some secret power to overcome the adversities that killed others, many believed. Such people cared less about his lifestyle. He did not drink alcohol, and his people read sinister meaning into it. He did not want to spend money buying alcohol for relatives and friends. He was a diabolical man and so did not want other diabolically minded people to poison his drinks.

The same cynics complained that he had married only one wife who bore him all his ten children. The woman had long died and yet Adogbeji refused to marry again, when every adult Okpara man had three or four wives, plus an undisclosed number of concubines. Adogbeji also did not smoke. When his young age-mates were taking to smoking, he had told them that he felt like throwing up whenever assaulted by the smell of tobacco. To his townspeople, he was a miser who did not want to spend a penny to treat himself.

"He will die without knowing the pleasures of life," such people said behind him.

Adogbeji had seen a lot in his life. He had experienced so much that, in the local parlance, he knew the footprints of a crab. He knew when the British sacked Benin and he frequently sang the song on every lip then: "Should I walk or run, when can I get to Benin to avenge the Oba of Uselu's capture?" He was a smallish man, a terra cotta figure in his strong demeanour. His wide nose had gone down the family line.

When he heard about the wedding, he chuckled in his cynical way, laughed, and shook his head. *"What time can do to humans!" he said to himself.* He knew that time could mend a rift. Time could heal the deepest of wounds. Time nurtures forgetfulness. Time, through memory, was also a cynic. How humans forget! And he knew that the Shegbe and Ituru families had forgotten so much in three generations. How could he as a young man then ever think that eighty years or so later the vendetta between the two families would ever stop, not to talk of being totally forgotten. In his wildest dream as a young man, there was no way he would have foreseen an Ituru proposing a toast to a Shegbe, as he was told by those who attended the reception party.

A Shegbe and an Ituru marrying! A mean-spirited creditor and a helpless debtor rising from their graves to witness the marriage of their great-great-grandchildren would not be a laughing matter at all! Two families that accused each other of secretly killing their members in their open quarrel for a decade or, more, had put those acrimonious years behind to celebrate the wedding of their son and daughter! Two Shegbe women were lost when they went to the market in Kokori and two weeks later two Ituru women who went to Ekakpamre Market did not return and were never seen again. The two families accused each other of kidnapping or killing their own.

What happened to the family honour that both had vowed to uphold by hurting the other family? What happened to the humiliation that the Iturus felt had been inflicted on them? What happened to the insolence and ingratitude that the Shegbes felt they had received for assisting Ituru with a much needed loan? Time performs miracles, Adogbeji mused.

Adogbeji remembered clearly what the great-great-grandfathers of the couple had been: creditor and debtor. All who had witnessed the bizarre happening had preceded him into the other world. And he was not going to tell anybody what he knew because there were many things that the elders knew but did not talk about. Most scandals were not passed by word of mouth from one generation to another. The Shegbe-Ituru scandal, though known by many, became a public secret and there were many such secrets not meant to be told to young ones. There were things seen or heard that should remain untold. What use telling children what happened three generations ago? He asked himself. Such happenings made him wiser and more thoughtful about life. "Anything is possible," he now believed. It was a pity that bearers of names do not even know their own history, he felt.

* * *

Shegbe's hard work had rewarded him with an abundance of wealth. Those who used to laugh at him for working too hard had stopped those snipes. In rain or sun, he worked. He had large farms of yams and also cultivated cocoa and coffee. During the palm oil production season, he was off with his climbing ropes and machete at dawn and would not return home till the early evening. He had no time to be at the men's-only *ohwarha* joint, where men gossiped about the sexual escapades of others. Some men hardly stayed at work for long so as to get to the joint by late afternoon and gossip till night. Shegbe did not show up any day at the *ohwarha* joint.

"He has the strength of ten men," many gossiped about Shegbe. "If hard work killed, Shegbe would have long gone," others said behind him.

But many people worked hard and yet remained poor. "He is a lucky man," the old said. "How many of us almost break down from working and yet do not become rich like him?" they asked.

A few people went as far as deriding his wealth—that it was not his hard work that brought him wealth but the *usigho* charm he procured from an Ijebu man. He had bartered his life or something special to him to become rich, some people said behind him. Those people waited for the death of his favourite wife or for the eldest son to die, as usually happened, to confirm their belief that he had derived his wealth from diabolic means, but nothing happened to his family. Rather, whatever he touched, like a good soap, started to foam magically. It must be something secret that ensured his wealth, those envious people proclaimed.

Shegbe had seized the opportunity of the coming of the white man to obtain a chieftaincy title, the cost of which only very rich people could afford. The colonial officer had given a staff of office to one of the rich men in the clan to be king. Of course the installed monarch wanted to create his own power base and amass wealth by granting chieftaincy titles to men and women in the community that could afford the high price he prescribed. To further their own ends, many rich men jumped at the new opportunity to have social leverage over others in the community. Descendants of low-born or servants rose astronomically to become chiefs. In their noble robes, they looked down on those who used to deride them as lowborn. Those descended from once noble families but now without money were demoted to the bottom of the social ladder. Shegbe shot up from a moderate family stock into prominence in the clan.

As the Osiolele of Agbon, Shegbe attracted money, wives, and children. His wealth redoubled within a short time. With wealth and the newly acquired title, Shegbe began to wield much influence in the community. Nobody murmured that Okpara was only his mother's side and that his father had come as a guest to Okpara and stayed for good.

Nobody in town took him to be an alien as they derided Saduwa with the same background. His hard work, wealth, and chiefly title had absolved him from being seen as a stranger. He built a big house as had not been seen in Okpara before. He married two other wives to show his superiority over others with one or two wives. His family was large—there was always noise of children, as expected of a big man's house. His house was a beehive of activities—friends and relatives came in to pay homage or just fraternize with him. Drinks and kola nuts were always plentiful. Food was also there for the hungry.

With time those who were financially strapped asked for a loan to do one thing or another. A feverish child needed APC, M&B, Codeine, or Aspirin to get well. A wife needed a new wrapper or some other type of dress for the traditional festival, and the husband came to borrow money to purchase her needs to avoid ceaseless harassment at home and denial of favours. Some men wanted to buy hooks and nets at the approach of the rainy season. Others wanted to buy a gramophone or a bicycle to live a more comfortable life. There was so much that people needed money for and only one person around was rich enough to assist with a loan. And that person was Chief Shegbe, the Osiolele of Agbon.

Chief Shegbe had a mental record of whom he loaned money. He knew how to calculate money very well. In the loans he gave out, he did not ask for interests but you had to pay back his loan at the specified time. Once you were indebted to him, your entire household was his. Your children were his, if you continued owing him beyond the agreed date. Your wife and daughters belonged to him, if you broke your promise to pay back his loan on the agreed month or season. In a way, you ceded all you owned to him if you failed to meet your terms of payment.

"Loans are not gifts," he warned those who came to him. "You have to pay back for others to be also helped and if you fail, you have to forfeit what is dear to you."

"I agree," his desperate creditor would reply.

"Do you understand the implication of your agreement to my terms?" he asked.

"I do."

Such a desperate person had very few options to choose from and so had to succumb to any terms offered.

Every transaction was done by word of mouth between Chief Shegbe and whoever was asking for the loan. It was an agreement based on trust and nobody in the community expected the most bizarre of happenings to take place as a result of the loan taken to meet a need.

Most people kept their promises and paid back their debts on time. But one day Chief Shegbe demonstrated that to remain rich he had to be strict. "Soft people can't get rich," he once told his friends. "It's because you give out what you have out of sympathy that you are left with nothing to boast of."

Ituru's debt was up to one hundred and fifty tins of palm oil or fifty pounds. The agreement was based on the cash value of palm oil at the time. It would take a very hard worker more than five years to produce that amount of oil. Ituru realized with time that he had to work himself to death if he would be in a position to pay off the debt to Chief Shegbe by the agreed time. Every morning he was out with his climbing ropes to harvest ripe bunches of palm fruits or gone to the palm oil press. In other seasons he was in his farm planting yams. He also fished during the rainy season.

Nobody complained that he was lazy. He worked and worked but there was not much to show for his industry. He could only pay off about thirty tins of oil each year, if he was to sustain his small family with what he earned. He was no longer in his prime and his productivity had gone down with age. Ituru no longer had the vigour of one who could make sixty or more tins of palm oil a year. He paid off some tins, but he still had many years ahead to settle the entire debt, which he had chosen to settle with palm oil rather than pounds. He could not imagine his ever amassing fifty pounds to settle his debt. After paying the British-imposed head tax that every adult had to pay or be thrown into jail, he did not have more than five pounds in a year. He had made peace with himself that slowly he would produce the tins of palm oil that he needed to settle his debt. He worked towards freeing himself from Chief Shegbe's debt or ownership of his family and property if he failed to meet the terms of their agreement.

The poor man could not settle all he owed Chief Shegbe before he fell ill and suddenly died. Fellow townsmen said anxiety over his heavy debt killed him. Too much work to defray Chief Shegbe's debts killed him, many Okpara people also said.

"Ituru has no wife that will please Chief Shegbe!"

"Ituru has no daughter for Chief Shebe to take in place of the unpaid loan."

"Ituru's mud house will not entice Chief Shegbe!"

Everybody in the community waited for what the rich man who was also a chief would do after the death of his debtor.

"Chief Shegbe never forgives," people said.

Nobody ever contemplated the surprising manner that Chief Shegbe handled the death of his debtor.

Chief Shegbe was a very forceful man. Nobody dared contradict him in his actions. Though he was kind to give out loans, he was a fiery man that nobody who did not need financial assistance would come near. Like the *Iphri* god, he could roast a defaulter of his debt without pity. He could protect you by giving you loans at difficult times, but he also could destroy you if you failed to meet the agreed terms of paying back. As long as you owed him, you were at his mercy. And this power he exercised over the living without being questioned, he would exercise over a dead debtor.

He had got news of Ituru's sickness and had already contemplated what action he would take should he die. It did not take him time to act as soon as the news came of his debtor's death. He ordered the corpse of his debtor to be brought to him and be buried in some patch of land in his own family land unless his debt was paid. He pointed to some bush that was his land far behind his house. Everybody knew that Ituru's case would be a test of Chief Shegbe's strictness in order to remain rich.

The people believed that one came back to the world from where one was buried; hence in death bodies were taken back to the family home. If Ituru were buried in Shegbe's land, their family would be depleted by one adult; dead or alive. In addition, the stigma of indebtedness would cling to the family like a badge of dishonour for generations to come. Anybody born into his family would, by association, be infected by the shame of indebtedness.

Ituru's family surrendered his body to be taken to Chief Shegbe's compound and laid in a corner by the bush. Nobody disputed Ituru's debt. It was public knowledge that he owed the rich chief. Nor did any one dispute Chief Shegbe's right to claim the body. A promise had to be kept, the people knew very well. Up till now they had thought that only the living had to keep their promises. They learnt from Chief Shegbe that the dead had to pay their debts too or be held as a hostage whose ransom had to be paid to be released.

At first some of Ituru's family members took it as a joke.

"Let him bury Ituru and save us the trouble," one said.

"Chief Shegbe should invite us to the wake and burial of Ituru. Let him buy the drinks we need for the burial ceremony," another family member said.

"He has more than enough money to take over our responsibilities," someone said.

"Let Shegbe and the dead fight over money that he so much likes," one man said.

However, sober reflection soon came in. The death of a poor relative was not a joking matter at all. Blood relationship exacts its toll, Ituru's family soon realized.

"Ituru might be poor when alive but in death he must be a free man," the deceased's cousin said.

"He has thrown his burden at us with his death," another relative said.

"We cannot shelve our responsibilities. He was ours and still ours. Let us save our man from the disgrace—he cannot be a worthy ancestor buried in the bush belonging to the chief."

"Did you hear that Shegbe says he will spit at the corpse before it is buried in the bush?" a relative, who claimed to have heard this, told his kinsfolk.

"If he is buried in the bush, as Chief Shegbe will likely order his men to do soon, Ituru's spirit will continue to haunt us," another said.

"Where will his children commune with him, if he is buried outside the family land?"

"How are we sure that he will be buried as a whole human being?" Odede asked, fuelling fears that none had contemplated saying out.

They feared that some of his body parts could be removed to make powerful medicines. The unclaimed body could be an opportunity to make Shegbe even richer because he could do anything to the body that he now owned.

Many of the people believed that medicine-men sought the hair and genitals of the dead to prepare strong medicines for those who wanted them. Such medicine-men would hit a bonanza with such vital human parts very hard to come by. Of course they would buy them at an exorbitant rate and also charge their clients cut-throat prices for medicines to solve desperate problems.

This dimension added a sense of desperation to recovering Ituru's body from Chief Shegbe before it was tampered with. They wanted their deceased relative's body intact and whole. They could not imagine an Ituru in later generations being born without some body parts such as ears, eyes, and hands. They did not want to contemplate a penis-less man in the Ituru family!

"What can a rich man not do to increase his wealth?" one man asked.

"We should not allow this to happen," another in the family gathering said.

"Let everybody go home and search for every penny hidden anywhere in the house and bring it," the eldest in the extended family ordered.

"If Ituru does not in his death come back to our family ground, the shame is on us the living and not on him."

"We are all debtors by association," the oldest man said, drumming the seriousness of the matter into their heads.

"We must all come back before taking supper," the old man told his extended family. "We cannot eat with the weight of this debt on our heads."

The gathering broke to reassemble by late evening.

By evening the family had rallied and collected the amount that Ituru owed, and were ready to settle the debt that would enable them to reclaim their kinsman's corpse. Raising the money to pay back the debt had brought almost everything each of them had. Those who kept their savings under their mattresses brought everything as those who kept money in big jars dug into the floor of their bedrooms. Everybody related to Ituru took the challenge of reclaiming his body seriously. The announcement to all in the family had gone far and wide and fortunately they made the remaining forty pounds of the original debt of fifty pounds.

The family members did not care what the burial ceremony would cost, after they had spent all they had to reclaim the body. One has to get relief from what is biting one first before what is merely irritating one, the oldest in the family said; they all concurred.

The oldest in the family and a five-man delegation took the money to Chief Shegbe, who smiled at seeing them placing down the correct amount of money.

"Here's your money," the eldest told him.

"Thank you for helping out your dead brother. As relatives inherit property or other forms of wealth, so should they also inherit debts," Shegbe told him.

"Now that you draw debts from the dead, let them also deal with you for the humiliation you have caused them," the Ituru elder told him.

"Are you threatening me in my own house?" Shegbe asked.

Ituru's relatives walked out of his house. For the generation that knew what happened, no Ituru had gone to a Shegbe house and vice versa.

At home Ituru's extended family members thought of the burial expenses of the body they now had in their hands. They had stripped themselves to pay the ransom of Ituru's corpse.

“We saved him from a big disgrace already and it doesn’t matter now how we bury him,” one of the Iturus said.

“At least the earth will not reject his body,” another relative said.

“Now that we have brought him home, he is always welcome no matter the manner of his farewell.”

That night they buried Ituru in the dark.

5

The Captain's Apology

It was a humid evening that brought no respite indoors or outdoors. A crowded room was too suffocating to bear. When Captain David Segine alighted from a taxi in front of his rented off-white painted house that Monday evening at dusk, his wife and her friends and family members commiserating with her were sitting outside. The dampness of the weather and the deep grief told on those gathered there. Though it was twilight, it was not difficult to see the taxi painted with the yellow of taxis that plied the city's roads. On top of its roof was the red-lit TAXI for easy recognition. Those gathered to console the bereaved young widow were distracted; they turned to watch the yellow taxi pull up at the right curb of the road in front of the house. An undeveloped plot stood between the house and the road. Since the owner of the plot had died in a motor accident, his relatives had not arrived at who should own the plot.

The gathering of mourners saw the passenger at the back seat fumbling with the right back door for a moment before the driver came out to open it. The mourners watched. They thought of either more friends or family members who had heard the sad news coming to console Edirin, David's wife. There had been a stream of people coming and leaving the past two days. It all began almost as soon as the bad news broke out. The young couple's house had turned into an open house which men and women came to and left when done with their commiserating with the grieving young wife.

"Have a strong heart," many told her.

"Everything is God's will," others said.

"Only God will help you to bear this sad loss," the religious ones told Edirin.

Words of wisdom poured from many mouths.

The death of a young man was sad enough, but David Segine's was even sadder. Here was a young man who had a good chance of rising to become a major-general in the Nigerian Army, if the unexpected had not happened. David was doing so well in the Army that he had good prospects in his career of becoming an army commander or a military governor at a time when coups were so common. He had shown smartness in his job to endear him not only to his senior officers but also to his colleagues and friends. In his Second Division, he was among the few captains expected to be promoted to the rank of major when the list would be published in three months.

But Captain David Segine also had a young wife who had just conceived after three years of marriage. The conception had brought joy and relief to both husband and wife, who were both beginning to question their ability to have a child.

"You will be fine with time," some elderly relatives told Edirin Segine.

"Have faith in God and pray for strength," her church members added.

"Everything that happens is God's will," others said.

The taxi driver opened the right rear door, pulling it wide towards his side so as to give enough room for the passenger to come out. Those sitting and facing the street turned their gaze to who was joining them to grieve and console the young widow that fate had struck a terrible blow.

In the half-light a man came out clumsily and balanced himself on both legs, as if he was unsteady on something or had a disability. The figure then stepped forward, and all eyes gazed at him as he moved towards them and his profile gradually became fuller and clearer. It was like a thick fog lifting from a hidden figure. Soon that figure became recognizable as the man they had come to mourn.

After his profile became clear, there was a sudden blackout street-wide. It happened so fast that everybody was in struck dumb and felt immediately cold with fear. As he took his next step, a soot-black blanket was thrown over everybody. The air turned eerie and the bold amidst the frightened group let out a simultaneous fearful shout of "Who's this coming?"

A stampede broke out. Some circled their fingers round their heads and snapped them.

"Not me!"

"You didn't meet me in your house!"

"Go back to where you belong!"

These frightened people were all addressing the ghost they believed they saw.

Edirin and everybody else took to their heels. David Segine's ghost was on the loose, they thought, and each ran away so as not to be on the way of the ghost of the young officer they believed had burnt to ashes with his many colleagues in a plane disaster, three days earlier. It was a bad omen to see a ghost, but worse still to encounter closely the ghost of one being mourned. Nobody wanted to be struck dead by the ghost of the person they were mourning.

Captain Segine was dressed in army fatigues; the same dress that he had worn on the Friday when he had left the house and said he was going to catch the army plane to Kaduna. Without blinking or looking at those fleeing from him, he went straight into his own house. He was dazed by the act of people running away from him, but he did not know how to react. It had happened so quickly. Was he to shout at them to stay or run after them? He did not know where they were running to and he could not run after them shouting his name. He was not crazy, he knew. His steps were heavy but sure for someone come to his own house. He noticed the confusion outside his house. There was an assortment of drinks, beer, Coke, Sprite, Fanta beside glasses. The place smelled of beer; the drinks had spilled from glasses and bottles, as those drinking them scrambled out to be out of sight of the person they thought was a ghost.

David walked through his wake and stepped into the parlour that was almost bare of chairs. He went straight into his bedroom. He crumpled into the King-size bed that was not made and appeared not to have been slept in, in the past day or two. He knew how Edirin used to be so meticulous about the bed. She liked making the bed neatly with colourful bedspread, sheets, and pillow cases. The house appeared to have changed from its warmth into a solitary cold place. However, he knew he was in his own house and not somewhere else. That realization gave him confidence not to worry about himself.

Alone and quiet, he looked at himself in the bedroom mirror. He saw himself as the same person who had passed by the house three days earlier to tell his wife that he was going to the airport to return to his base in Kaduna. That reflection made him real; hence he did not think of changing clothes.

David fell asleep in his army fatigues and had a series of dreams. In one of them, he was piloting a plane to bomb a building in which the military president and his armed forces ruling council were holding a meeting. In another, he was in a battle trench waiting to ambush an enemy when a snake emerged, and he had to jump out into a circle of prisoners of war.

He left the dark curtains down. To him, it did not matter whether it was day or night. He slept and had dreams until it was already daybreak.

It took a whole day before a medicine man that his wife and family had consulted and asked for help in the strange case went into the house in the late afternoon. The medicine man, whose name was Ojokoto, had come with the intention of exorcizing the evil spirit of the deceased from the house so that his widow could return and live to bear their child. He did not promise a miracle.

He told Edirin and members of the Segine family how dangerous the ghost of a young man could be after an untimely death. He explained that old people did not have ghosts because they immediately joined the ancestors. But not a young man like David Segine who, according to popular belief, had so much life left in him, after dying in a plane crash.

Ojokoto had some trepidation when he entered the house. But he realized that he had to impress those who expected some answers to a supernatural problem. As an experienced medicine-man, he put on his bravado to perform his duties. He started to chant some esoteric argots to drive out whatever evil spirit lurked in the house. He became more emboldened the more he chanted.

Going into the bedroom, he saw a man on the big bed.

"Leave, all evil spirits. I command you to leave. Leave!" he shouted.

Captain Segine turned around in the bed and saw a man costumed in cowries chanting and waving a flywhisk. Sunlight was filtering into the bedroom from a side window.

"Are you the owner of the house?" Ojokoto asked.

"Yes," he answered.

"Are you well?" he again asked.

"Yes."

"Why did they say that you had died?"

"You can see that I am alive."

David Segine got out of the bed. He shook hands with Ojokoto.

"Wait for me. I'll be back shortly," the medicine-man said.

Ojokoto went out with a swagger that only a successful medicine-man could muster. He realized what he had just achieved. It was a miracle to turn a ghost into a living human being.

In front of the house were gathered Edirin, relatives, and friends waiting for Ojokoto to come back and give them instructions on what to do. They were all downcast and thinking of not only dealing with the grief of David's death but also being threatened by his ghost. They were surprised by the manner that Ojokoto swaggered out of the house, as if he was a clown and not a medicine-man dealing with a serious issue.

"I've done my work. You all will be very pleased with it," he announced.

"What do you mean?" an old cousin of David asked.

Ojokoto placed his right palm over his mouth. He would not answer any question, and that confused the people even more. However, he went to Edirin, held her by the right hand, as a few immediate family members looked on, and led her into the house. As they went into the house, Edirin thought Ojokoto was playing pranks with her so as to charge enough money to live on for the rest of the month. Before they entered the bedroom, Ojokoto paused.

"Your husband is now alive. If he died, he is now alive," he told her.

When Edirin first saw her husband, she took one step backwards and wanted to run again. However, Ojokoto held her tight and David beckoned to her to come to him, as he himself moved forward. In an instant Edirin's fear disappeared. She sprang forward to embrace David who had already opened his arms. They embraced and remained glued to each other.

David spoke first.

"I'm sorry," he told his wife.

He realized she now knew he had gone somewhere else instead of going back to Kaduna that fateful Friday.

"Let's thank God for your survival," she told him.

David could feel the warmth of her pregnancy. Three hearts were beating. David and Edirin appeared to be studying each other's eyes. At this moment, the family members came in to see the couple clasped to one another. They were dumbfounded and just stared at what was before them. A miracle had happened.

Ojokoto became instantly famous for confronting a ghost and solving a bad case. He had turned a ghost into a living human being. With such confidence, he told Edirin and the rest of the family that they should pay him what they thought he deserved. He was not going to charge them a specific amount. He said he would give them time to reacquaint themselves with David Segine and he would return for his fee in three days. The members of the family around begged him to accept what they could collect from those around. He made ten thousand naira for confronting a ghost. And he expected much more when he came back for his fee. And that upon the publicity this single case would generate!

Only Captain Segine knew the story of his miraculous survival from the military plane that blew up in the air and disintegrated into ashes.

* * *

Captain David Segine had been happy about a free trip and the opportunity to be in Lagos. He had not had the time to visit Lagos for almost four months. His wife of three years was still there and had informed him that she was pregnant. He had hoped that his transfer to Kaduna would be short, part of a rotation of troops that made no sense to him. The military head of state had asked his army commander to transfer his junior and middle-rank officers as often as possible to prevent them from plotting coups against him. Leaving them for too long in one station offered them the chance of acquiring close friends with whom to plot coups. So David was not surprised at his transfer to Kaduna.

But after he had settled in his job there, the posting had become almost permanent. He believed that once he brought his wife to Kaduna, he would be transferred somewhere else again. He thus dismissed the idea of bringing Edirin to Kaduna. He had paid the rent for two years in Lagos and if he left the house before the two years ran out, that money would be lost. He decided Lagos would be his main home while Kaduna was temporary for now. He lived in a one-bedroom flat in Kaduna.

The last time he had flown to Lagos, he had travelled with Ebisan, who had then invited him to visit her in her Suru-Lere residence. They had met at the Kaduna airport's departure lounge on a Friday evening flight. She had introduced herself as a businesswoman. She looked comfortable. Ebisan was a very beautiful and cheerful woman. They had sat together in the plane and chatted all the way. It surprised both of them that they had talked as if they had known each other for months, if not for years. Ever since that flight, they had been phoning each other. A week barely passed without their keeping in touch. To Ebisan's persistent question of when he would visit her, David always replied "Soon."

"This your soon go be another year or two. You wan make I die before you go come see me?" she once asked.

"Just be patient. I go come," he told her.

"Lie-lie man you be. Na so you dey say you go come soon and three months don pass. Na so be soon?"

"You think say if I get the chance, I go stay for Kaduna? I go come Lagos quick quick!"

"When I see you for my house, I go know say you no dey lie," Ebisan told him on the phone.

The chance for Captain David Segine to be in Lagos came four months after his last trip, when he had flown in with Ebisan. He informed Ebisan that he was coming to participate in a workshop and would do his possible best to see her after his official task was done.

The workshop of the junior and middle-level officers on "Vigilance and combat-readiness" was very intense and there was barely any time to visit family or friends before returning to Kaduna. It was intense not because the participants were learning much but because they were kept occupied all the time. The military dictator was scared to death about the possibility of a coup against him and he asked his Army Commander to arrange the workshop to hammer it into the heads of possible coup plotters that anyone caught would be executed by firing squad. The participants were promised a heavy allowance for taking part. So, in the workshop, unknown to the majority of the officers, spies listened as they discussed coups, counter-coups, and the military in politics. Every participant took notes to be seen as attentive and serious. During the many breaks, there was plenty of cake as well as tea and soft drinks to wash it down, as the catering officer put it to them.

When the week's workshop in Lagos ended on Friday at 12 noon, Captain Segine felt he needed to use his time wisely. It would be difficult for him to get the opportunity to visit Lagos again soon and spend time with Ebisan. He did not want to apply for a pass to travel now that junior and middle-rank officers were being watched. Unauthorized travels would lead to suspicion, and he did not want to be marked for special attention.

Every participant in the workshop was expected to take the flight back to Kaduna.

"The flight back is at 6:00 p.m. All officers must report at the local wing of the Murtala Mohammed Airport at 5:00 p.m. prompt. If you are late, you are on your own," the brigadier in charge of the workshop had told Captain Segine's group of mainly lieutenant colonels, majors, and captains.

Captain Segine interpreted what it meant to be on your own in his own way. He was not the poor officer that a mere seven thousand naira of airfare could stop from having his fill of what he wanted. There was no threat of any disciplinary action against an officer who failed to arrive at five o'clock. After all, he could plead that the notorious Lagos traffic jam had prevented him from arriving on time for the flight. He could take any flight he liked afterwards. That was no problem for him. All that was necessary was for him to show up at his desk on Monday morning at eight o'clock. That he could manage conveniently with either a late Sunday night flight or a very early Monday morning flight. With so many flights to Kaduna, there would be no problem being at his desk on Monday morning. After all, officers could arrive late in the office "due to heavy traffic and domestic emergency," he knew from experience. And so to Ebisan's flat he headed.

Ebisan had called him while still in the workshop at Bonny Camp that she was preparing a special gift for him and promised him something she had not given to any other man before. Captain Segine wondered what Ebisan's gift would be. He thought of a thousand possibilities but could still not imagine what that gift would be. When a woman who he believed was not a virgin promised you a gift she had not given to any other man before, what should you expect? He asked himself.

Thoughts of Ebisan made him not to concentrate in the latter part of the workshop. His mind was not at the military workshop sessions but in Suru-Lere with Ebisan and the special gift she was keeping for him. On the flight many months ago, he had inhaled the fragrance of her perfume. He now wished to immerse himself in her sexy smell. He was fixated by the features of a woman in her prime. He saw in his mind Ebisan's velvety black skin that shone. He imagined what she would look like when she was prepared to receive him.

Captain Segine had been startled when asked a question in the workshop while daydreaming about Ebisan.

"Are you sleeping, Captain?" Brigadier Adedoye asked.

"No sir, I am listening to you sir," he replied.

"Be more attentive. This is serious stuff," the brigadier counseled.

"Yes sir," he said and saluted.

His other colleagues were jotting down whatever was coming out of the brigadier's mouth. Captain Segine wanted the workshop over as soon as possible. His mind was far away in Suru-Lere, in a house he had never visited.

* * *

Captain Segine left his pregnant wife in Akoka and went to see Ebisan in Suru-Lere, in another part of the city. It was the new woman that was a magnet. He gave the excuse to Edirin that he had to be at the airport on time—better to be there very early than get there late and miss the flight.

"You can't predict Lagos traffic," he told her.

"When will I see you again?" Edirin asked.

"Soon," he replied.

"But you rarely have the time from work to come this way," she protested.

"You'll see me soon. I'll look for an opportunity to come and spend some time with you."

"Okay-oo!" Edirin said cynically.

Captain Segine took a taxi to 38 Ovu Street, Suru-Lere. The taxi driver, who had been working in Lagos for many years, knew his way through the labyrinth of roads. In forty-five minutes, the driver dropped Captain Segine at his destination.

Captain Segine was welcomed warmly to Ebisan's flat. She was wearing a beautifully designed boubou, and had prepared and rehearsed a welcome ritual for her visitor. She took him first to her bedroom to put down his bag. Once he saw her bedroom, he would crave to be there, she believed. It was a cozy room that a man would like to pass the night in. The curtains, bed sheets, and everything in the bedroom were very stylish. Captain Segine had not seen a bedroom as beautiful and splendidly decorated as this one before. Not even the five-star hotels he had slept in were as cozy. Ebisan turned on the blue and red bedroom lights which produced a cozy atmosphere. She clapped her hands and the lights went off—the blue first, then the red.

She led him back to the sitting room. She showed him a sofa to sit in. The sofa took two people but she did not sit there with him. She believed in the gradual process of doing many things and being intimate was one of them. Then she brought out a bottle of red wine, which she said she bought specially for him. She opened the wine bottle and filled two special glasses. She handed one to him and then took hers. She raised her glass.

"Let me toast this to the success of your workshop," she said.

"Better toast it to our meeting in your house," he said.

"Okay. This is to our health and happiness," she said.

"To our health and happiness," David repeated.

They clicked the glasses. They smiled at each other.

Ebisan was self-assured and methodical. She asked David about the workshop, and after his description of the whole exercise as a waste of time, she went to set the table. She had already prepared a special vegetable fish soup with semolina. She had gleaned from him what he liked the most and David had told her about his love of fish. They ate, talking and looking at each other. David had told his wife, when offered food, that he was not hungry; now he ate voraciously.

The air-conditioner blew cold air.

"I didn't know you will really come," Ebisan told him.

"Here I am," David replied.

"I am happy you are able to make it at last. Now you no be wayo man again."

"I no be wayo man at any time," David told her.

"Make I dey call you Captain or wetin you want make I call you?" she asked.

"Call me David or Captain. All na the same thing," he told her.

"Okay. I go call you Captain. You be officer. If you command me I go obey," she said.

"Here na your house. Make you command me," he replied playfully.

"You fit obey woman command?" she asked.

"Why not? Woman strong pass General?"

"If you no know you go know woman power," she said, laughing.

Captain David Segine stood up and saluted Ebisan, who rose from her seat to embrace him.

What happened after would not only forever please David but save his life. He had come not quite sure of how things would go between Ebisan and him. Now her house was so cosy that he followed her when she said, "Let's go into the bedroom and relax."

David was treated to sex as he had never been before. An unmarried woman, or rather a single woman, was different from one's wife in bed, he mused. A woman in love did so much in bed to impress her lover, he discovered. No wonder, she had been asking me to visit, he told himself. This woman really knows how to treat a man. She fills me with excitement and joy, he mused.

This was not an experience he wanted to give up just like that. Instantly he decided to stay a little longer and go back on a commercial flight very early on Monday morning. He did not care whether he would be late for work or not. He knew the excuse to give. Traffic was always a problem. Every army family could have an emergency any morning to keep him late for work.

"What's money meant for?" he asked himself.

He had more than enough money to take care of his flight back and join his colleagues on Monday morning. After all, the entire workshop, he and his colleagues knew, was a fat bribe not to rock the boat of General Ali Mustafa Dongo, the president.

* * *

Flight NA00 did not take off at 6:00 p.m. as had been scheduled. Army engineers in the process of inspecting and servicing the plane before take-off discovered problems with the fuel tank's gauge. It was not working and they could not tell how much fuel was left in the tank. There was no time to place an order for a new fuel gauge. Things took time to procure in the National Army. This would take a week or more of filling forms, signing them, and getting them to and from the Quartermaster-General's office.

One engineer used a stick to test the gauge. The stick was too short and was of no use in determining the amount of fuel inside the tank.

"There must be enough fuel. Is it not Kaduna we are flying to? Are we flying to London?' he asked his colleagues.

They laughed hilariously at his joke.

Officers had been drinking in the special waiting hall and conversing loudly. Some were already drunk when the call for boarding of NA00 flight to Kaduna came.

"Na here we go sleep?" Lieutenant-Colonel Izobo asked.

"Make we go," another Lieutenant-Colonel shouted.

The senior officers had spoken.

The plane took off at 8:05 p.m.

On the following morning, the news of the plane crash woke the nation. The BBC, VOA, local radio and television stations and late-edition newspapers splashed the tragic story. The Army announced that all one hundred and fifty on-board were killed—it did not take any count of who was in the plane; there was no manifest. One hundred and fifty officers had attended the workshop and all were presumed to have taken the flight and perished.

It took some time to know where the military plane had crashed. By the time rescue teams arrived at the crash site on late Saturday morning, they could only see shredded flesh, blackened bones, luggage items scattered everywhere. There was no corpse that could be identified.

The shock of the crash brought a cold to the whole nation. It was like the feeling when a firing squad had taken the lives of Major Dabang and his group of coup plotters about ten years earlier. The old remembered that time when they imagined even the fish underwater had caught a cold! To respect the memory of the crash victims, the Federal Military Government declared a week of national mourning. It also ordered that the national flag be flown at half-mast.

Mrs. Ediri Segine collapsed in tears when she heard of the plane crash and the news of no survivors. Only yesterday afternoon her husband had stopped by for a brief hour to tell her he was on his way to the airport to his post in Kaduna. Much as he knew that she wanted him, he had listened to the call of duty and headed for the airport, she reflected.

"Why did I not stop him?" she wailed, as if she ought to have had premonitions of the crash and stopped him from travelling.

She regretted her shyness that had not allowed her to tell him that she wanted him. Had she told him, he would have listened, she believed. She knew how weak he became after they made love. He would have fallen asleep after and missed his flight.

She thought of other things she should have done to stop him from going. Now it was too late, and had resulted in tragedy.

* * *

It took Captain Segine more than two days to figure out what to do. Officially he was among the crash victims. To his wife and family, he was dead, without a trace in the ash-ridden site of the crash.

He had heard the news of the crash in Ebisan's bedroom and did not leave there during the rest of his stay. Ebisan brought food to the bedroom for them to eat, but the Captain was like a paralysed man whose body lacked mobility. He who the previous night had eaten voraciously, and almost stayed awake with excitement, had suddenly lost his appetite and desire for food and everything else.

"You no happy say you no die? Make you celebrate with me," Ebisan told him.

At night he still made love with her but he had lost his zest for the woman who had attracted him like a magnet from the workshop. The woman whose call he had listened to like a spell was there but not quite the same woman again. His body was heavy.

It was easy for Ebisan to detect the difference between the Friday night and the subsequent nights. On the first night she had shouted "Captain" over and over again. She had met many men, but Captain, true to his name, was a real captain. The military power and the woman's power had cancelled themselves out and, when tired, both had fallen asleep at the same time. They woke up when the sun was already up and the sad news of the crash in the air.

"See me see trouble-o. Make you happy say you no die," Ebisan shouted at him. "Which one you dey do like you be ghost. Make you thank me say I save you from death," she again told him.

He was silent. He could not tell whether he was alive or dead.

It was on the third day of his refuge at Ebisan's flat that Captain David Segine decided to face the reality of his situation. He was alive. He had to go home. He wanted to tell his wife where he had been and how he had missed the ill-fated flight. He would apologise to her for his lies and deceit and hoped she would forgive him so that together both of them would thank God that he was alive. He told himself that anyone who had escaped death as he had done must become a new person, which he swore he would. His survival needed rejoicing, the manner of which he would arrange with Edirin. He put on the army dress he had worn on his way to Suru-Lere and took his bag. He was on his way home.

6

Under New Pastoral Management

In Effurun, the Pentecostal churches had mushroomed in the streets at a weekly regularity that amazed many residents. A banner, bell, or crusade would invite passers-by to such new churches. Often presided over by a single pastor or a couple, each new church took the form of a private or family business. However, a majority of the new churches that made Effurun look like a Christian town despite the many public shrines to native gods did not grow beyond their first few months, before becoming stunted. But there were a few exceptions.

The Church of the New Dawn had established itself as the most popular of the many new Pentecostal churches in the town. Nobody made fun of it as a family business centre, as they did of the very small ones. Its congregation was a mixture of Christians from other faiths such as the Roman Catholic, Baptist, and Anglican, as well as converts attracted by the charismatic evangelist's heart-warming sermons about here and now.

Those stricken by malaria too often, and who believed it was not caused by mosquito bites but some sinister power, came to Evangelist Peter for a permanent cure. So did those who believed they were working very hard and not becoming rich, but sinking deeper into hardship and penury; they came to the Church of the New Dawn for special prayers, for an upturn in their fortune. And many young women who could not find husbands, as well as married women whose husbands were philanderers, also came to the church for answers to their problems.

Men and women who dreamed of riches did not go to work on the days that Evangelist Peter wanted to say prayers about personal breakthroughs. Women who found it difficult to conceive came to break the curse on their wombs in the Church of the New Dawn. Such women left their men at home to attend regular all-night prayer vigils so that the Evangelist could crush the demons making them sterile. Since most of the people suffered from diseases, hardship, and broken hearts, they came in droves for relief.

"It's always never too late to get a cure for your problems," Evangelist Peter would exhort his attentive congregation.

He often characterized his work as that of a spiritual doctor.

"You are currently besieged by dark forces of night, but you will certainly come into a new dawn!" he would tell his new converts.

"Alleluia!" they chorused.

"Whatever you want God to do for you will come true in the Church of the New Dawn," he said.

"Amen!" reverberated in the church.

There was so much enthusiasm for this church that wives disobeyed their husbands and left the churches they had married in for the Church of the New Dawn.

Evangelist Peter was in his late thirties and still single. He was rather chubby but very agile in movement. He was the only single pastor of the many Pentecostal churches around. He had in one sermon wondered out loud why men and women hurried to marry when Jesus died still a bachelor at thirty-three. His congregation believed he wanted to give his whole energy, time, and attention to God's work.

Evangelist Peter also cited the many mature women such as Martha and Mary Magdalene who did not marry, but assisted Jesus in his mission. Members of his congregation did not know how to interpret his many reflections on marriage, but felt he was biding his time to get a wife suitable for his pastoral mission. Better to be patient to catch the right woman than be impatient and be ruined by a Jezebel, such people reasoned to explain the marital status of Evangelist Peter.

He was always dressed neatly in a white, blue, or black suit and appeared well groomed for every service, which was an opportunity for him to show how kind God had been to him. His choice of the type of suit to wear for service was informed by the spirit of the time. On happy days, thanksgiving services, and the annual harvest, he wore immaculate white. Dark blue was for ordinary times, while the black suit was for sober moments.

"God is so kind, God is so good; my God is fantastic," he asked his congregation to repeat.

And they did so with rebounding passion. They expected so much from God and they believed that, through Evangelist Peter's intervention, their hopes would be realized.

"My God is a trustworthy God," he sang.

There is nothing a good Christian wants that God will not give to the person; through prayers the human and the divine can dialogue, he told his church members.

On Sundays, as Evangelist Peter railed against witches, wizards, and demons from the pulpit, loudspeakers, specially mounted on the church's rooftop, would blaze his message of defeating evil forces with special prayers. Every passer-by heard his holy message. The neighbourhood heard him.

"Jesus will make you vanquish all sorts of demons. No witch or wizard can penetrate one covered by the blood of Jesus. You in the arms of Jesus are the winner. Say 'I am a winner!'"

"I am a winner!" the congregation would chorus.

"Praise the Lord!"

"Alleluia!"

Those who felt vulnerable before suspected diabolic forces holding them down in life or threatened with poverty, accidents, sickness, or death flocked to the church for protection. Evangelist Peter was their shield against evil forces. His church would also ensure their salvation. These salvation-seekers had something to hold on to so as to be secure and safe from a myriad of perils. In Evangelist Peter's view, Jesus was a giant that his flock held to or just came to for protection. The presence of a giant or his proximity was great protection for the neighbours. Jesus was their family man or neighbour, he explained.

"If now you have no food to eat, Jesus will fill your plate with enough yams to last you all your life. Believe in the Son of God and He will work miracles for you!" he preached.

The frequent split and subsequent breakups in the Baptist and Anglican churches benefited the Church of the New Dawn. Every personality squabbles in the other churches left a group drifting to Evangelist Peter's church rather than suffering the humiliation of their faction being defeated.

Also those Catholics who felt that their church was too rigid and took no cognizance of modern life found it convenient to become members of the Church of the New Dawn. Among such were divorcees who could not remarry in the Catholic Church but were allowed to have new partners in the Church of the New Dawn. Evangelist Peter was silent on polygamy.

"Only God the Father is the judge," he told his congregation on this issue.

That opened the way for a few polygamists in the church to pass the word to others outside who needed a church to worship in. Evangelist Peter welcomed everybody who wanted to know God into his church.

The rather tall and smooth-faced evangelist was happy. He glowed. He walked with a swagger, which, though looked natural, came from confidence in his pastoral mission. His crowded church was the envy of other new churches that could barely draw fifty people into the rented or uncompleted buildings they used for Sunday worship or service at other times. Two nearby mushroom churches whose services used to be drowned by the loudspeakers of the Church of the New Dawn closed to join Evangelist Peter's congregation. He praised the Lord for His kind mercies.

Evangelist Peter practised what his congregation called humility and modesty. He had a Mercedes Benz 280 and not a Toyota Land Cruiser or a Lincoln Navigator that other pastors of the few bigger churches around drove. Besides, he drove himself. He had rejected pleas by his congregation for him to have a driver.

"What do I need a driver for when I can drive myself?" he asked those who made such a suggestion to him.

"Maybe when I become older, I'll need a driver. Certainly not now," he told them.

He often took along one or two of his church members as he desired on trips that were described as "church mission". His congregation so revered him that whoever was chosen for a "church mission" felt blessed. Others yearned for such a blessing but discovered that Evangelist Peter tended to select the same woman or others for his trips to advance the faith.

* * *

The church building was imposing not only because of its size but also because of its sophisticated architecture. It was oval, rather like a dome in shape. Perched on the hilly part of town and surrounded by lush green vegetation it stood alone, dominating the landscape. From the low surroundings, the valley that was the main town, one could not look up north without being captured by the spectacle of the oval house of God. It was grand even from a distance. It was like the huge mansion of a rich man with refined tastes. And it held in its precincts a solemnity comparable to any cathedral that the Evangelist had entered in Rome in one of his several pilgrimages there.

The church compound was floored with concrete and the roads were tiled. From the spacious parking lot to the church was laid a red carpet of shiny tiles. Different types of plants and flowers beautified the landscape. Eucalyptus, whispering pines, hibiscus, crotons, and exotic palms brought a certain natural harmony to the church compound.

The floor of the church itself was of terrazzo and glazed when cleaned, as was often done by a group of women volunteers led by Magdalene, wife of Elder James Ogbe. The seats were the most comfortable of any church around and had cushions; the evangelist's special chair was of imported Italian leather and burgundy in colour—he was, as head of the flock, a special shepherd and his seat was comparable to a monarch's throne.

The eye-catching building had imitation fresco windows at the upper level and real frescoes at the bottom. The ceiling was a splendid work of art. The heavy cross hanging above the altar shone day and night, displaying the suffering Christ with blood splattered over his body. It was heart-rending to look at this image for too long. Suffering such nerve-racking pain that He could have avoided as the Son of God was the ultimate sacrifice, Evangelist Peter told his congregation, mindful that in the society no son of the king would suffer for the sake of his father's subjects.

Five years earlier, Evangelist Peter, moved by missionary zeal after waking from a dream of one day becoming a saintly man, after years of debauchery, had gone to the United States to raise money to convert the many pagans that still frustrated God's work and needed to be converted into light, as he told his various white donors who lavishly contributed towards his church in Nigeria. He felt he needed the American connection since his country men and women respected what came from outside rather than what was home-grown. He had seen how American and European pastors drew mammoth crowds in their crusading missions all over the country.

"The Devil is having a field day among my people. I need to bring God to rout Satan and his evil angels from their midst. Today my people live in darkness; they need God to see light. Your dollars will bring light and God to them," he had pleaded.

The pastor of the American host church he had visited saw a cause that needed to be pursued with vigour and so challenged his congregation to come out with a sufficient amount of dollars to make God proud of them. It was just after the Thanksgiving Holiday and everybody was looking forward to the Christmas season.

"Instead of spending all your money in buying gifts in a few days, let your gift go to God," he said.

"Amen," the congregation chorused.

"This is the only opportunity we all have to contribute our little quota to the building of the house of light in dark Africa. Do you want to be counted out of this noble cause?" he asked.

"No!" was the thunderous response.

"Let your best gift this season be given to the needy people of Africa," he admonished them. "God will reward you a hundred fold for the saving of lives that your contribution will bring about in Africa. Let them in Africa see God and light!"

"Amen," the congregation chorused.

"Let the lost people of Africa be saved!" he shouted.

"Amen!"

And the American Christians gave what pleased the visiting pastor and his host church. Those who had inherited money from slave-owning parents saw an opportunity to be free from the moral burden that was always weighing heavily on their minds. Such donors gave out hefty sums. Those who gambled regularly and made it, but knew that Jesus had condemned gambling in the temple saw the opportunity to relieve their minds of that age-old sin. Many whites who had felt guilty in their racist treatment of blacks throughout their lives wanted to redeem themselves by being supporters of the cause of Christianizing Africa. Different groups for their own reasons gave out so much money to free their minds from excoriating thoughts and deeds of the past.

It was enough money to build a fine church. Peter felt contented because his foreign mission was worth the pain of the physical exertion and personal humiliation at European airports where young men in uniform questioned him as if he were a drug smuggler or someone running from his country for residence in Europe or North America. His youth and boyish looks fitted the profile of drug traffickers and illegal immigrants that airport security worldwide screened thoroughly; that caused so much embarrassment to a man wearing a golden cross and a pastor's collar.

The American donors would not have been disappointed with what the African evangelist did with the money he had raised from them. The impressive church building spoke loudly and clearly for itself.

The pastor had from the inauguration of the church taken the name of Evangelist Peter. He had become the rock upon which the new church would stand and grow. The church would be the beacon of light in a dark landscape, he had envisaged.

Five years later the church was as solidly rooted in the community as if it had been there from the beginning of times. Even the older churches did not have as passionate and devoted a congregation as the Church of the New Dawn's. No service in any other church in town could boast of more numbers. No church event elsewhere in town was more crowded than anything done in the Church of the New Dawn. No congregation was more loyal and more generous than that of the Church of the New Dawn. Members of the church took literally the paying of tithes and did so without Evangelist Peter beating it into their ears as other pastors did, but without success. The Church of the New Dawn had become a model church in the area. All other Christians looked to the church on the green-clad hill with envy and admiration.

* * *

One Sunday morning, in the season of Lent, only two weeks to Easter, at 11 a.m. the congregation of the church came as usual to their place of worship for their weekly service which usually lasted from late morning to late afternoon. The church members looked to the service as to a great event in their lives and had dressed as for a popular festival. The Sunday service was a weekly festival that they waited for to fulfil a strong yearning that was at once social and spiritual and so compelling. Despite the five hours of service, they looked to the hours spent there as the time they had dedicated to God. The drumming, singing, and dancing brought spiritual energy that radiated into every pore of the body. They were too busy the rest of the week to think of God. The rest of the week they put into practice Evangelist Peter's recommendations about achieving wealth and fighting diabolical forces that stood in their way to success. During that period they sought the breakthroughs that their pastor told them to expect from God.

Evangelist Peter had always kept the main door of the church shut on Sundays until fifteen minutes before the service began. Members of the congregation who came early had to stay in a line and, as soon as the door opened, would rush in to occupy the front seats. They were usually in their fine clothes and jewellery, and would converse and shake hands. The men would shake hands with the women, and the women had the same opportunity to shake hands with men, which was not common practice outside the church premises. Sometimes Evangelist Peter would shake the hands of the first fifty people or so in the queue before they were let into the church. He would hug a few women who often took responsibilities for church activities. Magdalene Ogbe always came early and often received a hug from the evangelist; her husband would receive a handshake. Many members of the congregation believed Evangelist Peter was a modern-day prophet with his hands soft like a ripe banana.

This Sunday the usual humming of conversation could be heard. Many women showed off the latest fashions. New head-ties, new styles of blouses, and new fabrics bought from Lagos or imported from Marks & Spencer in London or from Dubai. They wore the different types of gold they craved for—Saudi, Italian, English, Dubai, or Indian. The men talked about where they had visited or the new contracts they had got from government agencies. This was a good part of Sunday, the showing-off time before the service began.

However, those coming late could see that the crowd had grown and there was no line to fall into. It was a large crowd but in groups of threes, fours, and fives—a forest full of clumps of trees.

This situation was because the early birds had found out that the church door was still shut even when it was already eleven o'clock. Was Evangelist Peter, always punctual to the minute, late this morning or why were people still outside? The latecomers wondered. He had never been late for service and they did not think that he was late that very Sunday morning. The evangelist had the mind of God and so could not forget time, more so the time for worship on Sunday. He would not want to keep his flock waiting to worship God. Something must be amiss, they thought, but could not guess from a distance. There had been no word that their pastor was sick or that he had travelled. Evangelist Peter was always well especially as he had boasted of being covered by the blood of Christ that repelled all physical and spiritual ailments from him.

The Sunday service attendants who had come first, and so were in front, saw what they thought was a prank. Who would intrude into the church premises at night to do this? What they saw were not only one poster but many. Could this happen? They asked. Their church building had been sold to another pastor. On the hand-carved huge front door was posted the boldly written "Under New Pastoral Management." The same poster was pasted on different parts of the front wall of the church.

The new pastor, an imposing man like a tall boxer, and his wife, both dressed as if they belonged to royalty, introduced themselves as the new owners and pastors of the church, which they had bought from the former owner—Evangelist Peter.

"I am Pastor Emmanuel and my wife is Magdalene," the new pastor said.

They showed the signed agreement to those close enough to read the paper they flaunted before the crowd and asked the people to go in for worship.

"After all, the house remains the house of God. I am only God's messenger to bring you good news," Pastor Emmanuel said.

He was wearing a black suit as Evangelist Peter did on some Sundays. It was humid. He brought out a white handkerchief from one of his pockets and wiped sweat from his face. The sun was bright and one could feel the intense heat it had in store for the rest of the day.

There was division among the congregation as to whether to go in or leave.

"Let's go in for worship," one member of the congregation said; "you never can tell that this is God's working and we have to accept it—He definitely works in a mysterious way. If the Almighty deems it necessary to give us a new pastor, let's accept him. He may well be what we truly need."

Adam had never liked Evangelist Peter and had felt he favoured the pretty women over other members of the congregation.

"A church is not property that you sell for profit and then disappear to buy a cheaper one somewhere else," Samuel argued.

Samuel was one of the few men that Evangelist Peter took out on church missions. He was in the Church's Finance Committee that rarely met and only to approve Evangelist Peter's accounts, but still felt favoured by being in the committee.

"We came to worship in Evangelist Peter's church; now we are asked to be in Pastor Emmanuel's church. It is only one God in the churches, really one church," Adam said.

"Why did you leave the Catholic Church for the Church of the New Dawn if it is all one church?" Samuel asked Adam.

"We have put in so much energy and tithes into this church and whether or not it is sold, it remains our church," a church member added.

"I can't imagine myself worshiping in another church," Adam told them.

"But the building alone is not the church. The pastor matters as well as the type of church," another church member said.

"Evangelist Peter and I are both men of God chosen to minister to you. Let's not argue before God's house. Don't be a doubting Thomas! Go in and you will be satisfied that God never fails in His mysterious ways," Pastor Emmanuel told the gathered crowd at the door of his newly acquired church.

He could not imagine the people leaving. The failure of his take-over of the much coveted Church of the New Dawn would be disastrous for him. He had invested so much money into this new church and wanted it to continue to prosper so that he could give praise to the Lord for His kindness. Eighteen million naira was a huge sum of money to pay for a building and its congregation, but without the congregation the investment would be ruined, he pondered. The building was designed as a church and could not be converted into a block of flats, Pastor Emmanuel reflected. He just had to succeed by all means, if he was to avoid a business disaster.

Pastor Emmanuel had acquired the art of persuasion from a source that would remain a secret all his pastoral life. He believed that to fight the devil, he had to use all means necessary, including devilish techniques. That was how he justified to himself his going to a medicine-man to make the charm of persuasion. The traditional healer had used a needle to poke his tongue to bleed and rubbed it with some medicine as he chanted an esoteric invocation. That, he assured the pastor, would make whoever listened to him accept what he said as truth and also carry out what he asked to be done. What was important in the end was his ability to convert more people to his church and exercise authority over their lives. With that Pastor Emmanuel felt he could enforce the paying of tithes without any hassle and preside over a prosperous church.

Pastor Emmanuel's wife, Magdalene, was very supportive of her husband. She used to be called Grace but he made her change her name to Magdalene as soon as he became a pastor. That was a better Christian name than just Grace, he felt. Magdalene was the woman who had stood by Jesus even after his death. She had anointed Jesus. If Jesus had been an ordinary human who wanted to marry, Pastor Emmanuel felt, the Son of God would have married no other woman but Magdalene.

Magdalene was a very charming woman whose dress, face, and smiles were as persuasive as the pastor's words. She was tall and had a well-proportioned shape. She walked with grace and whatever she wore gave her a unique charm. Pastor Emmanuel remembered what it had taken him to succeed among her many suitors. He had spent hundreds of thousands of naira in cash and kind to earn her attention and affection. He had planned ahead his successful life of a God's servant. Emmanuel and Magdalene formed a good partnership in the crusade against darkness and demons. Each found the other's company fortunate, as their partnership became strong with an ever-expanding beatitude.

At the end of a long debate, which each side thought it would win or lose, depending on their tenacity to their viewpoint, the congregation was swayed over to enter the church by the new pastor and his wife.

"Can't you give me the benefit of the doubt?" he asked, when he saw the opposing argument as gaining more support.

"My husband is a man of God that makes things to really happen. He knows how to pray, as a warrior knows how to fight his enemies" Magdalene interjected.

The congregation, feeling guilty for arguing so noisily with a man of God beside his newly acquired church, decided to give him the benefit of the doubt that he asked for and went in. Though the old order of entering the church was not respected, they sat in their usual seats.

Nothing in the church had changed. The altar section, like other parts of the church, remained in the way they used to be arranged. Only one thing was absent and none there noticed it: the rose or other flower that Magdalene Ogbe used to place at the altar before Evangelist Peter started service. But that beautification only took place when Peter was there.

It was as if it was a normal Sunday service but without Evangelist Peter, whose baritone voice always held them spell-bound. He could sing and he could dance. His lilting voice would rise to a crescendo as the percussion instruments brought his dance steps to a staccato movement. He had been the lead singer and the rest of the congregation the chorus. Similarly, he had been the lead dancer and his congregation followed his graceful and agile steps. In their minds, they wondered if Pastor Emmanuel could match the evangelist's dexterity and talents in song and dance.

This first service at the Church of the New Dawn under new pastoral management proved to be a great success and more than pleased all present. There was something in Pastor Emmanuel's voice that made them feel he could be trusted. Though he was in his forties, he preached like a wise old man who knew life and could advise others. He had a different voice from the evangelist's, but his was like a river running leisurely towards the ocean, sure of where it was going and dissolving itself into the wide waters.

When it came to preaching, Pastor Emmanuel performed the sermon he had practiced meticulously at home for weeks. He knew the consequence of not doing his utmost best in his first sermon in the new church.

"Alleluia!"

"Praise the Lord!" echoed from the pews.

"I say Alleluia," he repeated in a stronger voice.

"Praise the Lord!" the church reverberated thunderously.

"Al-le-lu-ia!"

"Praise the Lord!"

He was now primed enough to start to perform his sermon.

As his sermon progressed, many people began nodding approval of his lessons. Some rose to shout "Amen!" to his prayers. And the whole church was on its feet to dance with Pastor Emmanuel and his wife. The congregation did not want the long service to end. It was as though they were suspended in a planet of pleasurable spirituality.

Pastor Emmanuel was an artist and knew how to weave functionality and beauty into his craft. He was an experienced performer who took the cues from his enthusiastic audience. He knew how to connect with his audience and did wonderfully with the new congregation.

Pastor Emmanuel and his wife felt his first day in his new church was a huge success. The three offerings accompanied by drumming and dancing fetched a staggering amount that made them smile. No wonder, they thought, Evangelist Peter struck a hard bargain with them. No pastor who made so much money every Sunday would sell his church unless he really had to, they now realized.

* * *

Once back home, some members of Pastor Emmanuel's congregation started to hear strange things about Evangelist Peter. They started to add so many things together. It started as a rumour, which gossip easily transmitted to every attentive ear. The absence of Elder James Ogbe's wife at church the past Sunday fuelled the rumours and gossip. Some women had looked out for her when Pastor Emmanuel introduced his wife as Magdalene, the same name as Elder James' wife. The Magdalene they knew, Mrs. Ogbe, was not in church that day. Now they remembered that the ritual of the flower being placed on the altar was not performed. "Where was Magdalene today?" many started to ask. They imagined she had not heard about the change of ownership of the church and might still be on an assignment that Evangelist Peter had arranged before he sold the church.

"Did she get wind of the sale of the church and had stayed home in protest?" others started to ask.

It was common knowledge that Magdalene Ogbe had been a favourite of Evangelist Peter. At thirty seven, she was much younger than her husband in his late fifties. She had had no child in their ten years of marriage and looked very much in her prime in beauty. She was the leader of the women's group and reported to the evangelist their discussions and resolutions. She had travelled many times with Evangelist Peter on church duties out of town, and to conventions out of state that lasted many days.

Evangelist Peter had complimented her service publicly in the church. He always embraced and hugged her on Sunday mornings before worship, when he came to her; he shook hands with most other women.

Magdalene, the name that the Evangelist had given to her, stuck. She had been Agnes, which the Evangelist said was not as Christian as Magdalene. Unknown to Elder James Ogbe, his wife and Evangelist Peter had been having a secret relationship and she had received numerous favours from the Evangelist—always in the delegation travelling on behalf of the Church. Rumours had started, but none wanted to imagine that the Evangelist could do such an immoral thing as sleeping with his church member's wife.

Magdalene went often to see Evangelist Peter to pray for her at different times of the day. Church members noticed her frequenting the pastor's office and home but their minds did not wander beyond her not conceiving all the years of marriage. They pitied her and her husband—such a gentle and godly couple!

There were rumours too that Elder James Ogbe was either impotent or weak as a man, but again, nobody wanted to imagine such a beautiful woman married to a eunuch.

"How could that beautiful woman have married such a mature man without a taste of the thing first?" They asked many questions.

When such rumours first came, the bearers were seen as agents of Satan.

"Don't defame a man of God," one member of the church had said.

"The good ones will always be smeared by the rumourmongers of this world," another had added.

"Those who perjure the Evangelist will roast in hell," another swore.

* * *

Magdalene Ogbe had conceived. It was a miracle that only she and Evangelist Peter knew about. They did not expect it, but it happened. They accepted the crop whose seed they had been planting.

The two secret lovers went underground for a few days. Only Pastor Emmanuel and his Magdalene knew that Evangelist Peter and Magdalene Ogbe had migrated to the United States to start a new life. As part of the contract that included the sale of the Church of the New Dawn, Pastor Emmanuel had secretly married Evangelist Peter and Magdalene before they took off. That was after they confessed their sins to Pastor Emmanuel who forgave them. That also was part of the contract. Only his wife, the namesake of the new bride, was witness to the ceremony that took place in Pastor Emmanuel's house after midnight.

"We are entering a new dawn," Evangelist Peter quipped.

"God bless both of you!" the pastor pronounced.

"And God also bless you with the Church of the New Dawn that I hand over to you," Peter told the pastor and his wife, as he handed to them the keys of the church.

That night Evangelist Peter and Magdalene headed into darkness not to spend a conjugal night in bed but to travel fast to catch their plane taking off from Lagos later that morning. Their minds were focused on where they were going and the new life as husband and wife they were going to live in God's own country.

No member of the Church of the New Dawn, including Elder James Ogbe, knew where they had emigrated that night. Magdalene had told her husband that she was going for a retreat in Lagos and would be away for a week. He did not ask her any questions about her travels for religious events, including this one for which she had filled a big trunk with clothes, shoes, and jewellery.

To the congregation of the Church of the New Dawn, Evangelist Peter and Magdalene might as well have died or gone to heaven. Or hell, if members of the church knew what had really transpired between them in the many years they had been under the pastoral leadership of Evangelist Peter! As for Magdalene, the women would say, "She was looking for more than conception or a baby from God under cover of prayers—a new and virile man!"

7

The Women's Final Solution

While her man volunteers information to her, other women are not as lucky because they are unable to extract any personal financial information from their husbands. She is said to be the only woman in the neighbourhood who knows how much her man earns at the end of the month and yearly. The women know that she has a joint account with the man even though it is really only his earnings and not hers that go into it. She has a separate account that she does not share with her spouse.

Other women don't know how she is able to do this; more so, as she is married to an Agbon man like the rest of them. It is not only that her fellow women do not know how much their husbands earn but also do not have access to their men's accounts. They learn from the elderly housewives that the men fear that should the women know about their wealth, they could poison or kill them by any means and gain possession of the money. The women know that such reasoning, as killing their husbands, is just an excuse to hide their true financial situations and protect their egos because most of their husbands might not really have as much money as they would make one believe. In that case, the men keep their wives in a guessing game as to how much they are really worth. The women consider Lydia a unique woman in many ways.

"See her! She is called Lydia," Ufuoma says, as she points to her to Tobore.

Lydia dresses gorgeously and gracefully. She has a knack for dresses that fit her very well, and she draws compliments from women as well as men. The colours of her wrappers, blouses, head-ties, handbags, and shoes blend into a harmony that makes her figure a beautiful work of art. She has a good shape and she is pretty, but cannot be said to be extraordinarily beautiful. There are women who are more beautiful than her but do not draw to themselves the lust of men and the envy of women as Lydia does. She exudes the composure and confidence of a woman who gets what she desires. She is tall and on the slim side. She walks like a model in a rather coquettish manner that the other women cannot imitate however hard they try.

The women, also married, who point to her, do so without bitterness and malice. They don't know what to make of her—condemn her or be like her. But it is very difficult, if not impossible, to live Lydia's lifestyle, they know. She who can tame men, they call her. After all, their men are like goats on heat. They return to her, the men she makes friends with. Also, she is the one who commands men and gets from them her desires. She is more like a man in the patriarchal society in which the men dominate the women. She dominates. In fact, some women gossip that she always stays on top of men, what they will like to do but cannot prevail upon their men to do without being called prostitutes. Nobody, man or woman, dares call Lydia any nasty names. She is the lady who must be complimented.

Lydia is married, yes, but she is as free as, if not even freer than single women. Umukoro, her husband, works offshore for Chevron, the second most important multinational oil company in the country after Bell Oil that has been operating there for over four decades. A safety expert in offshore rigs, he earns a hefty sum and lavishes his salary on his flamboyant wife, according to gossip. She lives well, whether her husband is around for the two weeks he takes to spend at home or on duty at the oil rigs offshore for six weeks. His is a dangerous work and he is paid very much for it.

Her partner, as she often calls him, dotes on her. She is much younger than him; fifteen years separate them. He flaunts her like a prized trophy wherever they go together. He wears the same fabrics she wears, though sewn in their respective male and female styles. He takes her to parties and there are many, especially on weekends when he is back from the sea. He takes her to nightclubs, where they drink expensive wines, dance, and make acquaintances. Often she goes on tirelessly. The more she dances, the more the energy in her becomes apparent. As for the man, he cannot cope with her inexhaustible energy at all. She often wonders why he gets tired so soon whenever they dance. After the man takes his seat, she dances on and has the opportunity to have other dancing partners. She no longer complains to him why in bed he sleeps facing the wall rather than her. She has to look for a solution to whatever problem they have, she tells herself, and she has solved many of such to her satisfaction.

In his partner's presence, under his nose, as the women gossip, at such parties, she signals to her men friends that she freely associates with. She dances with other men and asks her husband to dance with other women who want to dance with him. Other married women dance with only their husbands or close relatives and with no other men. They marvel at how Lydia is so free and comfortable dancing with strangers and does what will be scandalous to other women: holding another man tight in a dance, while her husband is seated or dancing with some other woman. Other women cannot come close to other men the way Lydia gets away with it. Her partner does not seem to mind his wife's rather flirtatious manners in a society where men are so jealous that they wish to tie a leash to the waists of their wives and concubines.

The women have been socialized to believe that their ancestors or some spirit will strike them with afflictions if they come close to a man who is not their husband or relative. Nobody has ever caught her but many of the women do not only believe but also gossip that Lydia sleeps with the men she fancies whenever and wherever she chooses. That is supposed to be an abomination, which supposedly draws the wrath of the ancestors. Not with Lydia, who is buoyant and vibrant all the time. *Why do the ancestors not strike Lydia with an incurable disease for her dalliance?* the other women ask in their gossip group.

"How does she do it?" Tobore asks Ufuoma.

Ufuoma and Tobore are outside the hairdressers' complex by the Warri-Sapele Road in Effurun. They have both done their hair and are exchanging pleasantries before leaving for their respective homes.

"Have you not heard what is said about her?" Ufuoma asks in a low tone.

"I want to know, my sister," Tobore pleads, like one who needs to know an interesting formula that she will try for herself.

"I don't have her courage," Ufuoma says, more of a lamentation than a condemnation of Lydia.

She holds her breath, looks at Tobore in an intense manner as if to assure herself whether or not she can be trusted. She raises her forefinger, closes her lips with it, and drops it. She gives a long sigh that Tobore cannot interpret, but waits eagerly to hear something about a fellow housewife whom they look up to but will not openly acknowledge.

"If I do what she does," Ufuoma resumes, "I would have been caught by my husband or shamed for my deeds by the ancestors."

This she says with a tone of regret. She wishes she can do what Lydia does without repercussions. Why is she always afraid of the ancestors who are dead and gone forever? She asks herself this and other questions about her temerity over living freely.

Tobore waits anxiously. She believes, as a woman, she has to learn from other women. Marriage, to her, has been a big burden that she cannot shake off. Being single is a curse in the society, much as marriage is hard. However, if there is anything she can do to ease the burden or totally relieve her of it in a way that will not bring shame, she will go for it. She wonders in her mind how one can continue stealing without being caught someday. That is a skill that she will find difficult to master. She praises any woman who gets her wish, however secretive the pleasure comes to her.

"I beg, tell me, my sister," she pleads again, anxious to learn a craft she may find useful.

She wants to know how to use the craft of womanhood effectively. After all, that is what Lydia has been doing so successfully to the amazement of other women.

"Don't say I told you-o, but everybody knows her ways anyway," Ufuoma tells her.

"I will keep it to myself," Tobore promises.

"They say Lydia has the 'the dead don't see and hear' medicine," Ufuoma starts to explain.

She pauses a bit, inhales and exhales, and continues her gossip.

"They say she either met a medicine-man who prepared it for her or she did it herself. She must have used the soil or sand from the top of a gravesite in some concoctions to bathe herself. She may even have done the strongest of the medicines, procuring the water used in bathing a corpse in the morgue before being dressed for burial to prepare the medicine. She may have made a special arrangement with the mortuary attendant for a good price to get what she wants. Once she has the medicine, she communicates with her lovers only in English. That medicine neutralizes the power of our ancestors, who don't understand English anyway! You see that her husband does not mind and nobody will catch her doing what she does because to her the rest of the world is dead people."

"That's terrible!" Tobore exclaims.

"But you need something terrible to counter our terrible situation," Ufuoma says, as if in defence of Lydia.

"I don't think I can do that," Tobore admits.

"It will not be so terrible to me if my man will dote on me and I can be free with my life as I want. Look at Lydia! She drives a First Lady car. See her Toyota jeep? Her husband has also built a house for her from his huge income. How many of us can compare with her?"

Ufuoma has given birth to seven children already, and has no control over the number she will get. At the rate she is going, she could have ten to eleven children before her menopause. Now she does not want her husband but still gives in to him whenever he wants her plus his secret dalliances. "My husband is worse than a goat," Ufuoma sometimes tells herself.

Tobore already has five children and her husband and his people expect her to fill the house with kids and noise because they still measure the wealth of a man with the number of children he has. Her last delivery was through a Caesarean section which was not a pleasant experience at all. The attending doctor had to resort to that procedure when he found out that she was very weak and could not push. She had felt she was going to die from that delivery, but thanks to the doctor's expertise and her good luck she survived with the baby. I am scared of being pregnant again. I just feel I may not be able to make it through the next conception, she tells herself. And yet she cannot deny her husband the pleasure of her body.

Lydia looks very appealing. She exudes sensuality with her body. Her breasts are still erect at thirty-eight. Her hips are as sexy as a twenty-eight-year-old woman's. She makes up and there is enough money to procure her needs. She has two children, five and eight; both girls. She has put a stop to her procreation. According to gossip, she boasts that she wants to enjoy herself without being distracted by pregnancies and so has undergone a medical procedure to avoid pregnancy. Such gossiping women even quote her words.

"Who enjoys pregnancy?" she often asks her fellow women.

"For me," she continues, "the nine months and the labour period are times spent in hell while alive. I won't like to condemn my friends to that hell."

Other women listen to or hear about her, amazed at her forthrightness in the open. They cannot let out of their mouths such utterances that really reflect their feelings. They cherish what Lydia says but are afraid or shy to proclaim it the way she does with abandon. Lydia is the bold one. She is the shameless one to the other women. She does not care about what others say about her but says and does what pleases her. To other women, who gossip about her, it is because she feels immune from ancestral repercussions. The dead don't complain. The living and the dead are mute and blind before her actions and utterances.

"She must be taking contraceptive pills or wearing a curl," Ufuoma tells Tobore.

Other women believe this. There was the scandalous rumour that Lydia delivered the second daughter with a curl attached to her forefinger. She must be using some devices to prevent pregnancy but it failed in that instance, the women believe. These women also want to be free of the anxieties and problems of pregnancy but do not know how to go about freeing themselves from the perennial obeisance to the whims and caprices of men who do not suffer the pangs of conception.

"My husband wants many children, but can't understand the damage to my body," Ufuoma again says.

"They always want more children, our men. I wanted only two or three but my husband started to preach why one must have many children," Tobore says in response.

"They all do the same. Did my husband not ask me that if I had only two children and if one or both died wouldn't I be a childless woman? I was not convinced but had to agree to have more because there was nothing I could do to stop him from coming to me to have as many children as God permits, as he puts it."

"The world is changing but our society does not seem to be aware of what is happening. We are still having too many children that we cannot adequately take care of," Tobore tells Ufuoma.

"Can't you see that our women are either nursing babies or pregnant?" Ufuoma asks.

"I think only Lydia has found the final solution. I think I will be bold enough now to enter a cemetery and take the soil or sand from a gravesite to be free to live my life the way I will like to. Or maybe pay a mortuary attendant his month's salary to give me a half bottle of that water. It is nauseating, but what can I do?" Tobore confesses and asks.

"Yes, women do bad things because of their suffering. I can do anything now short of killing my husband to achieve my freedom to control my body," Ufuoma tells her fellow housewife.

Lydia joins Ufuoma and Tobore by the mango tree where they are standing and talking. She has been chatting with a young handsome man, both smiling and looking free and happy with each other. Her husband has gone to the rigs the past four weeks and has two more weeks to work offshore before coming home.

"My sister, good evening," Ufuoma hails Lydia.

"Good evening, my sisters! How una dey?" she responds.

She is so composed that she does not care that she is with another man, whom she appears to be having a good time with and following perhaps to a hotel for more fun.

"Take care of yourselves. See you at our meeting on Sunday," Lydia says, as she waves goodbye and goes her own way in the twilight.

They hold their Elegant Ladies Association meeting once a month and will meet next Sunday afternoon. Ufuoma is a member of the association.

As soon as she disappears into the dark distance, the two women slap the palms of their right hands, as if showing solidarity with the bold one.

"I won't blame her," Ufuoma says.

"Of course, none of us should blame her. Why should women condemn themselves or one of their own for what men do without qualms or the least thought of us?" Tobore asks, concurring with Ufuoma.

* * *

The next day Tobore feels she has to do something. She will not go to the mortuary attendant nor will she enter a cemetery. She needs neither the odious water nor the special sand to change her lifestyle. And she will not go to a medicine man, many of whom are quacks and around even in the city. Her life, she suddenly realizes, is in her own hands. She can live the way she wants to live by practicing it. There is much she can do on her own. Without being shy, she walks into JJC Pharmacy on Ginuwa Road and asks for a packet of condom, which she pays for and takes home.

She knows that her goat of a husband will come to her at night and, without fondling, will like to charge into her.

It happens as she has predicted.

"I bought condom for you to use. I am having discharge and won't like you to be infected with any bad things," she lies to him.

"What is happening to you?" he asks.

"Do you want me or not?" she asks back.

The man is taken aback. He is not used to his wife talking back to him at bedtime.

"I will not wear anything," he says.

He leaves their bed for the sitting room to mull over his wife's sudden stubbornness, as he sees her action. He falls asleep there and saves Tobore from succumbing to spousal rape.

Tobore thinks of another strategy. She cannot tell her husband every night that she has a yeast infection or some discharge. He may soon conclude wrongly that she is sleeping with somebody else, which will bring trouble to the home. She knows that her husband flirts, but he will not accept the thought of his wife sleeping with another man. She cannot withstand the hell that will be let loose in the house.

She thinks and acts fast. She goes on her own to a private clinic in Ovie Palace Road to install IUD or coil into her body. All she wants is to start to enjoy sex without the burden of conception or the monthly anxiety of whether or not she will have her menstruation.

Her husband is soon happy that the infection is over. She holds him back for foreplay that he is not used to. She teaches him what to do and he follows this time, beginning to enjoy squeezing her breasts, kissing her, and complimenting her body. It takes quite some time before she draws him to herself and leads him on. She moans as the man also moans, but the man does not know what has taken place in the woman he has lived with as his wife for so many years.

Their love life changes for the better. After about six months, her husband wonders why she is not yet pregnant again, but he keeps his surprise to himself. By another year, he can no longer contain himself with his fears or suspicions. One night, as they sat on the bed talking, a preamble to foreplay and sex, he holds her right hand and draws her close to himself.

"Darling, why are you not getting pregnant?" he asks her.

He had started all of a sudden, since their sex life improved, to be calling her Darling.

"Am I the one to ask? Why not ask God, my dear?" Tobore boldly asks back.

He goes ahead with the preliminaries of lovemaking both of them have now got used to. She has won a battle and feels she will map out how to win the war at home that will continue to make her a happy woman.

* * *

Ufuoma decides to take her revenge on her husband. He comes shabbily to bed, often not taking a bath. She always goes to put warm water in the bathroom and tells him to have his bath but he appears too lazy to bathe or feels he needs to resist his wife's order for him to bathe before going to bed. He comes in a hurry, as if he will lose his erection if he takes time to get her ready. She is not happy with him. She has complained to him many times that he needs to prepare her with foreplay, but he will not change. If he will not change, maybe she has to change, she tells herself.

She starts dating a younger man who makes her young and excited. She prepares carefully to meet him at times they agree on. She selects her best dress and provocative perfume to wear for the tryst. The day they first made love, the young man plays with her for a long time, touching parts of her body where her husband has never touched. She is ignited like dry leaf aflame in the harmattan. She is possessed once the man comes into her. She gets her first orgasm and a long one for that matter. No wonder, nobody can stop Lydia. Nobody can deprive me of this anymore. I have now tasted the true fruit of love. She talks to herself as one out of control of her senses.

That day at home she behaves strangely. The excitement, the sense of fulfilment, and her flushed body tell a story of contentment. Absent-minded, she seems not to hear what her husband is saying.

"Are you OK?" he asks.

"Why do you ask me that type of question? I am very OK," she replies.

She fears what will become of her if she experiences more of this special elation that love for the younger man brings to her. Must she go and prepare that medicine, which, according to rumour, Lydia uses, so that her husband and everybody else will be blind and deaf to her transformed being? She sings in the house as she is not used to doing. She fears she is becoming crazy. She has to do something to stop being caught or tormenting herself with fear of the joy she now experiences.

* * *

The two friends meet about a year later. They have started a new life that they hope they can enjoy without disruption. They promise themselves to go to any length to protect their interests like Lydia does her things. Even if they have to go to the graveyard to take the soil to prepare medicine that will make them free! Or pay the medicine man or morgue attendant to make the dead see and hear nothing as the living do what pleases them! But they will not go to Lydia to ask her about the potent medicine that gossip among many frustrated housewives says she has. She lives on so naturally, without other women really knowing the solutions she has chosen for her unbearable problem of having a husband who had become impotent and with whom she has made a devil's pact.

8

Nobody Loves Me

The handwritten note on the bed simply read: "Nobody loves me." A big nail cutter kept the white sheet of paper from flying off. The writer wanted the note to be read, it appeared, because of the clear way it was written and the effort to make sure it remained easily visible on a neatly made bed. There are people, dead or alive, who do not want to leave others guessing their personal intentions; more so, on such an important matter as love.

The shock in the compound and neighbourhood was unprecedented and spread cold shivers to everyone who knew Ngozi or any of the other tenants. Ngozi was one of the many single young women who lived in this self-contained one-bedroom complex in Alaka Quarters of Effurun. Chief Kemukemu owned the residential buildings, which he had built with the windfall from a highly inflated contract to supply sandbags for military checkpoints in cities during the General Buraimoh military regime, which he defended and praised as the best military administration in Nigeria's history despite its blatant repression and corruption. Civil rights activists said that Chief Kemukemu was capable of selling his own mother to make money. That told how much he cared for money; he would do anything to get it, including singing praises of vultures and hyenas.

The chief specialized in renting his flats to single young women, who ranged from twenty-two to thirty-seven years of age. With three storey buildings of eight self-contained flats on each floor, the compound, well secured with an imponderable gate manned by a kola-chewing Hausa man, was a beehive of visitors. It looked like a hostel for rich university students. And the tenants lived like youthful students with the exuberance of those free from parental watch and stretching freedom beyond traditional limits.

Some of the tenants had friends, like them single, living with them. The tenants were workers, and mornings and evenings, as they went to and returned from work, the spacious compound was a parade ground of beautiful ladies. Some of them stood out for their features. Rather, some were popular, as one would expect in this type of place.

There was the stylish slim, tall, and model-walking Ebi that everyone acknowledged as a stunning beauty. She walked with a conscious gait and was as seductive as she possibly could to attract attention. Lola spoke with a British Cockney accent. She was born in England and her parents repatriated her to study in Nigeria with the hope that she would get a Nigerian man to marry rather than remain single in London. Her rich parents spoilt her because they did not treat her as a worker but as one who should be sent pounds sterling to live a comfortable life in Nigeria. Marho was known for singing religious songs. She was beautiful, but spent much of her free time and weekends in the Church of the New Dawn, where she hoped to get a man to marry. She expected whoever would marry her to be "born again" like her and they would sing hymns before going to bed at night and upon waking in the morning.

Ngozi was beautiful and at the prime of womanhood. She was already in her early thirties. At the University of Jos she had been a very sociable lady and was known for that. Ever since she completed her national service in Takum, Taraba State, she had calmed down, hoping to get a worthy suitor to say goodbye to spinsterhood.

Visitors kept the gateman busy on week days, but more so on weekends. Men, young and older, were constantly going in or leaving the compound, sometimes escorted by those they had visited. On Friday and Saturday nights, in particular, cars parked along the entire Egbo Street, and pairs of men and women could be seen chatting before driving off or after returning from their outings.

What surprised the gateman was that no man slept in any of the flats. No man was considered intimate enough with any of the young ladies to warrant sleeping in her flat. It was an unwritten agreement among the young women, it appeared, to keep men out of their flats at night.

It did not take time before a pattern emerged of the visitors and those visited. Some of the tenants constantly received visitors, sometimes more than two men at the same time. Such tenants with multiple visitors or partners either stood or sat awkwardly talking to their friends, as if each of the visitors was not aware of the other visitor's relationship with them.

A few of the ladies did not receive visitors at all and some did occasionally, even as there was the heavy traffic on a daily basis. The gateman and the landlord praised those young women who did not subject themselves to immorality or sex trade, as they saw the nightly transactions. Ngozi and Marho were two of such, often contrasted with Lola and Ebi, whom they called shameless prostitutes.

The gateman overheard many things and saw much drama that he kept confidential. Sometimes he listened to the haggling going on just beside the gate, where he sat waiting to open or close it. He usually spread out a mat by the side where he sat, watching.

"This money is not enough!"

"That's all I have with me," the man would reply.

"Why did you not tell me you had no money before I followed you," the young woman would reprimand the man.

"You be meat I dey buy or wetin you think you be?"

"How you no go talk nonsense? You don get wetin you want," the lady would say.

She would wave her forefinger.

"Don't do this to me again. I am not cheap," the woman would add.

The young women looked prosperous as they had expensive electronic gadgets in their beautifully furnished rooms. Many had plasma television sets and cable service that they could not afford with only their salaries. Each knew that their boyfriends had to "foot the bill" for whatever they wanted. They bought expensive dresses from what they were given by their men. Many were not satisfied with only one man but had to date multiple partners to live well enough to outshine others in the tacit competition that took place in the complex.

On weekends, many of the ladies came from outside drunk and barely knowing their flats from others. Some ran into their bedrooms and vomited into their toilets. They smelt of Guinness Stout, hard liquor, and strong wines. It was a boisterous atmosphere in which they looked happy.

In the two years he had been hired to guard the place, Haruna had noticed the young women change their tastes in fashion. At the beginning, they dressed in mini-skirts and sleeveless blouses. The spaghetti blouse was in vogue. Many were even half-naked. Lola and Ebi flaunted their bodies, especially their legs and breasts, and appeared looking for handsome or rich men to launch them at.

However, in recent times, the women were changing, as was their taste in dressing. Many were consciously or unconsciously losing weight. He knew some jogged in the morning to lose weight and keep fit. Some that were plump had become slim in a sickly way. He had heard through rumour that some, despite the money they had, almost starved themselves to be slim because many men did not want fat women. Everyone wanted to be a "hot cake," as they put it in their slang, and so they had to be thin.

All of a sudden, many of the girls were wearing long dresses, almost covering themselves in jeans trousers and long-sleeves. Some literally wrapped themselves and could barely be recognized. A few wore dark glasses at all times. It was a riot of fashion, Haruna observed, as he manned the big gate.

He had also observed other young women who returned sick from clinics, where they might have gone to commit abortion after appearing plump and obese. Others suffered from infections and their regular visits to clinics told their condition. Condoms often littered the compound or the backyard where the chief planted flowers and kept some loveseats. Marho realized she was living in Sodom and Gomorrah, but felt she could control herself from not slipping into the immorality she observed surrounded her. She sang her church songs to remain strong in the adulterous environment, as she realized where she lived had become.

By the fourth year of Haruna's watch, some young women were very ill and a few others dying from unknown diseases. Still the floodgate of men remained open. Nobody mentioned HIV or AIDS, as if doing so would make one get infected by the dreaded disease. But the landlord and the gateman observed that those girls dying like malnourished figures and coughing into their handkerchiefs must be infected by the unmentionable disease. After all, these young women were all workers and they had men friends who took them to expensive restaurants and hotels and so were not starving to lose weight at that alarming rate. The number of the popular ones was diminishing, almost month by month. Some did not die there but went home and never came back. Since they paid rents on a yearly basis, the landlord was not bothered by absences until the rents were due.

Still Ngozi, for reasons she could not understand, received no visitors in a town of goats on heat. How could one live in Sodom and Gomorrah and not be approached for sex? she wondered. It bothered her immensely. She bought new clothes sewn fashionably. She wore the attractive dresses and paraded Egbo Street nearby, but no man beckoned or talked to her. "What is wrong with me?" she asked herself.

When Ngozi attempted to chase one of the men she felt was loitering to talk to any woman he saw, she did it so clumsily that the man walked away. But also, unfortunately for her, one of her fellow tenants saw her trying to chase her man.

"Na my man you wan take? You no fit get man for yourself?" Vicky asked Ngozi, who felt ashamed of herself.

"Sorry, I was trying to ask him whom he was looking for," she lied to Vicky.

"Just be careful with other people's men," Vicky admonished her.

From that night Ngozi could not sleep well. She thought of her condition. "Am I not a woman?" she asked herself.

She looked into the mirror in her bathroom after stripping. She looked at her eyes, lips, breasts, face, and all parts of her body. She was not an ugly woman, she assured herself. Her eyes twinkled and she cropped her eyelashes at the salon. Her lips were thin and they looked fine when she put on lipstick. She had full-size breasts that many ladies would envy, and she went for the most expensive imported bras in the market. Her face was oval and smooth, unlike some other ladies around with pimples taking over their faces.

Ngozi searched for a reason why she did not appeal to any man with so many men there seeking women. She knew that men drove round Effurun and stopped to pick girls on the street. She had walked, two weeks earlier in the evening, instead of taking a bus, but no man in a car stopped for her. She started to feel that she was not a complete woman or fate was unfair to her. Every other woman she knew in the compound had a boyfriend, man friend, or suitor. She wanted to be chased. She was tired of looking forward to a man and not having any; she wanted to make love like she knew the other young women were doing. She was tired of fondling her own body and however long and hard she did, it never gave her the pleasure that she expected from a man. She needed the warmth of another body. She wanted her body to be admired, wanted her expensive bras to be complimented by a man when she undressed for him. She wanted to be embraced, she wanted to be kissed, and, above all, she wanted somebody to share her life with.

She remembered that her elder sister was still living a spinster at forty-five in Aba. Is it true that the female children of her mother were jinxed not to have men? Did anybody place any evil charm on her to be loathed by men? An old aunt had died after confessing that nothing could be done to remove the curse she had placed on her mother's female children. Could prayers not annul the curse? She prayed and prayed, after which she went out dressed to test whether the curse was gone. Still, no man came to her. She had noticed that in her university none of the male lecturers had come close to her, as if she had a repulsive odour. She used designer perfumes but did not still attract compliments from any man.

From gossip in the housing complex, she had heard that a particular medicine man in a remote part of town made medicines for women to charm men. She constituted a court in her own mind in which she condemned and absolved herself.

"If you are a Christian, why would you go to a medicine man?"

"I need help because I have tried all means and failed?"

"Why do you think going to the devil will help you?"

"I won't mind if the devil will make me a complete woman."

Ngozi, on a weekend evening, when her fellow tenants were being picked up by men, took a motor bike to the renowned medicine man in a part of town without street numbers. Fortunately for her, the bearded gaunt man, reputed to produce the potent medicines for women to charm men, was in. After Ngozi had explained why she came to him, the medicine man prepared for her what he described as the most potent of the love medicines he could offer.

"Don't come back to tell me that every man wants you," he warned her.

"No, I won't mind men competing to have me," she replied.

Ngozi rubbed the medicine over her body, as she was instructed to do. When she went out, it appeared that she was having a despicable and repellent odour because men kept a distance from her. Those that came close by chance immediately walked away from her. Two weeks after she had paid the medicine man a hefty sum for the medicine that would make men compete for her attention and love, Ngozi had got no man chase her in Sodom and Gomorrah.

She started to lose interest in everything. She did not like the food she prepared. She did not buy food outside either. She picked any dress from her wardrobe and sometimes went out with awful combinations of dress, shoes, and handbags.

After the heavy traffic of the Friday, Saturday, and Sunday nights did not change her plight, despite parading like a real prostitute outside the compound gate, Ngozi decided to stay indoors. She knew that her mind was being destroyed by unfulfilled desires. She was not a lady, it appeared. She became weak and could not carry herself to work on Monday.

It was on Tuesday morning that her body, dangling from the ceiling fan tied with her wrapper, was found. The note was left on the flowery bedcover. "Nobody loves me."

Since she was dead, she did not know that on that very day too one of her fellow tenants died of an AIDS-related infection in the

General Hospital. Also a few others were too sick and embarrassed by their sores and coughs to come out to ask what was amiss when wails rent the air upon the discovery of her body.

9

Any Problem?

In their wildest dreams, both Mama and Papa Tejiri did not expect good fortune to smile so lavishly at them someday. In their early sixties, the man sixty-four and the woman sixty-one, they had suddenly been lifted into a new life they used to see from a distance. *So, this is how life is, an ebb that shrinks your possibilities and a flow that raises you to the height of your dreams?* they reflected. They had certainly been lifted to an enviable height in their society.

For many years they could barely have two good meals a day; then they lived in a shabby one-bedroom flat. They had left their hometown of Warri for Sapele where Papa Tejiri worked for more than two decades at the African Timber & Plywood Company. Papa Tejiri, like his fellow workers, lost his job when the company folded up because there was not enough timber in surrounding forests to feed the world's largest sawmill company's voracious appetite for timber and the world's insatiable need for plywood for buildings and furniture. For decades, poachers and sawmill operators had been devouring the forests of the Midwest Region and parts of the Western Region without thinking of planting more trees to replace the fallen ones. It was just a matter of time for the available timber in the forests to be exhausted, and it surely did to the amazement of the thoughtless and greedy managers of the big sawmill.

After enduring hardship for four years in Sapele, hoping against hope that the AT&P Company would reopen with some reorganization, Mama and Papa Tejiri left for Lagos in search of some other work. Lagos attracted jobseekers because it was not only the seat of the federal government then but also the commercial centre of the country. But Lagos had a way of attracting people there and then frustrating them with lack of jobs. There, their condition became even worse than at Sapele after the loss of the plywood company job. They had to pay high rents for the one bedroom, and the landlady was always there at the end of the month to collect her rent. Without any pension from the old job in Sapele, Papa Tejiri was in dire straits. It was getting very difficult to have one good meal a day. They had to take roasted corn for brunch and *eba* with meatless soup for late dinner. There had been days they had to take several balls of *akara* in the late afternoon as the day's only meal. The couple had become very creative in stretching the pittance they had to survive. They had begun to accept their plight as unchangeable when the unexpected happened.

After ten years of extreme hardship, their son, Tejiri, rescued them from their hapless situation. It was like a miracle because they did not expect it. If someone had told them that they would be freed from the dark, damp, and dishevelled one bedroom they inhabited in Ajegunle, they would have doubted it. If anybody had told them that someday they would eat well as human beings should, they would not have believed the person. Nothing in their lives at the time pointed to the relief that came from unexpected quarters. And it came suddenly.

Tejiri Akpome had suddenly become rich. His wealth came unexpectedly as a Niger Delta flash flood from a thunderstorm in the dry season. According to a common saying, once money arrives, one sees so many things to do with it. And Tejiri had plans to invest his sudden wealth. He built two impressive houses in adjoining streets in Warri. In Okpara Street stood a duplex into which he brought his mother and father to live. The building perched on an elevated quarter and with its off-white paint attracted every passer-by's attention. It had four bedrooms, and Mama and Papa Tejiri had more than enough space for themselves, as they never had before.

Their wealthy son provided adequately for them. They wore nice clothes, ate well, and looked every way comfortable. All they did was to live a good life because their son also paid them a stipend of fifty thousand naira a month plus the food and cook he provided.

Now they lived in a duplex at a conspicuous point of the street. Now they were proud residents of Warri, not shy residents living in slums and so did not tell you where they lived. Now they proudly described where they lived to anybody who cared to ask for it. After all, one wears ivory bangles to show off one's hands! Okpara Street was conspicuous in Warri, and when you said you lived at No. 48, people saw it when they came to it. It was not unnumbered or numberless, as many homes in parts of Warri or Ajegunle were. To be doubly sure that people knew the house they meant, they described it as the off-white-painted storied building. It stood impressively and nobody passing by would miss it.

The duplex had a spacious balcony up, and it was a favourite place for Mama and Papa Tejiri to relax. They installed five plastic white chairs, two at the centre where both sat. They watched the goings-on in their street and adjoining streets from their vantage position. There they saw children playing dangerously in nearby streets—somersaulting on top of tires—and fighting mock battles with toy rifles as they saw in American films. From their vantage position, they saw men and women's fashions and shook their heads at what young women now wore. They cursed modernity as responsible for what they saw as the half-naked appearance of young ladies in the name of fashion.

There on the balcony too Mama and Papa Tejiri could see far from them the slum they had experienced for decades of their lives. In their minds, one should run as far away as possible from poverty. It was so demeaning and inconvenient. They were now relieved and relaxed. The constant headaches both used to suffer had disappeared. They did not lack the basic things they needed to live well. There was always food to eat and leftovers thrown away. They had the type of clothes they wanted and liked to wear. They had the simple things, such as soap, pomade, and perfume that poor people had to do without for lack of money.

* * *

"Good morning!" a distant cousin greeted both Mama and Papa Tejiri atop their balcony lounge.

"Any problem?" Papa Tejiri asked back.

"I am just passing by and felt I should greet you," the middle-aged man answered.

"Thank God," said Mama Tejiri, as she looked away from the person who had greeted them.

When they first moved into No. 48 Okpara Street, both Mama and Papa Tejiri had been pestered by needy relatives and friends. They had many relatives, since they hailed from nearby Agbarho, though they saw themselves as Warri residents. As for friends, they had not as many. Not many people really considered them as their friends until Tejiri settled them on this lofty place. The relatives and friends believed that they must be very rich, who lived in such a fine house. And they came when in need to seek assistance or outright relief from Mama and Papa Tejiri.

After a few weeks of the pestering, the couple grew exasperated. They realized there were too many people having problems with basic needs that they could not solve with their stipend. At the beginning, saying they had no money convinced nobody who came to them for assistance. Soon, they started to have headaches from the shameless persistence of desperate people, who would not leave after being told to go. It was in response to what the elderly couple saw as unwarranted harassment that they soon began to dismiss whoever greeted them. They made themselves unreachable by now locking the gate to the fence surrounding their house. They believed one could only beg or ask for money from one who was accessible. They could not feed or assist all their relatives and friends, they told themselves. They rejoiced that they had got rid of their headaches.

"How are you Mama Tejiri?" an old friend of hers asked from below.

They now looked down on those looking up to them.

"Any problem?" she asked.

"I was passing and saw you outside," her friend explained.

"Thank God there is no problem," Mama Tejiri responded dismissively.

Soon everybody in the street knew them as the "any problem?" husband and wife. Their relatives also considered them as their "any problem?" blood kin. Friends also knew them by the same appellation.

Those who used to greet them felt offended by their cold and insulting response.

"Do you feed me?" one cousin asked.

"What do you think you are? Are you Michael Ibru because you live in your son's house?" Mama Tejiri's old friend asked.

Soon nobody was greeting them in their high balcony. They were surprised by the silence that surrounded them. Relatives, friends, and passers-by did not greet them as they used to do. When they saw the elderly couple, they looked down or to some other direction, and passed.

Mama Tejiri did not like this new silence.

"Why is it that nobody wants to greet us anymore?" she asked Papa Tejiri.

"How do I know? I am here with you. In any case, what do we need greetings for?" he asked.

"It's not that greetings sustain us, but don't you like being greeted?" she asked back.

"I don't really care. Those who pass by see us and that's enough," he said.

"I don't like the silence," she repeated.

"Do you like having headaches?" he asked her.

"Of course not, but I don't like the silence," she answered.

Mama Tejiri decided to remove the lock from the gate. Let whoever wanted to see them come in, she told herself. Papa Tejiri did not oppose her and allowed her do her wish. However, no friends or relatives came to visit them.

* * *

Mama and Papa Tejiri did not know how their son had become rich. They did not ask him the source of the wealth that had made him to build many houses around. They had just been contented with the lift he had brought to their lives.

When Tejiri could not meet the deadline for his loans, his bank did not mince words.

"If you don't pay by the deadline, we'll have to seize your houses that you placed as collaterals," they wrote him.

"Just give me a little more time to clear the debts," he pleaded.

"You know we can't wait for too long," they wrote back.

The second building was the first casualty of the bank's tough policy on defaulting on business loans. Even the tenants of the building did not know that their building had been seized by the Atlantic Bank. One Friday evening, notices were posted on their doors that they must leave their separate flats by the next Friday. "Defaulters will not be permitted," a flyer announced on the same doors.

No. 48 Okpara Street was next in the bank's determination to recover its debt from Tejiri Akpome. The Atlantic Bank's General Manager had written to the Economic and Fraudulent Crimes Commission office in Warri about Tejiri Akpome's loans and debts. The Commission had sent in two of their officials to photograph the building, No. 48 Okpara Street.

Mama and Papa Tejiri were sitting comfortably in the porch on a humid day. It was an early dry season afternoon with the sun blazing. Once in a while, Papa Tejiri succumbed to the urge of taking gin, and this early afternoon was enjoying with his wife glasses of the Schnapps that his son had sent to them.

"This drink is losing its spicy taste," Papa Tejiri said.

"Don't you know that it is no longer imported but made in Nigeria?" Mama Tejiri asked her husband.

"That's true. I am not surprised that Schnapps has lost its original flavour," he said, nodding his head.

"Still, it's better than our *amreka*," she told him.

"Of course, *amreka* cannot be a match to Schnapps," he affirmed.

They were certainly enjoying the now milder but still valued drink and did not know what those men in black suits meant by taking photographs of their duplex. They clicked many shots, taking photos of the building from different angles. The couple put down their glasses to fix their gaze on the men in their grounds.

"They may be journalists and will likely publish our building in the newspaper," Papa Tejiri told his wife.

"That will be nice. God bless Tejiri for providing us this beautiful building that everybody will like to live in," Mama Tejiri said.

"I believe in future we'll be able to charge those who want to take photos of our home," Papa Tejiri told her.

"We are going to be much richer than we are now. Let nobody come to us with their problems pretending to greet us," she said, proud and believing that their home was the cynosure of every eye.

No other photographers came to No. 48 Okpara Street before a series of catastrophic events started to unfold.

Meanwhile, as both Mama and Papa Tejiri awaited more photographers to come to take photos of their homes and even imagined foreign tourists coming to have a tour of their duplex, they thought of wealth that would make them the richest family in Warri. In their imagined status, the Akpome family would displace the Edewors, the Sokohs, the Odibos, the Obas, and the rest whose names had become legendary in Warri.

They continued to sit in their favourite position upstairs. Once in a while they sipped their Schnapps. A few times they placed an empty bottle of the gin on the table as they sat in the porch for every passer-by to see them. Whenever anybody greeted them, they turned their eyes to a different direction. When such a person persisted, as if they did not hear well and greeted again, Mama Tejiri asked "Any problem?" in a very cold voice.

"No, Ma. I just want to greet you. I am going to the market," the young lady, a niece, told her.

Mama Tejiri could not explain why passers-by had resumed greeting them. It did not occur to them that no relative or friend visited them in their lofty home anymore. They did not want to be bothered by poor people. They had left the low class and would not like to be reminded of it. They did not want to be pestered by demands for financial assistance. Everybody should work for his needs, they now believed.

One of the men in black suits, who had taken photos of the house, came as early as nine o'clock one Monday morning. He entered through the gate that had remained unlocked since Mama Tejiri decided to have it so. The man in a black suit did not greet anybody. He only posted an announcement on three spots on the house walls. "House Seized by Atlantic Bank. All current residents must leave in a week!" The black suit man left without talking to the residents of No. 48 Okpara Street.

Upstairs, after breakfast, Mama and Papa Tejiri thought the tourist industry that would make them even richer was about to begin. This must be the final phase before their house became a tourist attraction.

"Let's go down and see what the man posted on our wall," Mama Tejiri said.

"Go and read it and tell me whether what they wrote there describes the house well enough," Papa Tejiri replied.

"You are too lazy," Mama Tejiri chastised him.

Mama Tejiri held his hand, and he followed her downstairs. They stepped down with the dignity of first-class chiefs, one slow but steady step after another; their heads erect and not looking down. They had the confidence of residents familiar with their house and its steps. Mama Tejiri jumped down at the bottom of the stairs and Papa Tejiri did the same to show that, though slightly older, he was as agile as his wife.

They were dumbstruck by what they read on the posters. Could this be true?

"I have to read this with my glasses," Papa Tejiri said.

"Let me hurry up to bring them," Mama Tejiri said in a loving tone.

She came back with the old pair of glasses that Papa Tejiri rarely used but made him look so avuncular. He used the edge of his wrapper to clean the glasses and put them on. He stared at the poster. It was what he had already read, even though now magnified into bolder characters.

Was this not a fraud? After all, Nigerians were so smart that they tricked people from their own property? Could this not be the 419 type of fraud that radio and television presenters talked so much about and warned people against?

"It's only Tejiri who can answer this," Papa Tejiri said.

"How can we reach him very soon since he is away on a business trip?" Mama Tejiri asked.

Mama Tejiri decided to lock the gate to stop anybody from coming in to post any more bills on their house walls. She went up and came down with a heavy lock they had never used for the door before now. They had to keep out fraudsters from their home.

Things were getting very tight for Tejiri and he had to be close to his home. He came back from his business travel two days later. His parents sent for him and he came. The father brought him into the parlour, out from the porch where Tejiri had wanted to sit. The parlour appeared to have taken a dark look despite the sun outside. The son did not sit down before his parents started expressing their concerns.

"Have you read the poster on the wall?" Papa Tejiri asked.

"What is it?" he asked back.

"Atlantic Bank is seizing this house. Is it true, and what really happened?" his father asked him.

"If they are seizing the house, it is true," Tejiri told his parents.

"We are as good as dead!" Mama Tejiri shouted, lifting her hands up in the air.

"Why should this happen to us?" Papa Tejiri asked.

"Take it easy. That's life," Tejiri pleaded with his parents.

* * *

The Catholic Church took pity on Mama and Papa Tejiri after they were evicted from No. 48 Okpara Street. They had no friends or relatives to go to. The Church could not look on while two of its members, and old for that matter, suddenly became homeless. It was a pathetic sight to see the two abandoned in the open in the rainy season, their belongings in black polythene bags. The Social Welfare Committee of the Church acted promptly by renting a one-bedroom flat for them in an area of Warri that Mama and Papa Tejiri would not like to mention as where they lived. Their cook and monthly allowance were gone. Their son had disappeared and nobody knew where he was. Rumour and gossip said he travelled out of the country to avoid being jailed for economic fraud offenses.

For weeks and months Mama and Papa Tejiri barely left their new home. Their headaches had returned. They could not believe that they had come down so low within such a short time. When time had made their new status a compulsory badge they had to wear, they ventured out more often. They often felt like leaving the heat and dirty surroundings of their new home to have fresh air outside. In the process, they met people—relatives and friends.

It was their turn to receive the type of shock they had inflicted upon others.

"Good morning, my son," Mama Tejiri greeted a nephew as he alighted from his car to go into the church.

"Any problem?" he asked, as if he did not know her, and went straight into the church.

Both Mama and Papa Tejiri remained silent. They realized the irony of the situation. They went into the church to pray for God's forgiveness and mercies.

10

The Priest's Dog Falls in Love

Many who saw Reverend Father Daniel would not believe he was a Catholic priest who had taken the oath of celibacy for the rest of his life. He was the sort of forty-year old man that single women would dream of dating or marrying. Five feet, eight inches tall and rather moderate in size, he exuded inexhaustible energy as shown in his walk and overall demeanour. His face was naturally smooth and he had a fair-toned skin that made him stand out in a group as the fair one. He was also the calm one, as he maintained a calm temperament at all times. His fellow priests called him Danny but his congregation would not go that far familiar and so called him Father Daniel. He had obtained his Ph.D. in Sociology, with a concentration in the subgenre of sociology of religion; in his case, traditional communities and their responses to new religions such as Christianity and Islam. There were no Muslims in the communities he studied and so he focused exclusively on Christianity. He flew his shirts and wore jeans to work. He also put on jeans or casual wear at home. He laughed a lot and was very witty and humorous, often provoking his company to spontaneous laughter. Many people also called him the laughing priest to distinguish him from other priests who looked glum and thus seemed not to be happy with their priestly vocation.

At the College of Education, Warri, where he taught in both the Departments of Religious Studies & Philosophy and Sociology, he was a popular lecturer; admired by students and colleagues for his professionalism and sense of propriety. Students used him as an example of a lecturer who favoured no student, was never late to any of his classes, patient, and an exceptional lecturer who maintained wonderful rapport with them no matter the level they were in. The students wished they could assess their lecturers and, if they did, would have ranked Father Daniel the best in almost every aspect of teaching. To his colleagues, he was always ready to assist. He was one of the few you could call upon to give you a ride or take over your class if you were going to be unavoidably absent. He asked of you by phone, if he did not see you for some time, and visited you if you were sick or admitted to the hospital. He was a good human being to everybody on the college campus.

Contrary to his outward un-reverend appearance or un-fatherliness in being seen as more of a regular lecturer and not showing off his priesthood in mantle, preachy attitude, or other aspects that marked the conventional priests, he took his priesthood very seriously. He took his respective duties as a lecturer and a priest as one of service. He saw himself as God's servant and serving his fellow human beings, young or old, students or congregation. Service, he believed, meant making sacrifices, which he did as both lecturer and priest.

Of course, he considered his priesthood uppermost. After all, he trained as a priest after graduation and only went for post-graduate studies after his ordination. He was grateful that he was allowed by the Church to continue with his studies and felt he had to repay kindness with more kindness, and trust with even more trust. He considered himself blessed and so should pay back in the form of service to the Almighty and His children.

Father Daniel got to know most members of his congregation, whom he visited for one reason or another. He was adviser, counsellor, and confidant to many members of his congregation, including those far older than him. He was the trusted one. What you told him ended with him. He did not use what a member of his congregation told him in confession to preach against sin. He believed in the fallibility of humans and encouraged his congregation to constantly fight against sin by doing their utmost. He compared sinning to falling down and getting up, dusting oneself, and doing the utmost to prevent falling again. Yet he knew that, as long as one is human, one was bound to fall again and again. What matters, he told members of his congregation was the determination not to sin again and admitting that sinning was going against God's wishes that one should avoid. His philosophy seemed to have been a marriage of Roman Catholic strictness and intellectual liberalism, which made him a very unique priest.

Father Daniel kept a dog that the older members of his church often teased him about as his wife. Billy looked well-fed and taken care of. It was rumoured that Father Daniel spent plenty of money at the veterinary doctor's office once in a while to treat the dog when it fell sick, and that strengthened their likening the canine to a loved one being taken care of with so much money. The rumour mill also had it that Father Daniel, the laughing priest, was moody whenever his dog was sick. On its part, Billy was very protective and possessive of its master to a fault because it did not know what the duties of a Catholic priest was to his congregation. It stood between him and others, men, women, and children, who came too close to Father Daniel with threatening barks that made them either stop on the spot or withdraw instantly.

To Catholics of the community, Father Daniel had to conduct the sacrament of matrimony, be involved in naming ceremonies, baptizing children, and performing burial rites. He was invited to many occasions and he usually obliged, if he did not have a prior engagement scheduled for that time or day. As counsellor to his congregation, he advised on issues ranging from infertility of one of the partners and backsliding Christians to flirting men who neglected their wives; common problems the reverend father had to deal with in a patriarchal community in which the men set strict rules for the women and no rules at all for themselves.

Mrs. Theresa Ede was a fairly young widow and a regular member of the church. Losing her husband of only eight years was a jolting blow to her. She always wondered why she married Mr. Ede who was not as educated or as rich as her other suitors. If she did not, she often mused, her life would have been very different and her husband might still be alive. But she did not want to question fate and knew there was something charming in Mr. Ede which she did not see in the other suitors whatever their education or wealth. She had also felt that Mr. Ede loved her more than those suitors, most of whom wanted to have her as a possession or a trophy to show off as their beautiful wife. In any case, the unfortunate had happened and she had to accept her widowhood. She had no other choice.

Her late husband's family wanted to transfer her to one of the man's junior brothers but she did not accept that as a Christian or modern practice. The infuriated family took revenge on her by stripping their rented apartment of the man's belongings and the couple's joint belongings, including the bank passbook, chairs, beds, and Toyota Camry. She knew she was young at thirty-two years of age and had to continue with her life. Fortunately, she had gone to school and completed the National Certificate of Education, which made her qualified to teach in elementary or secondary schools in the state. She taught at Uvwie Secondary School and she was seen as a devoted teacher by the students and her colleagues.

Theresa had volunteered to do so many things in the church that Father Daniel knew her as a devoted member of his congregation. In fact, she volunteered so often so as to be noticed by the relatively young, highly educated, and charming priest. She joined the women who swept the church twice a week, Wednesday and Saturday evenings. They also swept the entire churchyard and weeded wherever was overgrown when necessary. Her service in the church did not interfere with her teaching at Uvwie Secondary School. When Theresa asked Father Daniel when he would be free to see her, he had given a matter-of-fact response.

"Come any morning or evening after Mass and you can join the queue of those who want to see me. I'll surely talk with you any day you come."

"I'll be there on Wednesday evening," Theresa told him.

"See you then," Father Daniel replied.

There were many issues that a young widow would like to discuss with her priest, Father Daniel naively thought. Theresa had only a daughter, seven years old, and she was attending the Catholic Primary School, Effurun. Was the widow finding it difficult to cope with taking care of herself and her daughter? With secondary school teachers paid so little and still owed many months' salaries by the Delta State Government, Theresa might be having a financial problem, the priest thought, and so might be asking for help from him or the church. Or could it be that men were harassing her for sex or even marriage? At thirty-two, she was very beautiful and in her prime with her oval face, large eyes, gap-tooth, tall height, and moderate size. Men around, he knew very well, wanted concubines or secret second or multiple wives to satisfy their lust. From his little experience in life, he knew a thousand and more things could be in somebody's mind. So, he did not want to conjecture what she wanted to see him about. When she came to him, he would know why; not till then.

Wednesday soon came. There was a thunderstorm that lasted from late morning till early evening. It was one of those storms when the sky seemed to be crashing on earth with relentless lightning flashes and thunder. It flooded most parts of town with debris strewn across the streets. The storm brought cold that kept people to stay indoors and to wear sweaters to keep warm. It was an evening that was not cheerful to venture out. Everybody knew that the cool breeze of the evening would turn to extreme cold later in the night.

There was prior agreement that whenever the weather was bad on a Wednesday evening, sweeping the church would be postponed till the following evening. This happened often during the raining season when it could rain any day at any time and schedules were not strictly enforced. Father Daniel did not expect many members of his congregation to attend the 6 o'clock Mass that evening, and truly they were scanty. Only the most ardent members of his congregation showed up. He was pleased that, few as they were, they came at all. If so few came to the Mass, he did not expect anyone to wait behind to see him, as was the routine after evening Mass. Of all those who had booked to see him, only Theresa came in through the waterlogged streets to the evening Mass. As the seven or so others who came for the Mass left, Theresa waited and followed Father Daniel to his residence, a bungalow in the church compound. He had a study where he did his counselling.

"Take a seat," Father Daniel said to her, pointing to a chair on the other side of his desk.

"Thank you, Father," she said, genuflecting before she sat down facing him.

There was silence as Father Daniel waited for Theresa to tell him what she wanted his counsel for. At first she waited as if also waiting for Father Daniel to start the conversation but soon realized it was she who had asked to be seen. She started trembling but managed to summon courage to start off.

"I just felt like coming to see you," she told the priest.

"Are you sure you don't have something troubling you that you want to discuss with me?" he asked.

"No."

"Always follow the path of Christ and Holy Mary, both of whom will give you strength to bear your condition," the priest counselled.

"What condition?" Theresa wondered in her mind. Was he praying for her not to be human or what type of prayer was that? She asked herself.

"Thank you," she replied.

The meeting turned awkward because Theresa did not say anything and continued staring at the priest who at first looked at her but later turned his gaze from her. Even then he could feel the woman still looking at him in a manner he could not understand but found distracting.

"Feel free to come and see me when you are ready to talk. I am a priest and whatever you tell me I keep confidential. And mind you, it is always good to confide on somebody and seek advice from a disinterested person. Maybe I can help you." Father Daniel told her, as he got up, signalling the end of their appointment.

Billy had stood beside Father Daniel, as if monitoring what he was discussing with Theresa. It stared at Theresa, as if ready to pounce on her should she make a move against its priestly master. In fact, when she was silent and staring at the priest, Billy had barked and startled her. But neither priest nor Theresa made any meaning of the barking before the dog sat down by the priest's chair and wagged its tail. Wagging its tail, Father Daniel knew, meant the dog was happy. He did not know what made it happy after the barking.

More visits followed. Father Daniel was not naïve. He might be a priest but he was an adult man and also had a doctoral degree in sociology. In subsequent visits, Theresa brought him gifts, ranging from food items to shirts.

"Theresa, I am a man of God. I can't refuse your gifts but I don't need material things. You know that I am OK with my salary from the College of Education and you should be the one that needs support."

"I felt I should give you from the little I have," she told him.

"Thank you, but I would prefer you to take good care of yourself and your daughter. By so doing, you will be assisting me in my priestly mission," he told her.

Theresa changed from giving material gifts to bringing only food to Father Daniel. He ate the first few times and knew that she must have exhausted her culinary skills and spent a huge sum of money to prepare such delicious dishes. Once it was fresh fish *banga* soup with *amala*. It had bitter leaf and an assortment of spices that would make one not even hungry to overeat. He enjoyed the food and even wandered as far as to think of men who had wives who prepared such sumptuous dishes for them on a daily basis. His mind went to Theresa because a woman had to really like or love you to prepare this type of food for you. One makes sacrifices for the person one loves, he knew as an adult man. Theresa was making sacrifices to please him with food. She must like or love him.

He knew he was straying in his thoughts and quickly crossed himself and said a "Hail Mary" for forgiveness. Temptations of things of the flesh often came and were routine but the good priest, he understood, had to fight back and overcome such worldly weaknesses. Father Daniel promised himself that he would be priest to his entire congregation and not be too close to only one woman, a beautiful one for that matter, because Theresa was extraordinarily beautiful; he was thirty-eight and only several years older than her from an earlier inquiry about her age.

One evening that there was no meeting, before the six o'clock Mass, Theresa came with another food - *jollof* rice and plenty of beef, oxtail, *shaki*, *kpomo*, liver, kidney, and some dried fish, she told him. In the "warmer," a flask-like container, one could smell the fresh spices that went into the food. The day before, Father Daniel had held court within on his relationship with Theresa. Was it proper for him to be receiving the widow in this manner and eating her food specially prepared for him? Did she not know that whatever man ate her delicious food would fall in love with her? Was food from a woman not a message of affection? As priest, could he refuse audience to any member of his congregation? Was he not getting too interested in this woman who now occupied his mind even as he did his priestly prayers? The other day, when he said Mass, as he faced the congregation, he saw Theresa and stared at her for a few seconds but it was an awkward moment that even the congregation would have noticed as not normal of him to hesitate in the rites he was so used to performing. He knew he had to do something, which he was not sure of. But he felt he had to remain a responsible priest that God had helped him to be up till Theresa came to confuse him with frequent visits and sumptuous food. "God, help me over this woman!" he prayed before he fell asleep the previous night.

"I am full now. Leave the food there for me. I will eat it when hungry," he told her.

"I hope you will enjoy it," she wondered.

"You are an excellent cook and whatever food you prepare must be very tasteful," he complimented her.

"Thank you, Father Daniel, for enjoying my food," she replied, smiling.

* * *

When Theresa came to visit Father Daniel the next time, Billy ran to the gate as soon as it saw Theresa entering the church compound with other women and men. It appeared Billy had sensed the woman coming because up to ten minutes before Theresa's appearance with other members of the church, it had run to the gate several times, looked out and come back to the priest's house. It stood facing the church gate and wagging its tail. Despite Father Daniel's call for it to come inside the house, it stood gazing at the gate and continued wagging its tail. And it sprang out towards the gate as the shadows of the people coming in appeared and only very keen eyes would have noticed that. Billy ran to Theresa and made gestures as it would do to a bitch when on heat and then started to follow her. It jumped at her in a playful manner, always wagging its tail with excitement.

There was some consternation as to how the dog would be so familiar with a member of the congregation and a beautiful woman for that matter. At first the group looked on at the spectacle of Billy and Theresa almost struggling with each other in a tenderly manner. She had to caress the dog's head and back, but it seemed the dog wanted more of her cuddling. The dog acted like one who wanted to be carried. She lifted it and later placed it down as they came to the front of Father Daniel's house.

"Her beauty is visible by humans and animals," an elderly woman remarked.

"Did gorillas not rape women in the bush in the olden days?" an elderly man asked.

Father Daniel had noticed the transformation in Billy after it had eaten Theresa's dish of *jollof* rice and assorted pieces of meat. Billy knew the person whose food it had consumed and was perhaps showing appreciation, Father Daniel at first thought. He had promised in his prayers to Holy Mary and Jesus Christ not to eat Theresa's food again and to succumb to temptations of the flesh and so had given the full big plate to the dog, which it ate voraciously, as if it had been starving for days. After eating, Billy rolled on the ground, got up and performed what looked like a dance. It started to behave weirdly, rather horny, afterwards. And the priest noticed the new behaviour of his dog.

Theresa had taken extraordinary steps to make sure that the relatively young priest fell in love with her. She loved him, lusted after him—the handsome face, the muscular arms, the charming smile, everything about him excited her and her nights and days had been reveries on Father Daniel's sensual body. She saw in Father Daniel what made her fall for Mr. Ede out of the multiple suitors before she married. She noticed so many features in physique and character that her late husband and the priest shared—from their gait to their liveliness. She felt possessed by the priest's body and presence. Many times she had fantasized their walking hand in hand in a lonely garden and kissing and later their sharing the ultimate intimacy in which she reached an orgasmic state shouting meaningless words. She liked and loved him but it seemed the priest was unmovable.

She had discretely asked for where she could find a medicine man to assist her in moving the immovable priest so that she could be the sole object of his affection; the apple of his eye, to put it in a cliché form.

"I want him to hunger for me as I hunger for him night and day. I want him to think only of me and have me!" she told the medicine man.

"Anything else?" he asked her.

"I just want him to have no fulfilment till we are each other's significant other!"

"So you want him to so desire you that he should not have peace unless he sleeps with you?" he asked her.

"Yes," she answered.

"You want him to overlook everybody else and have you as his only solace?"

"Yes."

The medicine man, who boasted about his total success rate in his prescriptions or preparations, had given her what to put in the food of the man she loved but who did not respond to her. She did not reveal to the medicine man that she was in love with a reverend father.

"Make sure, you prepare the food with wishes of your being in bed with him," the medicine man had exhorted.

She nodded.

"Spend a good sum of money to have a tasty fish, *eba* - every man loves that fish! Use the most expensive spices to awaken his manhood. Try to buy a pigeon and use it with corn and the fish. No pigeon leaves corn alone!" he intoned.

"Add one cube of sugar and a spoonful of honey. Once he tastes your special food, you will remain special to him. Once he eats your sweet food, you will be sweet to him and he will remain restless until he fulfils his intimate wishes with you," he also told Theresa.

She again nodded. He gave her three seeds of alligator pepper and seven corn seeds to blend with her ingredients in the food.

"Alligator pepper awakens one's manhood. He eats the food you prepare with these alligator peppers and he will seek a consummation with you!"

Again she nodded. She kept the items meticulously wrapped and tied to her wrapper and went home to do as she had been told. She felt the five thousand naira she paid for the consultation was nothing compared to what she would gain by being loved by Father Daniel, now the love of her life. As for the medicine man, he knew the efficacy of his medicines lay with the faith of those he prepared them for. Love medicine was fairly easy, he reflected, as he used his experience and common sense as an older man. This was one of such and he would not be surprised if, in another month, the woman so spent so much money on the food and became so seductive that she would get the man to bed and praise his medicine man's craft.

Theresa meticulously followed the instructions she had been given for the special dish to make her irresistible to the strongest willed of men. She foresaw the efficacy of the prepared food with the required ingredients and fantasized a sex orgy with the man she loved. She had starved herself since Mr. Ede's death two and a half years to this time and now she felt the time was close for a consummation with the only person she wanted to be in her life. He was the only man that stirred her womanhood in dreams and real life. She spent a big sum to buy the fish and meat for the food.

* * *

Once the priest saw how Billy behaved, he knew his dog was no longer his own. It stood by Theresa and did not even answer his call by wagging its tail as it was used to doing not to talk of coming to him. He was sceptical of exorcism and felt there was nothing he could do if a spell had been cast over Billy. He gave the dog to Theresa. He was not surprised that without hesitation Billy followed her home without looking back; the same Billy who before now would have died resisting rather than be separated from him. As for Theresa, she realized that her desire had been short-changed because instead of getting a man to fall head over heels for her, she got a dog in his place. Such was life, she told herself. As she often heard, one cannot say one has failed without having tried. At least she had tried!

11

When Pastors Took the HIV/AIDS Test

The order came directly from the Overseer himself at the Church's headquarters in Lagos. As the supreme leader of the Garden of Eden Assembly of God Church, his orders must be obeyed by every member. Every pastor of the Church, according to the order, must test for the dreaded HIV/AIDS. The disease had become such a scourge in the society that those who ministered to its victims or counselled others against promiscuous and unprotected sex must check themselves as to whether they were themselves free from it or not. "You must take the mote from your eye first before removing the one in another's eye," the message added, paraphrasing the Christian prophet's saying in the Holy Book. This would help pastors in praying for not only the afflicted outside but also those among them who carried the disease. The Church must grapple with the ugly reality of the disease and not be in self-denial, according to the Overseer, Bishop Julius Oyebode.

The church boasted of top professionals in different fields. Among the Church's members were eminent doctors who would supervise the test. It was too important a test, according to the Overseer, to leave to ordinary health technicians and nurses alone. Fortunately, the foremost expert in the country on sexually transmitted diseases that included HIV/AIDS, Dr. Ola Latunji, was a fervent member of the Church. He was among those who had volunteered to serve when called upon to perform the screening exercise. The Overseer got some other members of the Church that had private hospitals to voluntarily offer or donate their screening equipment to be used in the exercise. The pastors and staff of the Garden of Eden Assembly of God Church in Lagos had undergone the screening, with the Overseer himself and his wife, the beautiful and indefatigable Ronke, popularly called Mama Oye, among the first batch to be tested and come out negative. It was true that the

Overseer, Bishop Oyebode, wanted to lead by example; hence he and his wife had joined the queue for the testing like every other pastor in the Lagos area.

Ronke had heard rumours, which she had passed to her husband, about some pastors who were having affairs with members of their congregations. She knew that Nigerian men expected their wives to be faithful to them but they did not feel obliged to do the same to their wives. Of course, the cardinal law that the Lord handed over to all humans is "Do to others what you will like to be done to you!" It is a simple injunction that every human being should understand, she believed. With her husband travelling all the time, most times alone, outside Lagos, only God knew what he did in the name of evangelizing. She knew her husband very well; he could not do without her for a half week, and yet he was away sometimes for over two weeks. He had travelled without her to Britain and the United States of America a few times and stayed a month each time. He was a man of God but God made humans to be fallible, she believed. Upon all that, her husband was a very handsome man who dressed very well and was a great orator. So, much as he was a man of God, he was still a man with desires that needed to be filled when they ran riot. And she knew what women could do to get a man they so desired. She knew what it took her to commit the then Pastor Oyebode to marry her. It was a lot of sweat, cash to buy gifts, scheming, and more things she would never disclose now as a bishop's wife. That was after she had observed that many women were so much interested in him, with some scheming to her hearing the extent they would go to get him to marry them. To her, if your rival threatens using powerful means, you have to use more powerful means to overcome them. Now she thanked God that she was not naïve that praying alone was enough to secure her wishes. After all, God helps those who help themselves. God had helped her as she helped herself towards achieving her goal.

She was thus very pleased that her husband had listened to her to compel all pastors to take the HIV/AIDS test. And she was personally pleased that both of them had led by example by being the first to take the test publicly and had come out negative. For her, she had cleared a nagging doubt about her man of God. She had to do it for other wives of men of God to be assured of their partners' fidelity.

It was now time for pastors of the congregation of the Warri Diocese of the Garden of Eden Assembly of God Church to do their screening. Onome Efeludu was a female pastor of the Effurun branch of the church, a vibrant part of the Warri Diocese. She had converted to the new church from the Catholic Church and become "born again" before training and ordination as a pastor. She was single though she was in her early forties. She had had a child while in secondary school, a situation that had complicated her life and had not afforded her to be a real single woman. However, she made up her mind to devote her life to God and so trained for two years to be a pastor. After being an assistant pastor for a year, she had become a full pastor.

There was trepidation among the pastors. Whom did the Overseer get this idea from that he was subjecting every pastor to? Was it his idea or his *shakara* wife's? They had come to realize that the Bishop's wife was as strong as the Bishop and many members had for long suspected some orders of the Church coming from the Mother of the Church, Mama Oye. This was an order none could disobey publicly. Only through cunning could they deal with the situation. It was a wild card that could go either way, many believed. Nobody was sure of what could happen because nobody was sure of himself or herself. The fear of the test caught all involved—it was better not to know than to know the positive condition, many felt. Bishop Oyebode and his wife were becoming dictators for ordering all pastors to mandatorily undertake the test. How would the Bishop be railing against military dictatorship and still issue this edict? These pastors now felt they would obey their Bishop as they did military dictators out of fear. Fear of being singled out as not doing what others were doing. The consequence of disobeying the order was not talked about publicly but everybody knew what it would be.

Onome had thought of not taking the test, but how could she among so few women pastors be absent without being noticed. She had heard of people who had contracted the disease in inexplicable circumstances. That is, it could be got not only through sexual intercourse, nor through cuts. It was sometimes a mysterious disease that could strike at random and for no just cause anybody whom it wanted to afflict, she believed. Or it could be contracted without knowing in so many ways she could not think of at the time. She had had sexual relations before, but she had for the past three years been without a man friend and abstained from sex. She had promised herself that she would not make love again unless with a man she could call her husband. Until then, she would not abuse her pastoral mission and also free herself from any of the sexually transmitted diseases.

But she feared for her past and not for her future. Her present condition was thus uncertain. What, if in those wild years in which she was almost a sex addict, she had contracted the disease? It was after an elderly female pastor who lived near her told her that she was not only ruining herself with so many men she blatantly dated but was doomed to hell that she had a moment of reflection that set her on the pastoral path. She learned that the disease took time to show—from as short a time as two years to ten or more years. She was very afraid of what she had carried in her body from the past when she indulged herself in so much pleasure of the flesh. She feared a terrible disease was incubating in her. Her heart beat a loud anxious drum that she felt others close to her could hear from her chest.

"Fall into line!" ordered the chief epidemiologist, who came from Lagos to supervise the exercise for the branches of the Church in the Delta area. There were more than fifty branches of the Church in the state and some big churches had up to four pastors with one designated as the Senior Pastor. Onome's branch was a small one that had opened only two years ago. Her congregation was small but that was not the problem now. The test with what it would result in grabbed her to the present reality. There was no way of escaping this test now that she was here, and she had been compelled to be here by the order of the Overseer. She wished she could be out of the scene but that by itself would not be an answer because of the roll call of the pastors of the Church in the Delta.

A queue was soon in place and it ran the length of a football field. Male and female pastors, young and old, were there. So were their spouses, for those who were married among them. It was the atmosphere of a trial by ordeal, even though this was a modern medical procedure—extract drops of blood after piercing a finger with a lancet and then drawing the blood into a vial for the screening. Each person's blood was clearly labeled to avoid confusion and to show that everything was being done professionally.

As they stood in the line, Pastor Onome's heart continued to beat a loud and arrhythmic drum. Among those standing on the line of men and women of God were those drawing lines with their toes. Others, who took pen and paper to the exercise, doodled. And many others stared into blank spaces, unsure of what the results of their tests would be. She could only think that many were like her praying not to be disgraced by a positive result.

Some three men slipped out of the line in quick succession; no-one was sure of where they went to, toilet or home. After all, they had registered in the big book that they had come for the AIDS/HIV test. Whether the results would be written beside the names, nobody knew at this stage but from the seriousness of the order from above those without results would be dismissed or publicly reprimanded and would still be compelled to do the test at their own expense. Many were praying silently for their past dalliances not to be discovered. The Lord is a Merciful Father and should make them come out victorious. It did not matter to them that there was no war or battle involved in the simple medical test they were about to take.

Onome was among the few unmarried female pastors of the church. Her baby while in her fourth year in secondary school was now a postgraduate student of petroleum engineering at the University of Benin. She had wanted to marry but somehow her relationships with men did not go far enough to talk of marriage. In a few cases, the past twenty years, whenever she brought up the issue of marriage the relationship broke down immediately. This was one of the main reasons after her sexual escapades for two decades that she became "born again" in the Lord Jesus Christ. She could not continue in that course without heading for disaster. Now she would not allow any man to come into her again unless he had married her. But she remembered the decades of free love that she had experienced. She did not want to give a number to the men who had slept with her before she gave herself to the Lord—it was quite a number for a woman who was not a prostitute.

Onome's turn came. She had come to the table where two nurses sat on plastic chairs with their tools ready for the finger-piercing and blood collection. Each person was asked for the mother's name.

"Mine is Umukor," she said, and wrote it down.

She wondered why she was asked for her mother's name. After all, she had written her full name on the form of consent she had to sign. She did not want to bring her mother into this test. She remembered when she got pregnant while in secondary school and her mother's disappointment and calling her a prostitute for not having self-control until she completed her secondary school education. They remained on poor terms before she died without their reconciling. Her mother had refused to take the baby when she delivered it and her aunt in Igbudu Quarter of Warri did later to allow her go back to school. She saw anything involving her mother as a bad omen. She blamed her mother for her not having a husband up till now because she broke up with any man who was very interested in her always after such a man asked about her mother and she told them lies about what a great relationship they had before she passed away. Since they had failed to reconcile before her mother's death, she wanted to keep away from that name and the bad memories it evoked.

Though the test was supposed to be voluntary, despite the Overseer's order, she felt it was under duress. How could she not obey the Overseer's order? She stretched her hand trembling. She steadied it so as not to be seen as afraid. Was she already an AIDS victim or why should she be afraid of the test? She knew too well the trial of those suspected of possessing witchcraft among her people in the olden days. They were taken to Uzere to be thrown into the Eni Lake and those who swam out were considered innocent, while those who drowned were witches and deserving of their deaths. But this screening was a different thing she had to go through with courage. Only God knew the secret of those already infected with HIV/AIDS. She prayed as she stretched her hand for the nurse to take the blood sample that would determine her fate. It was really her fate in the Church and in life. Who did not know among the pastors that whoever tested positive for the HIV/AIDS would eventually be removed from pastoral duties as showing a bad example to the flock? After all, every pastor was asked to preach the results of Bishop Julius and Mrs. Ronke Oyebode's tests. Yes, theirs was negative, but would the Overseer have ordered the announcement if their results had come out positive? Onome realized that she was venturing into rebel territory in the Garden of Eden Assembly of God Church. Even if not expelled from the Church, what a shame to be known as an AIDS victim and pastor at the same time! She continued praying to the Lord to forgive her past dalliances and give her grace. After all, she had already given up the loose life of old for one dedicated to Jesus.

Then she was tagged like every other person going for the test. She was given the anonymous number 64. Of course, she knew that her name was written beside the number 64 in the record book kept by the nurse. She was not deceived that she was not known as Onome Efeludu on the vial that would hold her blood sample and whatever happened to her would be public knowledge. There was no hiding in this test just as there was no hiding from God, the all-seeing. She did not even feel the lancet's prick that brought out the blood suckled into the vial already labelled 64; her mind was deep in prayers for God's grace.

The process did not last long. In a matter of about two hours, as results were compiled, each person was called individually. Every woman whose test was negative sprang out of the counselling room and shouted "Praise the Lord!" to the chorus of "Alleluia" from the women in the waiting room. Every woman so far who had gone for her result had turned out negative. Onome prayed that she should not be an exception to this trend of the past twenty minutes. The women, who were told that they were free of HIV/AIDS, danced and raised their hands in gratitude to God for saving them from the scourge. In their hearts, they knew they were saved from the highest form of embarrassment and humiliation. Even if their husbands, whom they could not refuse love, had slept with other women, they were at least free. "Everyone to his own cross," they had been told.

It was not yet Onome's turn. When she feared that she might be already infected with the dreaded disease, the clock on the wall moved too fast. Under such a circumstance she would like to be the last to be shown her result. Nobody would be there to know her true state. Within seconds she felt she would surely be like the other women who had received their results. In that case, the clock was too slow and she would like to be called next to the counselling room for her result to vindicate her negative status. She wondered why it was taking a longer time to call her now than when she came in for the test. She hoped she would not be jinxed by her mother's name. However, she realized that because this was done randomly, it would be a matter of minutes before being called for her result and counselling, if necessary.

The men that were coming out were all "boning," as they said in Effurun and Warri. They walked briskly but gracefully without showing any emotions. One could not tell by their strides whether or not their tests were negative or positive. And it seemed they meant it to be so. It was as if the men had had a meeting and agreed on how to come out of this confidential exercise.

"How now?" one asked, to Onome's hearing.

"I don do my own-o. I dey go home," and he waved like a triumphant politician with a made-up smile.

Another man was called in for his result and came out with clasped palms that gave no indication of the result of his test. One could guess it was either a sign of relief or a form of distress but his gesture could not be interpreted in a definite way.

Onome soon noticed a pattern. It appeared the results were being released according to their seniority in the pastoral hierarchy. Her turn came about the end of the exercise when her heart was beating such a loud drum that she feared those sitting close to her would hear from her chest and ask her whether she was well or not. She got up from the chair she was sitting on and walked to stand by the wall, as if she was tired of sitting. She knew nobody except God could read her heart and mind.

"Onome Umukor!" the senior nurse shouted.

"No, I am Onome Efeludu!" Onome instantly corrected.

"Yes, Onome. We use the mother's name here after the first name," the nurse explained.

Onome almost fell from the chair, feeling that her mother had taken revenge on her by smiting her with HIV/AIDS. She was surprised that the past few weeks, some old boyfriends had complimented her for losing weight and being in good shape, younger than ever. AIDS patients continued to lose weight till they became very thin and frail before succumbing to the monster of a disease, if no treatment was administered. She prayed. She wondered why the nurse was searching for some other papers. Did others spend as long a time as this? She asked herself.

"Onome Umukor's test is negative. So Pastor Onome Efeludu, you are free of the dreaded disease. Congratulations!"

"Praise the Lord!" she shouted before the nurse.

As she stepped out, she shouted "Praise the Lord!" so loud that she startled the only woman and about ten men still left to receive their results and looking down as if the delay meant they were already doomed and would be positive. Among them was Pastor James Igho, a married man, who had been making advances to her the past six months but she had been determined to dismiss him. His wife was friendly with her and had visited her once. Pastor Igho's wife was the only woman still left there.

Onome felt relieved that she had not been caught for all the sexual liaisons she had indulged herself in the years before she joined the church. She would ask from senior pastors and elders how to reconcile with the dead. Enough was enough. She had to make up with her late mother who had brought her good luck this time. The Lord had saved her. As for the men who did not show any emotions as to whether positive or negative, she realized that only God knew what was in the hearts of His children. After all, they were all naked before the Lord!

She stood a moment in the waiting room before leaving to salivate her victory. She went to greet Mrs. Igho whose husband had just been called in for the result of his test. As Onome and Mrs. Igho exchanged pleasantries, Pastor James Igho came back weeping and shouting "No! Not me!" He could not behave like the other male pastors who had "boned" in such a way as not to betray their real status. Apparently he had tested positive. A nurse led him out, asking him to seek treatment for his positive status rather than complain about the veracity of the result of his test. As Mrs. Igho joined her husband in weeping before she was called in for the result of her own test, Onome felt sorry for the man who had been seducing her with all sorts of fantastic promises. She felt vindicated in not yielding to any man who was not her husband after being "born-again" and more so after her ordination as a pastor.

12

The Whole Thing

When my friend, Vero, delivered a baby-boy, who weighed twelve pounds, the doctors and nurses, according to her, said they had never seen such a big baby in their maternity ward of Warri Central Hospital. They had also not seen a woman that looked that elderly compared to others that came there deliver such a big baby, as she had done, without a caesarean section. They had hailed her as a superwoman and she had acknowledged the compliments with nods and smiles like a heroine who had liberated her people. She wished, as she had seen in American movies, they had swamped her with balloons inscribed with "It's a big boy!" She realized she might have set a record, at least locally. And she displayed that bravado despite the fact that she had been so drained in the delivery as to have blood transfusion immediately afterwards. That was almost exactly three months after her daughter, Vicky, had a baby-girl that weighed seven pounds in the same ward. They had different last names, my friend returning to her father's name of Akporhono because she did not want anything to do with the former husband and his name again, and her daughter now Mrs. Vicky Esegine. Despite their names, the nurses and doctors knew them to be mother and daughter, and Vero knew that they knew them as such.

My friend had been so excited when she conceived that you would think that was her first time and as if she had never had the experience several times before. And that excitement was also despite my misgivings about her having a baby at her age. When a woman of forty-eight or more got pregnant, she was surely looking for health problems to wrestle with, I knew from experience. Not personal experience but from stories of other women around who had gone through pregnancy at a late age. But there was a limit I could go discouraging one excited with her pregnancy about what to do with it. After she had announced it with a fanfare, I would ask her if she had thought of an abortion, which she confessed to me she did not want to consider as an option at all.

"The God that made me to be menstruating till I became pregnant will see me through this," she had said.

"Amen!" I answered.

I knew she really wanted the baby and was set on going through the pregnancy experience. I prayed that her path to and through delivery be smooth. I also prayed that the Almighty protect her for being excited over a pregnancy that could pose a threat to her life. If she had been thankful for this pregnancy after praying to God for it, I prayed to God to give me what I really needed and not just what I wanted or desired. In her case, she wanted or desired it but did not really need it, I thought.

When I visited her in the maternity ward, she smiled broadly and said, "I made it!"

To me her statement meant she had some doubts about making it but had hidden her fears from me.

"We thank God," I told her.

"Alleluia!" she responded.

"You are a very strong woman," I complimented her.

"I thank God for giving me the power," she told me.

Vero was not the church-going type of person and it struck me how the pregnancy and delivery experience had brought her closer to God, whom she now invoked at every opportunity. She was now God's favourite child because of the seeming ease with which she went through pregnancy and delivered her baby without life-threatening consequences. She was exhausted, yes, but that was not unique to her; every woman, young or of her age, suffered exhaustion after labour and delivery.

After a nurse told me the weight of the child and the transfusion my friend had received afterwards, I had to hold back from telling her that she had narrowly escaped losing her life. To me, she did not understand the gravity of the situation she had just gone through. The room's fan was at its highest speed because the hospital authorities did not use their air-conditioners when their generators were on as now. The room was plastered with pictures of nursing mothers that were breastfeeding their babies, singing lullabies to them, or doing some other motherly things one could to babies. I looked at the cot beside the bed to see the baby but it was empty because the nurses had taken it away so that its mother could sleep and rest after her feat of delivering such a big baby. No doubt, my friend had put in all her energy into achieving a feat and she deserved sufficient rest after delivering the big, baby-boy.

After three days in the hospital, Vero was discharged and she had to leave with her baby to her house where she lived alone. I spent that her first night as a new nursing mother at her home with her. I observed her a few times singing in a very low tone to herself and smiling. Once or twice, she seemed to forget that I was physically with her there. I saw her shaking her head to an unheard music as she smiled at the baby in the cot in her bedroom. I wondered how she would have managed to take care of herself and the baby if I were not there to assist her. She was still weak despite her saying she was fine and strong enough to be home. I had to press her body with warm water and stood by while she showered. Her feet did not seem to be strong enough to hold the champion mother up for long enough to bathe. I had to encourage her to take the pepper-soup I had prepared for her. "I am fine," she told me when she knew I was worried about her. Of course, I had to take care of things at my home and, after the first night, had to visit her frequently because I could not move in to take care of her on a permanent basis.

It did not take long before she began to experience the reality of a new nursing mother, as she would later tell me. Before this baby she had had three children; two girls, including Vicky, and Victor, her only boy before now. None of the earlier children lived with her. Her former husband had won custody of the two other children who lived with him and they appeared to be happy with the arrangement because they did not visit her, even now that she had delivered. I tried to assist her as much as I could. I did grocery shopping for her and prepared different types of food, which she kept in her freezer. Fortunately for her, the electricity supply in the area she lived was fairly regular and she had no problem preserving her food. She had a microwave, and that made life easy for her because I served portions of food in plastic containers kept in the freezer. As my friend grew stronger, she knew the time was fast approaching for her to take care of herself and the baby-boy, who took both the liquid food formula and still sucked her breasts voraciously. It was as if the baby had escaped famine in another world and wanted to have as much as possible from the new abundance of life in its mother.

Knowing that I knew her excitement at her conception, I could sense now that Vero did not want to complain to me about her situation. At least that was the way I read things at the time. When the baby was sucking her breasts, she felt and showed it that this was too much a drain on her vital fluids. She often murmured what sounded like a curse and that made me cringe. When it cried sharply, she was startled as if she was not holding the baby or it was not nearby. It was clear that she did not have a good night's rest but she would not complain to me, her friend, who had dampened her excitement at conception. "I am fine," she would tell me, almost needlessly, considering her plight.

Only two months after her delivery, Vero called me very early in the morning and was talking in a manner that was not characteristic of her. She had a clear feminine sonorous voice and always talked straight. This time her voice and speech were different. I knew she might have thought about what she wanted to tell me all night to call that early. But still, she talked like one who was drowsy and at times sounded incoherent. She normally spoke softly and excitedly like a flowing clear river. I guessed she must have had a very bad night, perhaps without sleep with the baby crying and sucking her breasts non-stop.

"I am feeling bad about the whole thing," she told me.

"Vero, what are you feeling bad about?" I asked.

"I don't know, the whole thing—this pregnancy and baby thing. I don't think it was a good idea allowing it to happen in the first place. And now I am like a prisoner of my own desires."

She would have gone on talking but I felt she must be in a bad state of mind. I believe she had grown tired of covering her true feelings about the "whole thing" from me and was now opening up to what I had only been suspecting—that the delivery and taking care of the baby were exacting a heavy toll on her physically, emotionally, and psychologically.

"Vero, I'll be coming to see you immediately. Just be calm and take care of your baby," I said and dropped.

In a rush I took the *akara* and oat meal I had on the dining table, quickly made up, and took off for her place. She needed somebody to talk to, me at least, to console her because I feared for a mature woman, a grandmother for that matter, who was feeling bad about the "whole thing," as she had described her state. I felt "the whole thing" was very loaded with foreboding.

It had not occurred to Vero that this would be the case at the beginning when she realized that she missed her period after her daughter had told her that she had become pregnant. She had toyed with the idea that when they delivered, she after her daughter, they could breast-feed the other's baby and allow one to rest. She had known from experience the challenges of nursing a baby—the wearing out with the baby's sucking of her breasts, the sleepless nights because of the baby's cries at odd hours when she should be sleeping, and more. This time it would be fun if she and her daughter came to live together and took turns to perform the responsibilities of a nursing mother. Each would be the other's help in multiple ways. But that was then, when she was pregnant. She had told me these things excitedly.

"Are you dreaming at this your age?" I had asked her.

"Of course, I feel like a teenager with this pregnancy and I am excited by the fresh joys of motherhood."

"Do you know you are in your later forties now?"

"And then?" she asked back.

"I think your new love has blinded you. You used to be more cautious than this. Your last delivery was fifteen years ago and you still want to try it? Going on with this conception is a terrible mistake at your age," I had warned her.

"It is already there and I want it," she had said with finality.

I felt she wanted to make a point, irrespective of its consequences, and so romanticized the idea of conception in one's late forties. After all, she had told me, her former husband had married a much younger woman who was in her late twenties and had had two children the past four years. She did not realize that a man's body and a woman's were not the same. The man was not the one carrying about the pregnancies or delivering the two children from his new marriage. The man was not the one breastfeeding the children in their infancy. The man did not prepare food for himself or for the babies, knowing the sort of men we had in our patriarchal society. And, of course, her ex-husband's new wife was much younger and was having children for the first time. I joked with her, "You forget say you don drop three engines already!" And she always replied, "E no mean anything!" She and I knew that she was denying a fact of nature, since a woman who had delivered three children was not the same as a much younger one who had not delivered one. No one can cheat nature, as we often say.

Vero had for over ten years divorced her daughter's father. That was long before Vicky would marry Esegine and both she and her former husband had sat next to each other quietly in the bride's family pew during the wedding. She had moved on in her life, as her former husband had also done. But, unlike her former husband who had gone to re-marry, she had remained single to take control of her own life, as she wanted it. By taking control of her life, she meant she could have as a friend a man she felt really loved her or she loved but could leave the relationship when it became loveless or betrayal was involved. She had gone through many of such relationships, including with a man ten years younger than her, until she met Eugene Egbo, who had lavished her with so much love that made her mad for him; the sort of love any woman would dream of but could not have. She let down her guard because the love was so sweet and strong, as she would later admit to me, and consequently became pregnant.

Now that her baby had come, crying and demanding constant attention, she had lost the zeal for motherhood. I remember when I visited her several weeks ago after she newly came back from hospital with the baby. She lived in her own house since she did not want to live with a man in his house. Eugene, anyway, had a wife he had married according to customary law, and Vero was not going to live with another woman sharing one man. Better to share the same man without the two women seeing each other, she felt. In the days and weeks following her delivery, she had felt so relieved whenever the baby was crying and I took it to sing lullabies to calm it. She seemed to have forgotten how she raised her three earlier children because she appeared helpless before this baby. A mother of Vero's experience, I thought, should know how to instinctively calm a crying baby. This baby was hyperactive and would not allow her to rest. She discovered that this baby at her old age, as she would say, was more of a burden than a thing to be excited about. She was alone and Eugene visited but not as often as she would want after he closed from work. He spent time with her but left for his own house. He was not the man who slept in a woman's house however comfortable it was. This Vero had known over time even before she became pregnant. But now the arrangement irritated her. Why should only she be bearing the brunt of their baby's cries? Why did he say he loved her and wanted the baby too when she told him that she was pregnant? It was true that they did not discuss how to handle the baby when it came, but the man should know that everything from lovemaking through conception to caring for the baby should be a shared experience. To me, Vero wanted to renegotiate the terms of her relationship with Eugene. I could only watch her because it was their business.

Of course, Vicky was at her marital home consumed by her own task of raising a first child. She had no experience and was stuck at home with the baby. My friend's daughter did not come to her as she had wanted. It was the practice for the mother to come and assist when the daughter delivered, especially the first child, but this could not be the case this time because even at the time Vicky delivered, Vero was so heavy she feared she might have twins. She was not in a condition to go to her daughter to assist her. It would be laughable and weird if she moved to her daughter's home with her own pregnancy. My friend could not anyway because her daughter's husband, Mr. Esegine, who had got a woman help for his wife, would not allow such an arrangement. After all, he was married to his wife and not to both mother and daughter. More so, a mother who was consumed by her own pregnancy and anticipated baby!

Tormented by a late-age baby that she had thought would be a joyful experience, my friend became restless. She lost her sleep almost every night, since her baby chose that period to cry and be hungry. Even during the day, she could not sleep with visitors arriving unannounced to congratulate her on her safe delivery of a handsome boy. That went on for weeks after the delivery. Now she felt the visitors, some of whom she did not know, were coming to mock her, an old woman by their thinking, or just see the big boy, the biggest baby delivered in the hospital without a caesarean section, to feed their gossips. Whenever she looked at the baby now, her mind went to her daughter also nursing her baby-girl, she told me.

"Shit!" she would shout out, as if unaware that I was there with her.

"What shit is that?" I asked.

"Don't bother!" she would say.

"Vero, you must know that you are this baby's mother and are responsible for its welfare. Don't shit it!"

"I have to take care of it but it's a burden I am finding out that it was light to pick but now crushing to carry. This baby will kill me if I don't kill it," she replied.

"Don't talk that way!" I admonished her, wagging my right forefinger at her; "None of you will kill the other."

I was abhorred by the vehemence of my friend's voice. It appeared she now hated her baby.

"If you tell me so, I have to do so. Some evil spirit was telling me to do some bad things before you came," she admitted.

I knew that my friend would kill this baby if she remained in that mood where evil spirits visited her and gave her orders. A time might come when she would be so helpless as to take orders from them to slash herself or the baby. She had to be lifted from that state because she seemed paralyzed by the onerous weight of having a baby after her midlife. I had to call my husband and children to inform them that I was going to sleep over at my friend's.

That night Vero bared her mind, heart, and soul and I realized that she was overwhelmed by a plethora of problems. She was lonely, lonelier than at any time in her life. She needed her man's emotional support, which she felt she was not getting. And, of course, she wanted to be with her daughter or the other way around. She felt excluded from the life she wanted to live. She also felt excluded from the company she wanted to keep and she blamed the baby for her being abandoned. I told her that I had not abandoned her and would not do so no matter what happened. She was so touched that tears rolled down her cheeks as she smiled broadly at me. I picked a piece of toilette tissue to wipe the tears from her eyes and clasped her to myself. I knew she could come out of the dark hole where those evil spirits lived and from where they harassed her relentlessly. She could come out of that mood from where she saw her baby-boy as shit! But she needed support, mine and that of others.

We sat on her bed most of the night talking. I told her that life was not easy for anyone, including those of us who were married. However, each person had to make conscious effort to make life less of a problem for herself. By daybreak I had succeeded in asking Eugene to take my friend with the baby on a one-week vacation anywhere outside the state and also in persuading Vicky to come for a week to keep her mother company after they returned from the vacation.

* * *

By the time Vero came to spend three days with me four weeks later, she had turned the corner and was back in her cheerful self and filled with zest.

"Theresa, you have saved me and my baby," she told me, as I sat on the bed with her in our guest room.

"Only God saves," I told her, even though I knew what she meant by saying that I had saved her.

"Those dangerous spirits no longer visit me and I get no orders to do abominable things. Things are changing for me," she told me.

"I am happy you are coming back to your normal self," I replied.

Her complexion had changed to that shining black beauty that she was known for since her elementary school days. Her cheeks were full of excitement. Her spirit was of a bouncing woman who defied her forty-eight years of age. Now she was a spritely thirty-something or a woman in her early forties. Love can perform wonders. No wonder folks say that the mind is a mirror of the body. Vero exuded happiness. She now adored the baby, who all of a sudden had become quiet and did not bother her unless hungry and once fed played on its own. What only a few weeks could make in the life of a mother and her baby-boy!

Vero told me how she got the fun of her life when Eugene took her and the baby-boy for a vacation at the beach in Badagry.

"The baby was not a problem to us. The fresh cool sea breeze with its salt taste, the blue expanse that spread into infinity, the freedom of it all easily calmed and restored me to my normal buoyant condition. Of course, you saw my frazzled body and rattled nerves resulting from the burden of post-midlife womanhood and a baby. And give the devil his due, Eugene was fantastic. He served me food, did what he felt would make me happy, and took care of the baby too. I never knew he could take care of a baby. He performed wonderfully and the few times the baby cried, he sang some nonsensical rhymes to keep it quiet. I was amazed at his love for me and for the baby."

"I am happy for you. This is how it should always be," I told her.

"Ah, my friend, I know I have to put on a coil now, which in the first place should have saved me a lot of trouble. There's always a packet of condom nearby now. But I am happy that I have Godwin. I love him and he will grow into a great son. As for Eugene, he says he owes me two vacations a year from now on."

"I envy you-o!"

"Wetin man go do?" she asked, in response.

To top it all for Vero, Vicky came with her baby daughter to spend two weeks with her and Baby Godwin. I visited mother and daughter and their babies twice during the period. What I saw confirmed that

Vero was able to live the dream she had wanted, long in coming but not forgotten. She deliberately asked me to take her out and left her baby for her daughter to take care of while we were away. At another time, I had to take Vicky out for a half day leaving her daughter with Mommy Vero. My friend later told me that she felt good breastfeeding her daughter's daughter, her grandchild. She had heard stories of such in the olden days and there was nothing more loving than mother and daughter breastfeeding the other's baby.

We laughed as we ate or talked.

"You don enjoy well with your man and your daughter. As for you and Eugene, just be careful about another baby so soon," I counselled.

"No, I no get body for that again. The four engines I don drop reach-o!"

"So na only pleasure you want now?"

"Yes, now!"

"That's what you wanted from the beginning but you were either careless about or couldn't make him accept," I told her.

"That time don pass-o. We don enter new age! Who go reject good thing?" she asked.

We both laughed. I was happy that my friend had fully turned the corner in her state. I was confident she would not go back to that mood that invited evil spirits to encourage her to kill her own baby. I felt lucky that she became well without taking her to a psychiatric hospital. From her cheerfulness the whole thing had turned out right at last, I could tell.

13

The Pregnant Widow

Nobody saw Ojevwe travel out of town, several weeks or months after her husband's death and burial, and return, three or four months later a pregnant woman. This was a pregnancy resulting from a man and a woman's lovemaking. It could have come from no other way. Let all the doubting and gossiping folks wait and see. They would see her bring forth a baby. When due, she hoped to go to Warri Central Hospital where nurses and doctors would deliver her of the baby. Whoever visited her there and then would see the baby. She would not travel before her due time and return weeks later to town with a grown baby. Everybody knew that such so-called mothers had come back with stolen babies from only God-knows-where. People wanted to see to believe. They did not believe in the disappearing and reappearing acts of such women who became mothers. More so for a woman who had not conceived once in her life at her age before now! They knew when pregnancy was a fluke. Ojevwe vowed to herself that she would go to the local hospital so that those gossiping would know that her belly had not been pumped with gas or some contrivance all the while. Whether neighbours, relatives, and others gossiped afterwards about her conception, it was she, Ojevwe, who would have the final word about her child's name, Oghenerhoro Efebe. Let them spend their time to unravel the mystery that only she and God knew. Really, only God knows.

Ojevwe knew very well what the age of forty-four meant to a woman who had not had a child in fifteen years of her marriage. By the age of forty-four, things a woman had taken for granted at eighteen, twenty, twenty-five, or even thirty were no longer so. Hope is a blooming flower when young but will not remain so all the time, Ojevwe knew. Now some traditional sayings made more sense to her than before. As the day progresses, the palm wine gradually loses its natural sweetness. And freshness, she reminded herself. Freshness and sweetness go together with palm wine. Nothing remains forever fresh. It is the law of nature, she believed.

It was not just a matter of age to her. If she aged or rather ripened, as she saw herself, and there were things she could postpone till anytime in her lifetime, she would not be worried. But old age, the saying goes, is a kind of disease. It might not be a disease that wrecked or killed one instantly. However, it eventually took its toll on the body and was bound to disable, if not immobilize one. Age definitely slows or shuts down the workings in the human body, most especially a woman's, she reflected. She had talked with her fellow young women while in secondary school about the clock inexorably ticking on. Yes, the clock would always tick, she had felt. Now she knew the tick-tock was an affront to her womanhood, always fraying her nerves as she feared she might start her menopause at any moment. It was as if menopause was either stalking her or setting her up for a terrible ambush she feared she might fall into, and there was no getting out of its grip once caught. She did not want to fall into that inescapable position and live helplessly for the rest of her life.

Now she was pregnant and only five months after her husband's death! In fact, her pregnancy had become visible only a few months after she lost her husband. She knew what would be apparent to others: that her late husband had not been the one who had impregnated her because, if he were, such people would say, she should have been closer to term. Besides, it was common knowledge that the man had been incapacitated for three months before he succumbed to the complications of the stroke. They would add months together and come out with their own total of months and the oddity of her pregnancy. Odd her pregnancy surely was but it was something that she did not expect such people to understand. She also expected none of such people would know that even an incapacitated person was capable of instinctively seeking to fulfil his natural desires and in so doing also fulfils his marital responsibility. There are just too many things that people don't know about however closely they observe someone, she realized.

None of her neighbours had seen her with any man who could be said to be familiar in the sense of smiling or having any intimate relationship with her. She was still mourning, at least publicly, and that was bound to spurn gossips and questions that no relation or friend of hers could answer. She had many relations from her side and also from her late husband's side. She did not really have a best friend but only acquaintances. She did not believe in having friends in Warri where women competed for everything, from clothes to even their friends' husbands.

Nobody asked her any questions, or none of the gossiping or curious ones was bold enough to ask her whether she was pregnant, not to talk of whose baby she carried. She guessed they might be talking behind her but carried their faces in such a way as to ask, what have you done? She could read from the faces of acquaintances and relatives the question they were not bold enough to ask her. Still, she could sense their better-than-thou attitude as if she had committed an abomination. But she was not going to care about what people thought, felt, or even said. She had to live the life she had chosen to live. She had wanted the pregnancy badly for the past fifteen years, more desperately the past five years of the clock ticking so loud and fast in her body. Who knew her unanswered prayers the past years? Who followed her secretly to know what traditional masseurs she had gone to for treatment and the humiliation she was ready to suffer just to conceive? Who knew the temptations, arising from promises of conception, she had overcome to remain faithful to her late husband? Who followed her to hospitals for medical check-ups? Yes, she had wanted pregnancy and a child badly for so long and it was nobody's business how she became pregnant now. She had to be pregnant when it came even though she had sought it with a desperation she had not thought would bear fruit so soon after her husband's death. She had not expected it to come at all, but now here it was exposing her to the public. No woman could hide pregnancy in this society in which she had to be out, and there were so many nosy folks that pried into you for gossip materials.

The same people who were being nosy would be the same if menopause caught her suddenly and deprived her of any chances for pregnancy in her entire life. Those same friends and relatives would treat her like trash if she remained a childless woman or died childless. She feared the consequences of childlessness more than death and she had promised herself to do anything, even if scandalous or shameful, as she knew her case surely would now be taken to be, not to be childless. She prayed fervently that God would understand her desperation and its consequence that she now had to bear.

She would take things in good stride, living normally as if her late husband was still alive and she was a normal housewife who had conceived. When she woke, she would do her daily chores, and, if she felt like it, go to work. She was used to spending her time indoors anyway and would read or watch television so as not to feel bored at home and alone. Fortunately, there was a strike and she knew from the months owed teachers their salaries that there would be no school for a long time to come. It was one of those frequent strikes that could last six months or even an entire academic year. She went to her workplace, Essi High School, if she felt like going but there were hardly any teachers there. She believed most of them would be doing sundry tasks to make a living before their salaries would be paid. Several of her female colleagues must have been stunned to silence at seeing her pregnant because none of them congratulated her. Nor did any of them make any reference to her pregnancy which was very visible. And these were folks or colleagues who knew that she had had no baby before then. Her colleagues at Essi High School had been among those who attended her late husband's funeral at St. Patrick's Cathedral and must be carrying the memory of the sad event with them.

At other times she went to the market to buy foodstuffs from the same sellers she had known for so long. Igbudu Market was the largest food market around and she got what she wanted there.

"I am happy for you," the vegetable and fruit seller had told her, after looking at her closely, perhaps verifying whether the change in her body was real or not.

"Thank you," she had replied.

"A beautiful woman like you deserves a baby to round up your womanhood," the woman also told her.

"It's God's gift," Ojevwe said.

At least there was one who understood her situation that having a child was worth being desperate for and defying cultural expectations for, if necessary.

Another woman, the meat seller she bought beef from over the years, nodded with a smile at her. She smiled back; unabashed.

"Invite me to the naming ceremony when the time comes," the woman, herself past middle age, told her.

"I won't forget to invite you," Ojevwe told her, still smiling.

"I want to be with you when you present your child to the world with a name," the market woman added.

Only in the market, Ojevwe felt, did she receive some public approval for her current state. She saw some others in the market who knew her and also knew that she lost her husband a while ago turning away from her, as if she did not see them. She did not care for such people who did not have the courage to greet her or face her to be greeted. Still, the few warm hearts in the market made the life of a pregnant widow easier for her. That was why on days she had nothing doing and not really having much to buy she still went to the market to be greeted by the vegetable and fruit seller as well as the meat seller with whom she now chatted for longer periods even as they carried on their selling.

As for the sniffing folks poking their noses into her private life and looking for material to fuel their gossips, let them look stealthily at her to confirm their curiosity. Let those who chose not to accept her condition continue sniffing, she assured herself; she would not say a word on this. She owed nobody any explanation of her pregnancy. She did not need to tell anybody the man, dead or alive, who had made her a full woman by impregnating her.

Only God for sure and she perhaps knew how she became pregnant and she would not reveal that. It was a desperate and clumsy act that the sniffing folks would not even accept as what truly happened and so there was no need explaining. Would they accept as the true story that only a day before his death, dream or real life, she had placed her late husband on top of her and he penetrated her and had an ejaculation? Would they understand that even a sick man had feelings that had been bottled up that might explode at an odd time? Would they understand that that night his manhood had all of a sudden stiffened from excitement and that made both of them make love they had thought was all over in their relationship? But this story would give the unbelievers and scandal mongers more ammunition against her; they would call her a witch who killed her husband with her lack of self-control by forcing an already weak man to make love with her.

And would the gossips find truth in the story that the week of her man's death, even before the burial, a man who had come to commiserate with her was rained in at night and one thing led to another and they made love? And that man was so strange? And she could not confirm whether it was a dream or real life experience? They would still call her a witch who deliberately killed her husband so as to have the chance to sleep with a lover. Once she knew she had missed her period, it did not matter what happened. This was a secret she would carry to her grave, unless her child grew to a marriageable age before the Almighty called her away from this earth. Only then would she divulge to only her grown child what really happened that she was not even sure of. If that time never came, the secret would die with her. How would she abort the first and only pregnancy she had had up to that point in her life, no matter the strange manner of conception?

In her mind she had a mystery man who impregnated her. She herself could not tell who, her late husband, the man rained in, or some other elusive man, a kind of ghost.

"It will be hard on you," this man, more of a spirit than human, had whispered to her ears.

She discovered from the lucid voice and advice that her husband was only incapacitated in body and not in his mind. Or rather the resurgence of sexual desire had more than emotional impact on the man; his mind also clarified to him what she thought he was no longer capable of.

"I know but must bear whatever taunts in order to have the baby," she had told him.

"Are you sure you can handle it? You know our people and their way of thinking without sympathy for anybody whatever the circumstances."

"Don't worry," she had assured him, "I'll be fine."

"Are you sure?"

"Don't worry! I am the one going to be pregnant. I will carry the exhibit of our lovemaking."

"Fine then, good luck," he had said with finality.

He had died the morning after. She had become so confused for more than a week that she could not thread together the entire experience. Her late husband or a man rained in! Could the same person be a human and a ghost at the same time? Before her husband's burial, the weeks after his death, she had interacted with him in dream as if in life when they were younger. She gave him his favourite food which he ate with so much zest. They smiled and laughed and teased each other lovingly. Was the rained-in man not a ghost showering outside and later coming in to bed as a familiar man, her husband? But that was not important now that she had become pregnant. The mysteries in one's life happen for a purpose, she now believed. She accepted the pregnancy and would cherish the child for life.

Who will ever know how milk enters the coconut? She would keep her conception a mystery. She realized that some would say that her husband had not turned cold in the grave before another man mounted her. Most people had the luxury she did not have or could not wait for to enjoy. Her husband had not turned cold and might not have rotted in the grave when she stepped out of the matrimonial home they had shared, they would say. There was no way she could escape insults, pregnant or not; now that she was alive pregnant or if she had died without having a child.

Even when the husband had been sick and it was quite apparent that he would not survive for long, his junior brother had already started to look at her with such lustful eyes that she could feel his intrusion. His large eyes shot arrows at different parts of her body—breasts, buttocks, and she believed he must have penetrated her most private part in his imagination. He must have believed that she would be passed over to him as soon as the expected happened. She hated that sickening practice which she would not accept. Even at the time of her husband's bedridden stage, he would not have hesitated, she believed, if she had encouraged him by responding to his romantic or rather sexual overtures.

Even when the expected happened, within the week of her husband's death, the overtures were more brazen. His impish laughter, his offers of assistance in any way possible, his conscious brushing her physically when or where there should be distance, and more of such crude gestures. It was after one of such that she discovered the rained-in man in what should have been a dream. Her husband must have appeared to encourage her. That was before the burial which took place because of the rains five weeks later. She knew too well when a man was lusting after a woman and was testing her for more probing of a soft spot to exploit and eventual surrender. He must be one of those now gossiping and wishing to know the mystery of her pregnancy. Of course, he was trying to take over before his senior brother died and surrendered sovereignty over the marriage. Now she owed nobody any apology because she did not step out of the marriage when it was on and she did not break any vows to anybody in her action.

She knew the public would not understand her as a pregnant widow and so would behave like one who had a virgin conception. Some who did not wish her well might even think she was suffering from a very bad case of fibroid with a swollen stomach. There appeared to be an epidemic of fibroid among women around in recent times. She had thought it was a disease of older women, but it was apparently not so. She knew Kate, only thirty-three when she had it. Fortunately for her, she had had two children before her surgery and the removal of her uterus. Other women in their late thirties or of her age in their forties had suffered from it. But much as such evil-minded ones would think she had fibroid growing wild in her womb, she knew she was pregnant with a child. She did not care what her child would be, boy or girl; she was just happy that she would bear a child in a matter of months. She had escaped menopause's ambush with this conception. Whether beautiful or ugly, she would love her child. She knew that some of the gossiping folks might even think she was not pregnant but afflicted by something more terrible than fibroid growth in her womb such as a swelling disease that afflicted the stomach. Though she had not left home all the while, a few might even believe that she had gone to shop for a baby in Akwa Ibom or Cross River or some distant state in the federation and the big stomach was the beginning of a process that would lead to another travel with plenty of cash and her return with a baby! God knows she has no money for that expensive baby-swap trickery.

Yes, she liked the idea of a virgin pregnancy. Not that hers was so, since she was not a virgin. But hers could be explained as pregnancy without sexual intercourse or any medical enhancement therapies. She had heard of in-vitro fertilization but she had not gone for that. Efebe came down suddenly before they could think of trying it. However, thank God, despite his disability, they still managed to couple on the eve of his death. She always wanted to be sure of the father of her baby. She knew the father of her baby. To the public though, let her pregnancy be the first in the area of one without sex. They would not understand and she would not bother explaining to those doubters.

She expected none of her relatives or friends to know what haunted her like a ghost for so long. Not even the ghost of her late husband would frighten her. She had been faithful and loyal to him as any woman could be. Their marriage might not be a very romantic one but he and she had a good relationship. They hardly had a noisy quarrel and when there was a rare one, it spent itself out in a matter of a few hours or days. They had done the right things that a man and a woman did to have children but none came their way at the time for the so many years of marriage. Though one cannot trust a Warri man fully, she reflected, she believed her man did not have another woman by the side. As for herself, she kept herself fully for him. Fortunately, that ghost that tormented her for so long and would either drive her crazy or kill her had been laid to rest. Or rather, that evil spirit of menopause trying hard to stop her from conceiving had been exorcized. All the demons attempting to stop her from being a full woman have been vanquished. Thank God, she was now a full woman expecting her first child at forty-four.

* * *

Ojevwe's father had multiple wives and she had, before her marriage fifteen years ago, observed how Ayena had been mistreated. She was senior to her mother but had remained childless all the years of marriage. She had been taken as barren by everybody around because she had not been pregnant once. Ojevwe had not been aware of her getting pregnant or suffering a miscarriage, not to talk of her having a child and losing him or her. She had not been fertile and had no child to show for the years of marriage or years of her womanhood. Ojevwe remembered the song the younger women, her rivals, sang to her hearing in their constant taunting.

God, save me from a kola nut plant that cannot produce any fruit.

God, save me from being a desert patch in the forest.

God, save me from not being able to do what my mates do.

God will always give me a round tummy.

God will provide me names for naming ceremonies.

God, save me from the curse of a woman who is not a true woman.

God will always make my house noisy and filled with cries and laughter.

God will always bless me with a good number of children.

For some reasons, Ojevwe did not hear her mother sing the wicked song. Could she have done it when she was not around? The song scarred her mind irreparably and she would not be a sterile kola nut plant, if she could avoid it. Nor would she be a desert patch in the forest region. She wanted to be a true woman to experience noise, cries and laughter, in her home. She wanted to have as many children as possible. She did not know what happened to Ayena after her father's death. She must have left for her hometown and died miserably thinking of those wicked songs about her childless marriage and life.

Ojevwe's mind also went back to her youth. She must have been twelve years of age then. She would not forget what happened then because she had just started her first menstrual period and so had just become a woman, according to her mother, as if not always a woman before then. Her mother's sister had died and she wanted to accompany her mother to the burial ceremony in Kokori. Her mother had insisted that she should not follow her.

"But Auntie had been so good to me," she had protested.

"Yes, but you can't go to her funeral."

"She had taken me as a daughter and that is why I should be there. She has no other child of hers," she had argued in an attempt to persuade her mother to allow her go with her to Kokori.

"But that's why I don't want you to go," her mother had said back.

Maybe her mother knew something that she did not know, she had thought, and so did not accompany her to her aunt's funeral. She had wondered for so many years over that incident till she was much older, already married, when she asked her mother why she had insisted so many years ago that she should not attend the funeral of her aunt. That was long before her mother's own death.

"She did not have a child and you would not have liked what happened at the funeral," she had told her.

"But I would not have cared about what happened as long as I paid my respects to her," she answered.

"No, you are grown up now and so I can tell you. It would have been a bad omen for a young girl to go to the funeral of a barren woman. It is believed that her spirit of barrenness would seek a young woman to live in after the former carrier's death. I was uneasy about her adopting you almost as a daughter but I already had three of you and I was not going to be barren after that anyway. But I feared for you, I feared for your future."

Her mother looked away after telling her that. There was silence. She did not see the tears running down her daughter's cheeks and her wiping them off with her right palm before she faced her again.

"She was even buried in the bush because she had no house and nobody wanted her to rest eternally in his compound. I did not want her spirit to infect you with that curse," her mother resumed.

"That was wicked of our people to treat her worse than an animal," was all Ojevwe could say in reply to her mother, who behaved as if she did not hear what her daughter had just said.

Up till now her mother's "I feared for you, I feared for your future, I did not want her spirit to infect you with that curse" still rang sonorously in her head. As her mother's senior daughter, she remembered very well the celebration of life she organized for her. There was dancing and merriment as if it was not a funeral but a festival. She and her siblings wore the same type of clothes and their friends with their own friends and relatives came to make the place very noisy. She could imagine what her aunt's funeral would have looked like without any child of her own.

She would carry her pregnancy as a badge of honour whatever others might think of her or say about a widow conceiving before her late husband started to rot in his coffin. She needed a child at all cost and she would not wait to be a desert patch in a forest. Nor would she be the one at whose funeral mothers would ban their daughters from attending. She knew her late husband's brother would wish for her to deliver a goat from the way he now looked at her whenever they chanced to meet. She was ready for any child and would surely not forget to invite the meat seller to the naming ceremony of the boy or girl bound to be her child.

As for the child's father's name, that would be no problem. It would be Efebe. The child's name whether boy or girl would be Oghenerhoro because God had been wonderful to her. She knew her late husband's brother and other relatives would not be happy about the names, but she, as mother of the child, and God knew the father of the baby to be no other person than Efebe.

14

The Emancipation Walk

Efe had felt he was coming to the end of a road. All the signs of the landscape he was travelling within told him that. He was afraid of arrival at that unknown destination where he would become a deadwood. "A non-functioning writer is as good as deadwood," he told himself. Why he felt so was strange to him. It was like he saw before him a shrinking landscape that itself would end his career as a writer. He could no longer see beyond the end of the road and the prospect of his world totally shrunk to what he could not imagine frightened him. A vision that did not see beyond the immediate was poor, and he wanted to see far beyond the horizon. That was what his life as a poet had been—seeing through and beyond objects and material things. For more than nine months now he had not got a nudge of inspiration; no whisper into his ears from the god of songs. Not a lone poem, not an impressionable line, not even a fragment of anything that could be described as poetic; nothing floated into his mind when wandering aimlessly in his mental escapades. Things had gone smoothly his way the past thirty years when he wrote profusely, so profusely he was often described by critics as the most prolific poet in the country.

He who used to write as if summoning a flood from nowhere to drown rivals who could not swim in dangerous waters, he to whom words fell like ripe cherry fruits blown by an enabling wind to the envy of others who called themselves writers! He who considered himself the favourite of the god of songs had been silenced and his efforts to break the drought appeared to be failing. He wished he had been better known beyond the land with his poems on the lips of young and old in the streets, but still he enjoyed the modest acclaim. Above all, he enjoyed the fact that he wrote when he wanted, or rather he was always in a state of writing, a sharpened knife ever ready to do any cutting! A magic drum that played itself!

"How could I be this?" he asked himself. "I am sliding down a slope and if I don't arrest this, who knows where I will land?" he asked himself.

His house, though painted bright that was a combination of yellow and green, had become grey to him. It was enveloped in a lugubrious cloud only he could see that made him wonder if the greyness would not turn into something sinister and smother him. He lived alone in a three-bedroom bungalow at the dead end of Radio Road. You could not use the numbering, 78, to get to the house, since everybody chose their favourite numbers for their houses. He would not be surprised that there were many houses with the same number and that was why it was impossible to get to a house by its number in that part of Warri. He used to receive visiting poets who infected the house with laughter but for about a year now had not hosted anyone and the house had become very quiet like the cave of a hibernating fugitive.

Efe became a very worried man. He had been divorced for ten years in a childless marriage of twelve years. The marriage broke under circumstances he did not want to revisit. He consoled himself that there were many marriages like the one he once had and it was good for him to move on rather than pine over what he believed neither he nor Alice had the power to control. Everything had slipped off their hands like an eel that was lost forever into deep waters.

Recently his girlfriend of three years had left him. He took it too in good stride. There were many uncontrollable things chipping at his life and he wondered what would be left of him soon at the rate strange things were happening to him one after the other and without stop.

"How can I be naked in bed with you all night and we have not been together for a whole two weeks and yet you don't show any interest in me? Or have you been sleeping with another woman? You men, nobody can trust you!"

"So I have become 'You men'?" he asked back.

"I don't know but you will not see me in your unliveable house again," she said, and walked out, slamming the door so hard he was shocked at the vehemence of Cathy's rejection of him, since he could not raise himself to the emotional standard she wanted.

It was early, about six in the morning. Cathy had shaken him to be sure he was already awake. Rather than turn to face her, he did not know what made him turn to the wall side of the bed. That infuriated her into the outburst. Could a man not lose interest in what the woman wanted in bed for once? Must he be on heat at all times? He asked himself. And how could not showing interest just once after two weeks apart be the cause of this outrage that turned into an unforgivable breakup? Of recent, he had found Cathy too demanding of him and she was showing signs of exasperation that he could not cope with.

After she left, he thought for a moment about his house being described as unliveable. "Damn you, woman, I am living in my house and so it is very liveable!" he shouted to the empty house. He wished her good luck at her next watering hole.

Alone in his hermitage, Efe asked himself many questions that he did not expect to be answered because either he did not know or he was not sure.

"Can I still perform?"

"How can a person without inspiration perform?" a character he conjured up asked him.

"What has inspiration to do with love-making?" he dared ask the unknown character.

"Ha, ha, ha, so you don't know!" the strange character said and immediately disappeared from his mind.

"I never believed I would lose interest in love even if I lost interest in everything else," he said, as one confessing to a person whose expectations he had failed.

"Sure, sure, you get it yourself. You have hit the nail on the head, really hit it on point," threw in the strange character that had popped in from nowhere and soon disappeared as the words came out in the form of a prolonged dying echo.

Efe did not know where the character came from, the back of his mind or some spirit was speaking to him. He was scared more of what was happening to him than wherever the strange voice came from. He felt drained in a manner he could not explain to himself.

"If there is no life in a person, he is just a listless character. Passion enhances performance," the character chipped in again and of course vanished, voice and all.

"God, I don't want to lose what I have always had and had made me happy!" Efe prayed, like a spoilt child who did not want his privileges to be curtailed or punished by his parent after violating a parental order.

Not that he could think of anything wrong he had done to others or God to deserve the punishment of a shrinking landscape within him! He wanted to at least hold on to what he had enjoyed in his life and he knew God understood him without mentioning his desires. After all, he once wrote a poetic narrative in which a character wanted to know how to reach God and make demands and from nowhere God told the chap that he did not need to tell the Almighty what he wanted because He knew his needs!

If a jinx had suddenly been thrust upon him, he wanted to break it. He would spend as much time as possible of the next few days, perhaps weeks, or months, staying outside his house. He wanted to keep out of the greying rooms he had been confined to. He felt imprisoned in his own house where he had produced so many works that were acclaimed across the land as poems of emancipation. Now he wanted to just wander in town and seek what God or some benevolent spirit would give him to hold on to and continue with his life of seeing beyond the horizon. He called his project an emancipation walk.

* * *

Efe was doing the rounds of the streets to breathe fresh air after wondering whether Warri air could be fresh in any part of the town at any time of the day. But whatever that air was, smelly from sewage or other wastes or eye-twitching from fumes, it would be better than what he breathed in his own house which had become not just lethargic but stifling. Yes, Cathy had called it unliveable to mortify him. He was dying slowly at home, sapped by helplessness in his career. The other day he had stared at his writing notebook for several hours without putting a single word down. And that was not the first, second, or third time that words had refused to be summoned to his book. He had come to believe that he had lost the magic power with which he invoked a spell to summon beautiful words into a stream of verse as he wished. He no longer had access to the fountain that had fed his poetry for decades.

He had to leave his No. 78 Radio Road and just keep on walking. The condemned seek reprieve! Those enslaved seek emancipation! He wanted to expand his landscape rather than accept a shrinking one. The journey that would bring liberation must start with a determined first step. Now began the project he placed his hope on to reverse his shrinking life.

He did not take either side of Erejuwa Road, Lower or Upper. That was too busy for him to walk and leave his mind to also wander freely. Nor did he take Ometan Street that was always busy and he did not want to see the now ramshackle mansion that the late Chief Ododo, the *Olokun* of Warri, once inhabited. Taking Bazunu Road would be going in the same direction of where he had left—going deeper into Warri's greyness that he was trying to escape. Rather, he veered into Enemejuwa Road, still not tarred, dusty, and sparsely peopled as he had known that street from his early teens. He wanted to go through those streets whose names held a certain magic in his youth when life was exciting and you visited your age-mate friends as they also visited you. Yes, he passed Enemejuwa Street where you held the hands of your girlfriend and walked in the night because it had far fewer cars disturbing you. He by-passed Okoye Street where prostitutes used to beckon on any male figure shouting "Come make I make you happy!" The prostitutes were gone and he wanted to be happy. As a young man in those days, he and his friends did not want to be seen passing close to, not to talk of through that street. Mere sighting near there meant you had gone to meet your customers, and everybody knew what that meant. If they ever went there, it was deep at night when they expected nobody who knew them to be out at the wee hour.

He entered Mowoe Street and after a pole turned right. He reflected that nobody described distance any longer with the measurement of poles but now talked of meters and kilometres; poles had their magic because some short roads were not more than a few poles. He came to Igbi Street and a wave of old memories lashed at him. He remembered fresh BBC and WW 120. BBC was the madman who proclaimed himself "BBC London" in an affected Cockney accent some forty-five years ago. Some people then said he had gone overseas and come back mental but he did not look like someone who had ever left Warri all his ragged life.

All of a sudden Efe remembered one incident in those old days. He remembered how coming from Delta Cinema near Main Market in the business section of town in the night in a group, one of them, Godwin always naughty, shouted "*Onyeburu, Shiti Shiti* Man!" at the masked night-soil man. Upon hearing the insult hurled at him, the man took to his heels with a bucketful of excrements pursuing them. He felt hurt and had to wreak vengeance on them by splashing on them a broom dipped into excrements. Of course, as young spritely boys they easily outpaced the older man and they disappeared into some dark narrow streets. The man must have thought sadly about his humiliating job before taking his bucket of excrements into the truck numbered WW 120. Looking back, Efe regretted calling somebody bad names for working for money however dirty, and this was the dirtiest of dirty jobs! He quickly absolved Godwin from any guilt. They were young boys. It taught him how one person's action could affect the group. Any of them could have been fair game for the smelly broom splash. If he had children he would warn them not to demean any job.

He was now walking towards the Okere Road end of Ginuwa Road. De Luxe Hotel had shut down. All these streets had histories and legends that went untold and unwritten. Only a historian or artist could revive those streets into their glorious days when there was so much fun to every activity in town. That was when Warri was in vogue. Now he would walk on until he almost circled the old town of Warri. It was dusk; that time when night and day gracefully exchanged pleasantries before night suddenly fell. There was some light but it was a dull yellow glow that did not give much clarity. The light made figures look like shadows from a long distance. You had to be close enough to recognize anybody.

He came to the intersection of Igbi and Ginuwa Streets and the yellow light lost some of its dullness. The national electricity company was doing Warri residents a big favour after a five-day total blackout in the entire urban area. It was at this point of his wandering to kill boredom and win emancipation from mischievous characters floating in his mind that he walked into a dispersing crowd after one of the many open-air crusades that made Warri nights lively with a lot of people. There was noise of folks commenting on the crusade preacher's sermon about how only giving could make one prosperous. Giving in the name of God to anybody or the church, just giving would make one rich. Efe primed his ears to the air to hear more about the crusade which appeared to have just ended.

"Pastor Kolobia na my man! He know how to preach," a manly voice said.

"Na better pastor im be!" another voice added.

"If I bring better money, I for put-am for the collection basket. I want become rich. If giving the small you have fit make you rich, how I no go do the right thing," the louder masculine voice said.

"E good make we dey hear correct pastor."

Too many people were talking and Efe's ears could no more pick clearly the conversations summarizing what happened at the crusade. He had slowed down his walking pace and in fact stood for a moment to watch the crowd milling out and dispersing into all directions. He knew diverse problems must have brought the people to listen to the pastor in the hope of solving their problems. Life, he now realized, was a journey in problem-solving which took many forms. He knew the power of religion in the lives of his people and would not be surprised if the masculine voice would steal money even from a bank to give to the pastor so that he could be rich someday. That man would not take it that he was stealing or cheating, if he had any conscience to separate the good from the bad, for the sake of pleasing God to bless him. Yes, Efe reflected, Warri youths now asked to be blessed by elders they endearingly called "*Ose*" and that troubled him. While he loved their creativity in using words ingeniously, secular-minded as he was, he still considered it a sacrilege. The banality of it pained him as the Pidgin of his youth was so witty and ennobling.

In his front two young boys walking beside each other. They were looking around at the people dispersing into every available road, as if they themselves were not interested in leaving the grounds. The two boys, apparently in their late teens and wearing what looked like Arsenal Football Club's T-shirts and jeans trousers, were talking to each other in murmurs. The taller one nodded his head rightwards; a signal to action it turned out to be. Right in front of him the two boys shoved a woman to their left onto him. The sudden push made Efe to stagger backwards but instantly regained his balance to hold the woman as the shorter and slimmer of the two boys snatched her handbag. Fortunately, there was enough light for him to see fairly clearly and so saw everything happen in quick motion as if flashed for him to take notice. Summoned to action by an ever-alert guardian spirit, Efe grabbed the young man who had snatched the handbag and the robber easily gave up the booty to run away before he suspected Efe would cry "Thief! Thief" after him in a town where neck-lacing was the trend. Efe wondered why the shorter and slimmer one did the snatching because he believed he could not fight. In any case, the young man could not get away with his booty. Efe handed the handbag to the lady who had not fully recovered from being stunned by the robbery attempt. She took the handbag from him and pressed it to her chest. The fashionable Gucci bag held her purse and phone.

Efe knew the artist thrived on the unexpected; surprises that he invented in his poems. Real life offered such opportunities that artists seize upon. Inspiration came by chance. The world was created by chance. Things happen by chance. But does chance have any premeditation? Could a chance happening be arranged? He mused. He had expected the woman to walk away to her car or whatever direction took her home from this robber-infested crusade crowd.

"Thank you!" she said.

"You are lucky it was not dark here and I saw the boys clearly and they were close enough," he told her.

"Thank God they were not armed with guns or daggers," she said.

"Yes, some of these young boys could be dangerous."

"Yes, last week at Robert Road they killed a woman with a dagger for not surrendering her BlackBerry phone. Imagine somebody dying because of a mere phone or bag!" she told him.

"They are capable of doing anything. I must say we are lucky they did not resist; not the daredevil type of pickpockets or robbers."

"Thank you for saving me. This bag is a gift from my sister in Milan; she has been there for over ten years and visits yearly. I would have missed it if they got away with it. I don't know why I even brought it to this type of place."

"Very lucky, the attempt was repulsed without injury."

"I am Christiana," she introduced herself.

"I am Efe Tobore," he said.

"Are you the writer?" she asked.

"How could you have read anything I have written?"

"That was years back when I was an undergraduate at Ife. I was a Theatre Arts student but took some literature courses. You were one of the few poets we read in the course on Nigerian poetry."

"You gladden my heart to have read any of my poems."

"Do you live in Warri?"

"Yes. This has always been my home."

"How could I be in this Warri without knowing one of my favourite authors at school lives in the same town?" she asked, smiling.

"That's life!" Efe told her.

They soon realized that the crowd had melted to a few people trickling out. And these were carrying the loudspeakers and the other equipment used by the preacher into a van. They exchanged phone numbers. They would call each other because both of them would turn out to need company and somebody to talk to.

* * *

Christiana was built like those Urhobo women that Efe knew as a child in the farming countryside—never fat but not slim like a stick! Now forty, her body was taut; it was as if every excess fat had been taken away in her creation. She was relatively tall in her five-seven height, compared to the women around. She had large eyes, a rather pointed nose like the Fulani have; quite a surprising feature where most folks had flat-wedged noses. In her light chocolate complexion, she had a glistening skin. When she smiled, her beauty came out more as if a bright light shone from inside her. She was crowned Miss Federal Government College, Warri, before becoming Miss Moremi Hall while an undergraduate and a runner-up for Miss OAU, the supposedly most beautiful female student at the Obafemi Awolowo University at Ile-Ife during her second year of studies.

After graduating from Obafemi Awolowo University and completing the mandatory one-year national service, she felt ready to settle down, as she saw it at the time. She waited for the charming prince in her undergraduate plays and novels she had envisioned she would find to marry in real life, but there was no sighting of him for years and there was no hope that her dream partner would ever arrive early enough before it was too late. The real-life world did not bring any man to serenade her with poems as she had read of beautiful women in her literature courses. After many young men had asked for her friendship that she saw through as not serious, she had to diminish her expectations and settled for a politician, Ono Dudu, who had come courting her with determination.

If a man courted a woman with flamboyance, it was Mr. Dudu. He had completed his Higher National Diploma at the Auchi Polytechnic where he had read Accounting, which he never worked with except in the local branch of the national ruling party. There he would have made much money outside his moderate salary to live a flamboyant life that made him accessible to the so-called big men of the party. He soon established himself as an indispensable part of the local wing of the party that produced him for any important position that came up. He lived well by the standards of having a good house, car, and dressing affluently.

Christiana would learn later from the experience of living now with who courted her with such a flurry that she should have held back from him a little and waited much longer before committing to marry somebody she did not get to know too well. In any case, once engaged, things went very fast and she was soon Mrs. Christiana Dudu. She soon discovered that she was married to show off at home when her man received visitors, politicians from the entire state and sometimes from outside the Delta area.

Mr. Dudu bought her fine clothes and expensive jewellery and she looked stunningly beautiful when she wore them. He made her buy from the most expensive boutiques in town that brought clothes, perfumes, bags, jewellery, and other fancy items from reputable stores in Britain, France, Italy, and the United States. Many of her dress clothes that were not traditional were Western designer outfits that made Christiana look like a model.

Christiana had a house help, a lady several years her junior who assisted in going to the food market, the abattoir, the riverside fish market, and other places that spared the lady of the house dirt and inconvenience. All she had to do was to tell the help what type of fish, vegetables, and fruits she wanted to use to do the cooking. The help did the blending but Christiana had insisted from the beginning in doing the cooking for her husband and her guests. She needed assistance in cleaning the kitchen and the house but she would not surrender the task of cooking, which she enjoyed doing anyway.

The point was that while she cooked and dressed to entertain visitors, Mr. Dudu did not ask her to accompany him in his political tours which were many as he was the Vice-Chairman of the ruling party in Warri Local Government. Sometimes Mr. Dudu was away for not just several days but a week or longer and often did not care to call Christiana and check on how she was faring at home.

As soon as he found out that she was looking for a teaching job in one of the secondary schools in town, he queried her for trying to work for a pittance when he could adequately take care of her.

"Are you telling me that I can't take care of you or what?" he asked.

"It's just that I want to work. I have a degree in Theatre Arts and I need to use it so that it doesn't rust," she replied.

"Rust *ke*! Don't worry, I can give you as much money as you want and you can use this house as your theatre but don't cut my body when I am sleeping!"

Christiana was surprised at the ignorance of the man she had married. Could he not separate a surgery theatre from Theatre Arts? Or was he trying to be funny and mischievous? It was better for her not to explain the difference to him because he did not care.

"It's not the pay which I know is nothing to talk about but I just want to work and know I can take care of a few things myself," she argued.

"If you work, then I don't need to buy things for you other than the food we eat together," he said in a vehement manner. "Why work when I can maintain you?" he asked.

Christiana did not like the idea of being maintained like some property that has to be cleaned, reupholstered, or mended in other ways to look new or better than a worn-out state. In any case, she had come to know her man. Surely he did not like her working and so she had to give up talking about it. Give it up at least for now, she thought, because she believed marriage was an on-going dialogue between partners and her man could change his mind when she brought up the matter some other time. Soon Mr. Dudu was impressed that his wife was "born again" in a church he did not even know or care about. He did not go to any church but was happy that his wife was devoted to a church and trusted her as a virtuous wife.

She was very lonesome but believed many women envied her for just being wife to a politician. Such people did not know she was suffering, since her husband was always out for political or other causes. She was getting bored to death to the extent of being restless and just eating whatever she could lay her hands on from the fully stocked fridge. She knew that her husband took women along his many travels but she had no way of catching him. She would not have cared if he paid attention to her other than dressing her up for exhibition in his parlour when guests came in.

She had been scared from the moment her husband came home one day past midnight and woken her up to give her instructions:

"Don't come to my bedroom when you are under!"

"Don't prepare food for me from the moment you are expecting till you are fully dry!"

He could not even bring himself to pronounce menstruation because doing so meant soiling himself with it and he wanted to avoid it like contracting a fatal disease. He said these things in a matter-of-fact manner, knowing something important to his life could happen if she violated these injunctions.

In days of extreme lonesomeness, Christiana had thought of doing something to this man who did not let her into the secrets he must have sworn to in a cultic undertaking. There was proliferation of cults across the nation and in the Niger Delta in particular. The politicians that did not feel safe, even among themselves, joined these cults for protection. Part of their initiation involved taking oaths to do strange and sometimes abominable things. Christiana feared because some cultists submitted for sacrifice folks closest or dearest to them such as spouses or children.

"God forbid that bad thing!" she always told herself.

She did not know how to deal with a husband who had secrets and owed allegiance or loyalty to a cult rather than to his wedded partner. What if he swore to kill her and give to the cult her body parts as she had heard some men did to gain mystical or rather diabolical power? Sometimes she was at her wit's end on what to do to protect herself from any strange cultic attack by her husband. She drew up a plan to let him not know when her menstruation would start and still prepare food for him and see what would happen to him. Would he die after eating or start barking like a dog or just run mad? She thought of deliberately unleashing her secret plan against him to know what effects violating his cultic secrets would have on him.

After that night of don'ts, he had barred her from ever sleeping with him again in the master bedroom as they had been doing and asked her to be sleeping in a separate bedroom. Now he would go to her in her new bedroom when he wanted and when she was sure, more than a hundred per cent sure, that she was not "under"! She dismissed her plan which she felt was evil. She should not succumb to the temptation of paying evil with evil, she felt. She thought it would be better for her to leave him than violate his injunctions. His order asking her to leave if she was not happy with the arrangement, as if they were not in a marriage, stunned her. It took her a long time to reflect on what he meant and later when her lonesomeness was eating deep into her sanity, she took up the challenge and moved out to an apartment of her own. Mr. Dudu did not care that she was moving out. The challenge was not a joke but a take-it thing, Christiana discovered. He surely loved his cult more than his wife and so let it be, she told herself.

Much as she had moved from Mr. Dudu's house, she knew the society still identified her as his wife. Her people's men liked to tie a leash to a woman and, even after throwing her out, they would still want her to be their property that no other man should come close to, not to talk of touch. She had heard of many stories of men who not only separated from but divorced their women but still poke-nosed into their private lives. The other day, she heard, a Warri man who had married another woman after divorcing his wife went as far as going to the divorced and supposedly free woman in her own apartment in another part of town to raise hell because another man she was in love with came to visit her. He shouted obscenities at the lovers because his former wife now in denim shorts and a sleeveless blouse that she never wore in his house was sitting with outstretched long legs on the lap of the man who was cuddling her in a way he never did to her. Do men love women they have separated from more or they just want to make them feel miserable when no longer with them? Christiana asked herself. She knew that much as she was free that Mr. Dudu had not received back the bride price he had paid on her. She wondered when her people would abandon those antiquated customs of paying a bride price instead of just allowing any man and woman in love to marry. How long would the woman remain a chattel slave? For how long would a wayward man expect his wife to be virtuous even when neglected?

She had been going to the Garden of Eden Church of Christ for several months but ever since living alone had become more frequent in attending the church's many events. She was looking for solace and did not know where it would come from, and it might just be found in the church. She had freed herself or separated herself from the hoax of a happy marriage but she did not know what to make of her life. Time should settle that, she believed.

* * *

The Garden of Eden Church of Christ was a huge assembly of over a hundred thousand worshipers on service days. The house of worship was gigantic and built in such a way as to accommodate a big crowd as attended a major national football league match. Still, the crowd was such that it often spilled out into the adjacent streets of Igbi and Ginuwa and onto another side to Omashola Crescent. It was not possible for members to know themselves in the crowd that made the congregation and there were volunteers for everything in committees that ranged from sweeping the church floor to picking trash from the yard to other service assignments as organizing collection of food and other gifts for orphans, widows, disabled, and elderly.

It was a unique church in which baptisms took place beside an artificial lake in the vast church compound. Members were baptized by being pushed into the lake and expected to bathe themselves to be fully cleansed of their old sinful selves. The venerable pastor's main tenet for members of his uncountable congregation was "You can sin but don't be malicious to anybody! We are all human and should make each other happy."

Efe had to meet Christiana there. The Garden of Eden Church of Christ was almost equidistant from their respective homes. They had a spot where they met on Ginuwa Street, by a story building that had stores for expensive car parts sold by Igbo traders. Usually, by the time of the service by late evening, the stores had closed. Cars were parked on both sides of the road and gave cover to any secret tryst to look like a casual or chance meeting.

Christiana felt she should suggest to Efe to be "born again" like her, attending the church but not baptized in it. She knew it would be a tough sell because men of Efe's disposition did not go to any church but only criticized churches. It was as if a "good" Christian or regular churchgoer could not be a good writer. Or was it that the foreign religion benumbed their indigenous creative talent? She would ask Efe but he might not know or like to talk about his private faith.

She was very surprised at the ease with which she converted Efe, if his consent to be coming to the church was a conversion. She had expected to move a rock or mountain but it was a ball that rolled along with her tender kick! As for him, he wanted to try things and see what impact such things had on him. Why not go to church as an observer without any formal affiliation to it, if the woman his heart was throbbing for rhythmically wanted him to be there? After all, he had tried other sects or religions or what looked like forms of worship and abandoned them. Life was a continuous search, he believed, and he would continue the quest. It was part of the exploration of the human landscape, which should yield more discoveries the wider it grew for him. It might be that was what he needed at this time of his life. AMORC, the Grail Movement, and Eckankar at separate times had caught his fancy with their mysticism, but he found nothing lasting in any of them to sustain him. He would go to this church as an unbaptized member in the crowd to meet his woman and profess his faith in her.

"Make sure you pay your tithes regularly!" Christiana told him.

"Writer go pay tithes out of royalty from non-selling books?" he asked her.

"How they no go find out say you no be proper member of the church?" she asked back.

"Let's volunteer to do things together for the church! I like the service groups going to take care of the disabled, elderly, and homeless. Any of the service groups will interest me," Efe replied.

"Don't miss the evening service that goes on and on forever, sometimes for more than five hours. That will create the opportunity we need to take any days off to be wherever we want while you are intentionally at the service."

"I will follow your lead since you are the real member of the church," he told her.

Christiana knew that Mr. Dudu would be spying on her movements and whoever came to visit her in her apartment in Pesu Road in the manner of Warri men who would want to make her miserable by causing an unnecessary scandal.

"He is not home anyway and he will be happy I am stuck to a church and have remained born-again!"

"Have you flirted before?" Efe asked, as if his mind was on something else than Christiana's assurance of her safety to be with him when they wanted.

"Who has not done so, man or woman?" she asked back.

"So you have then?" he asked.

"What are we doing now? If I didn't, how would that dog of a man have got me into his pen?" she replied, answering his questions with her questions in the Warri manner of conversation.

* * *

Christiana was happy that Efe wanted her at all times, dirty or clean, in whatever womanly state she was in. Not that she was a dirty woman by nature but in whatever condition of womanhood she was. In her natural self as a woman! She was surprised when she told him that she was in her menstrual period and that did not hold him back a second from kissing and fondling her. He still held her tight to himself and she felt accepted and really wanted. She knew she would go a long way to gradually jettison her inhibitions and express herself in creative ways she dared not have done as Mr. Dudu's wife. She was overwhelmed and shed tears of joy that Efe still clasped her hands and led her to his book-clogged bedroom after she told him that she seemed to have started spotting. How many times had her womanly warm desires been killed with questions and orders barked at her? "I hope you are not close to your time?" "Don't let me come to you when you are not clean!" There were many of such warnings. And everything said in a very harsh tone that caused the warmth in her to evaporate and her body to turn cold. Whenever Mr. Dudu still went through with his desire after such, she felt violated, even raped by her husband. That period of her life was gone and she prayed it had gone forever.

When she forewarned Efe of possible spotting, what she heard gladdened her heart.

"And then?" he had asked.

"I don't want you to break any taboos," she said.

"What taboos do I have? I have already broken a taboo by falling in love with you!"

"That's no taboo. Love cannot be a taboo. It has to do with feelings. I love you and you love me and we are not breaking any taboos."

"Thanks," he said.

Mr. Dudu would not have done what Efe was doing—have any type of body contact and snuggling after mentioning "spotting"? No way! If she could not cook for him when she was "under," what of physical contact?

The build-up to the event fulfilled their expectations. They took their time in preambles to prime themselves for their first real physical intimacy. They explored the naked contours of their bodies planting kisses here and there. The poet saw twin hills to climb and a gorge to dive into. The theatre artist set up the landscape with a rich décor. It was a divine experience for both Efe and Christiana. They floated in the clouds of contentment and crashed simultaneously into the sea of pleasure. They clasped themselves together and murmured to each other sounds that conveyed their physical and emotional exhilaration. They had reached a peak they had never achieved in their romantic lives before. They remained swathed in a broad sheet and longingly looked each other in the eye, satisfied that things would not be the same again for each of them.

After that experience, their first of what Efe described as true communion, Christiana doted on Efe and he on her. Christiana knew changes had taken place in her body and feelings. She felt an awakening and her whole body had suddenly become so sensual that she wanted to be in Efe's arms all the time. She now experienced pleasure that she never dreamt was possible. At the same time the man who had doubted himself for a long time and could not be turned on by a naked Cathy a whole night after two weeks of absence had become so aroused that he could not now have a day without taking the special communion with Christiana.

After experiencing her uniquely sculpted figure, the writer felt like a once-dehydrated person drinking from an infinite fountain. It was a healing and invigorating fountain that kept him fully hydrated. A gentle wind appeared to blow inside him. Like a tall wiregrass, he swayed tenderly to the direction of the blowing wind. He and Christiana had become one being. His first poem came; an emblematic piece on the two of them appropriately in the Garden of Eden, their refuge! Then a flurry of poems and the writer knew that a floodgate had broken and he was back to his real self as a poet; an invigorated man of passion.

Efe discovered that his passion for Christiana and for writing were the same. He who had lost interest in life and everything was now a passionate man filled with zest for life. His love for Christiana was immeasurable and his desire for her intense. His excitement remained strong. He was like one carrying a gun ready to explode without firing. The keenly sharpened knife ready to cut! He now embarked on a love sequence. The tone was not euphoric but tempered with fear for their future. The poet imagined the politician was bound to revenge after he discovered his former wife was drunk with love for another person. Who would not notice the wiregrass dancing when the wind was blowing? Christiana was now like a lute that played enthralling music once touched. Her body had become a magic instrument. With their mad love for each other, they could not be discreet enough, as she wanted, in order to avoid eventual discovery. It was only a matter of time, he believed. Can a drunken person walk normally? He also feared that if the politician came back and experienced Christiana's body again, the way he did with her heightened awakened body, he might take her back to occupy her by taking her along in his travels and he, Efe, would be the loser. He would not deceive himself that the pleasure he and Christiana derived from each other would continue for the rest of their lives. Their paradise was too good to be true, too pleasurable to last forever.

He wrote in a frenzy to get the poetry sequence out before his fears came to pass. The readers, to him, would judge later whether what they did was right or wrong. As for Christiana, if the work turned out to be a masterpiece as he expected and he felt so, and the world knew she inspired it, she would live a glorious life. He was content that he was born again in many ways before any chance happening stopped him from living the poet's fortunate life! Christiana had made him a fortunate poet. If their lives remained uninterrupted, he did not want to commit the profanity of saying they would continue to live a divine life.

Efe now brought in Christiana who dared to defy any challenge to her pleasurable life with him. They both felt emancipated in No. 78 Radio Road that brightened with their love. The Warri Local Government had sent notice that it was streamlining the street numbers of major streets in the municipality, including Radio Road, and to Efe's triumphant pleasure against immeasurable odds, his house was assigned 78 Radio Road, Warri! Now one could get there without difficulty. He knew his house would return to a busier Mecca than it used to be.

15

The Director and His Deputy

In the large office complex at the national capital, Kofo and Dike were Director and Deputy Director respectively. Kofo Olufemi had made a name nationwide as an anti-corruption activist lawyer for almost two decades, including periods in detention for daring military dictators, before his appointment as Director of the national anti-corruption parastatal created with full legislative authority as Cleanup the Nation Directorate. After corruption had almost eaten up the entire fabric of the nation, the senators and members of the House of Representatives were compelled to pass a law establishing the Cleanup the Nation Directorate, which the President quickly signed into law. All three branches must have realized late in their stealing revelries that if the nation collapsed, they would have nothing left to steal from and would become like everybody else—destitute! They always wanted to be better off materially than those who voted them into power whom they did not care about. It was a case of thieves, after having stolen too much, suddenly realized that stealing more from the same coffers would bankrupt the source of their own thievery and so stopped—at least for the meantime!

The creation of the new directorate was therefore greeted by the public with deserved scepticism after so many of such bodies had been created since the Republic began in 1963 and corruption at national, regional, and state levels intensified. Who would believe that thieves and robbers would stop stealing and robbing because the Federal Government created a directorate and gave it powers to prosecute corrupt politicians and government officials? Once a veteran thief, always a thief! Once a veteran robber, always a robber! The left-handed will not turn right-handed through a legislative process. Nor will the goat stop its shameless defecating as it walks about because of a single legislation.

The public scepticism about the new directorate waned gradually as Kofo Olufemi was appointed its head. His name made cynics to rethink and give the directorate time to prove it had ferocious teeth in its bark. Really, Olufemi started to send some thieves to jail for the first time in the people's memory since Independence and that act further cheered the public. At first the people felt he was warming up to really lock up the big thieves. However, it appeared he had the ability only to convict small state and federal thieves. The people soon realized that it was the small thieves that were being convicted and the big thieves still stole with impunity. The real test, the people believed, would come when the big thieves started to be tried and convicted and given long sentences they deserved. Everybody waited till the Cleanup net caught really big fish—at least some of the numerous sharks running amok in the Niger waters: governors, ministers, government contractors, heads of boards and sine cure office holders at state and federal levels.

Nobody would know unless told when both Kofo and Dike were outside the office that one was the other's boss. Yes, Kofo was senior and boss to Dike in the office. They had worked together for one and a half years in the same parastatal and appeared to know what each expected of the other in the workplace. At least that was what it seemed to be. Over the period of working together, they had struck an enviable relationship. They played lawn tennis twice a week and on public holidays when they were in town. They visited each other at home and their families knew each other. They exchanged gifts during major festivals and had gone as far as visiting each other's ancestral home, what they described as country homes. Nobody was native to Abuja as such and though they worked there knew where their real homes were.

Kofo Olufemi came from Kogi State, which he described as the proud land of Princess Inikpi, legendary heroine who saved her people from foreign aggressors and exploiters with her life. That was despite the fact that he was really from the Kabba side of the state that the Igala felt was an unwelcome appendage of Yoruba people to their state.

On the other hand, Dike Okorocha was from Anambra, the homeland of Zik of Africa. He was not yet five years old when the Civil War started and his father had cleverly emigrated with his family of four to the United Kingdom when he foresaw looming war. It was there that Dike attended school and got his bachelor's degree before returning to Nigeria one and a half decades after the war's end. By that time the scars of the war had mainly disappeared through reconstruction efforts and Dr. Nnamdi Azikiwe, the Zik of Africa, had died, after being mistrusted by a majority of those who described themselves as true Biafrans and who saw him as abandoning ship when the going was rough and tough.

So Kofo felt he knew his deputy very well. He trusted him and believed in his ability. He felt he could not have had a better deputy than Dike. But that was until the worst case of embezzlement came to his office to probe. Of course, he was the chairman of the review panel probing Alhaji Ibrahim Danladi for the staggering amount of seven hundred billion naira in deals with the Federal Government that he really did not execute after being paid in full. After four weeks of thorough investigation, the review interviews and submissions were completed and the chairman of the panel had incontrovertible evidence condemning Alhaji Danladi of claiming payments for work not done.

Alhaji Danladi, according to those who knew him, was a juggernaut and was very capable of rolling a caterpillar over a black ant that was stubborn enough or dared to stab his elephant butt or, for that matter, mess up with his business. His concept of business or entrepreneurship, if he had a really thought-out one, was to get contracts from the Federal Government, get the payments without doing anything. "Who is government?" he had been quoted as asking. "We are the government!" he had answered. It was as if he believed that what the Federal Government had was a free-for-all booty. No-one felt that he had any morals despite having gone on the major hajj three times the past five years. That was in addition to sponsoring dozens of common men and women to the Holy Land of Mecca every year. Alhaji Danladi knew he had to nip the report in the bud. He had to squelch the nuisance of a probe report before it was announced. He was confident he could do what he wanted with his tons and tons of money.

He prepared himself to see this Kofo Olufemi that everybody said was incorruptible. He must bend before him, the Alhaji believed. What could he not do with his money? He knew he was the richest man in Africa and whether Forbes Magazine named him as such or not, he did not care. He knew he had more money than the sands that made up the mountains that straddled Nigeria and Cameroon. If he could buy the President of the Federation with personal cash gifts and campaign contributions, who was this Kofo Olufemi that he could not bend to do his bidding? He had asked himself, "Does he have eyes, ears, and nose? Does he have feelings? If he has them, he is human and I know how to handle him," he had assured himself. He had the power to put his money to work for him to eliminate a stubborn ant that wanted to stab the elephant's butt. He could pay some *almajiris* to do his bidding, remove the irritant from his way. However, he did not think it would ever come to that stage where he had to wield his ultimate weapon of asking money to do for him what stood in his way to becoming the richest black man on earth. He wanted to be richer than black rich men in America, the Caribbean, or Brazil. He now took an assistant along with him to carry the bundle of money with which he would talk sense into this Kofo Olufemi's head. He should better listen to him or face ugly consequences, which could be very bitter. It would be regrettable if things went that far before resolution.

* * *

Dokwase heard the multiple tapping on the door—three knocks that were unmistakably gentle but clear. The measured knocks appeared to be of one who was assured of entry or who knew the person he or she wanted to see. She did not hesitate to go to the door and see through the peep hole and the protector bars the one who was knocking at the door so early in the morning. Her husband was in the bathroom taking his bath. It was about six-thirty in the morning. Whoever came to visit at this time must have left home very early to catch whom he wanted to see. Also, whatever the message, it must be a very important one for someone to come knocking at this time before her man left for work. She knew though that one had to spit out fire burning inside the mouth. There were things or issues that just needed immediate attention and one could not wait longer before they deteriorated further. Of a moderate height of five feet five inches, she stood on her toes to see more clearly the profile of the person knocking. A lavishly-robed man stood in front of the door. He was huge, about six feet tall and on the weighty side.

"Who's that?" she asked in her thin voice.

"I want to see your man," the man replied.

"Whom do you want to see?"

"I say I want to see your man, Mr. Kofo Olufemi," the man said.

Dokwase heard the dignified voice and did not hesitate to open the door. They lived in an exclusive area and only important people came visiting most of the time. Unlike when they lived in Area One, now relatives from the village did not come to visit unless they were invited, and it was extremely rare to be invited here.

Once the door opened for him to enter, the big man flung his top *babanriga* piece upon his shoulders. He looked back.

"Bring in the things!" the big man ordered one who carried his briefcase behind him like a personal servant. The young man rushed back to the car to bring in cartons from the Toyota Land Cruiser's huge trunk. Up to ten big cartons were offloaded into the parlour. They sat piled one upon the other in two rows in a corner of the sitting room.

Dokwase surveyed the big man as she sat waiting for her husband to come out of the bathroom, dress, and come and see the early visitor. When she got up to go and remind him that a big man was waiting for him, she saw clearly the crispy new currency notes in the cartons, twenty naira notes, the highest denomination by then. In their cartons, the currency notes glittered seductively, fresh, and eye-catching. The crispness and sheer amount of notes piled there quickened Dokwase's breath.

Kofo did not even ask her why she thought it was a big man waiting for him. She knew that her man was always cool and never liked to be pressured or rushed into doing things; he usually took his time to do thoroughly whatever he was doing. She knew that he would take his time to sponge himself and enjoy his bathing as he did his eating and everything else he chose to do. She returned to the sitting room and sat on a chair at a corner observing, without doing it directly, the early-morning visiting dignitary. Her heart beat faster than normal. How could all these cartons be money brought to her husband? She was more than excited. So many things were running riot in her mind. Was Kofo she knew as a no-nonsense attorney be also a businessman and this man, his partner, had brought him his share of a joint venture? Men could be deep and difficult to know, she mused. However long a wife to a man, there are always some hidden parts of the man that continue to reveal themselves in the relationship, she also thought.

After taking his time to dress, Kofo at last came to the parlour. He looked stern, not the jovial person she had gone to bed and woken up with this morning casting jokes and laughing as they tickled each other. She did not know what to think of the relationship between this visitor and her husband. She decided to stay and witness what was going to transpire between the two men, with so much money there at the corner. Her husband had a way of brushing aside inquisitive questions and she did not want to bother him but she wanted to follow the story from where she had seen it start with the big man's door knock and entry. She only hoped her man would be fortunate to take in the cartons. She knew what this huge amount of money could do for her and her husband. Everybody liked and wanted money; hence it was difficult to make, she reflected.

* * *

"I am Alhaji Ibrahim Danladi," the big man said in a booming voice.

"What can I do for you?" was Kofo's lukewarm reply to the self-introduction of a man whose name was very familiar to him and whose photo he had seen many times.

"You, senior officer, you won't even entertain your guest before asking what you can do for him?" the visitor asked.

"Alhaji, you know I have to be in the office in an hour's time. What's the matter?" Kofo asked.

"I have brought you greetings and a gift," the visitor said.

It was as if Kofo had not seen the cartons of money neatly heaped in a corner, as he came from the bedroom. His face suddenly changed and he transformed from a polite host to a hostile one. One could not believe the severity of his voice as he ordered.

"Leave my house with those cartons! I say take those cartons of whatever is in them away and leave my house!"

"Why can't you allow me to talk?" the big man asked.

"Talk what? No, you can't stay here longer. You must leave now!"

Dokwase did not know that her husband could be so stern, a side of him that he did not show at home. He was of a medium frame and looking very fit. His voice was penetrating and there was a certain edge to it that must be unsettling to the listener. From the look on both men's faces, Dokwase knew this was a confrontation that was not going to be resolved in the big man's favour. She wondered which way the bags of money would go—stay in the house or be taken back. She got up and asked her husband to look at the cartons. He waved her aside in a very dismissive manner. She knew this case was not the same as an ordinary house talk between husband and wife. She knew she had to remain an observer and not a participant in what was going on before her.

"Alhaji, you must leave now with what you brought to my house!" Kofo ordered.

This time his voice was cold and conclusive. The big man realized that he was no longer tolerated in the house. However stubborn you were, it had to be in the right place and time. You could not resist leaving somebody else's house where you were a visitor. The owner of the house had a right to literally push you out of the house and you would not fight your host in his own house. This man said to be incorruptible by everybody seemed to be an exception, which was very rare in the Nigerian landscape. "How could somebody paid by the Government his little salary see so many cartons of money and not flinch?" Alhaji Danladi asked himself. He had to think of alternative methods to resolve the problem of a bad report soon to be published. Not every officer was like Olufemi and others would be surely easier to deal with than this big fool. Yes, he was a fool because only a fool did not take care of himself in a country that did not care about your principles. Alhaji Danladi reflected. He knew he had to accept the finality of Kofo Olufemi's order for him to leave his house and retrace his steps back to the car.

He got up, called his servant, and pointed at the cartons to him. The servant knew what he was supposed to do—cart back into the jeep's trunk the cartons he had earlier brought in. As the big man left, he shook his forefinger as a warning to Kofo, even though the sign he made was not clear. Dokwase was disappointed but knew her husband must have strong reasons to give up so much money. Of course, he cared about his good name which he did not want to soil with a heavy bribe.

Kofo arrived in his office at 8:30 a.m. There was much to do with the conclusion of his report, which Alhaji Danladi had wanted, through his early morning visit, to thwart or corrupt. He must know that there were folks around that would not succumb to any price however high it was in cash. He hoped to complete writing the recommendations by the end of the day's work. He was happy that after this case nobody would have any doubt about the Cleanup the Country Directorate. At least, in a corrupt nation, the people should believe in one agency that could bring sanity to the citizenry. He might not be rich but he knew he enjoyed an abundance of goodwill from the people who knew he was doing something to make his country clean. He congratulated himself for sending out of his house the powerful Alhaji. Yes, in the country rich folks were very powerful because of what they could do with money. It was not only rigging elections and killing political opponents that money was used for. Money was used to distort the rule of law; money was used to buy love and allegiance. Money could be used for good but in this country, it was used for too many evil things.

Barely three hours later in the day came an official note from Aso Rock. It was the Presidential spokesman's statement. He, Kofo Olufemi, had been transferred with immediate effect from the Directorate

Headquarters in Abuja to the Adamawa State branch in Yola. His deputy was to take over, also with immediate effect, as the Acting Director and Chairman of the Review Panel. Kofo realized how powerful Alhaji Ibrahim Danladi really was but he was happy that he did not succumb to the temptation of money and taint himself. He packed his personal files and left after hastily handing over to Dike Okorocha. He could only hope his deputy and friend would resist the heavy bribes that he did from the Alhaji to teach an unforgettable lesson. He would wait and see what happened as the final report and recommendations that were all but completed. Dike had little to do on the final report that he had to submit very soon.

Some things moved very fast in Abuja where others moved at a snail's pace or did not move at all but stayed dead like a rock. To Kofo's disappointment, his report was changed at the last minute and the following day there was the announcement that Alhaji Ibrahim Danladi had been exonerated of all accusations of corruption. He shook his head. He did not need to be told what must have transpired in the interim of his sudden transfer and that moment of the report's official release. His friend and former deputy did not call him to ask why there was that abrupt change in the Directorate. Nor did he show up for the tennis they were supposed to play that evening and which they always eagerly looked up to at the end of the day's work. No phone call between the former director and the former deputy director! He had to resume work in Yola two days later. He was sure that if he did not, he might be fired and he would lose all his benefits as a civil servant.

Barely six months after, there was the first correspondence from Dike—an invitation for the conferment on him of a chieftaincy title by his Uzoke community. Kofo knew he was going to show off his bribes and new appointment. His former deputy, now his boss, now felt secure enough in his position to flaunt at him and the public the "gifts" he had received as the acting head of the Cleanup the Nation Directorate.

Dokwase refused to accompany her husband to Anambra State, the home state of Zik of Africa. She had not recovered from the cartons of money taken back from the house into the jeep. She knew, as Kofo did, that Dike must have accepted the money and did what he was told to do. He had been paid to sing a tune composed for him! How would she go and witness the flaunting of that money that should have been theirs but her strict husband had rejected as a bribe. Kofo would tell her the story of the chieftaincy ceremony later. She could not believe what her husband told her about the man he had considered his best friend, his once able deputy director; now confirmed substantive Director of the Cleanup Nigeria Directorate. She understood life better now. She had been so naïve.

Her husband of course rejected the Ghana-must-go bags of money that the newly installed chief in a poor and needy community was doling out to his very important guests. While Dike had hurriedly built an imposing mansion within five months and furnished it lavishly, the roads to the house were pot-holed and not tarred. The house stood on a hill and there one could see the huts and rusty corrugated iron sheets of dilapidated houses around. The sharp contrast was clear to everybody to see at the celebration of Dike Okorocha's chieftaincy. The village people wore cheap clothes bought for them for the occasion while the celebrant's family and visitors displayed their affluence in the clothes and beads they wore and the cars and jeeps that brought them to this hole in Anambra State, the homeland of Zik of Africa. Dike Okorocha chose the title of *Eze Ego* of Uzoke and he flaunted wealth in the midst of abject poverty.

When the news came only three months later that Dike Okorocha was shot dead in the Maitama district of Abuja by a man riding a motorcycle who disappeared into the busy evening traffic, only Kofo and Dokwase knew what a mess he must have put himself into once he accepted Alhaji Ibrahim Danladi's gifts and got confirmed as Director after letting the shark out of a steel net into which it had been cornered. Who knows how many other deals Dike might have struck to let out sharks out of steel nets? It was not easy to extricate oneself from a mesh, more so a steel one. The Alhaji could perform wonders by getting out unscathed, but Dike Okorocha from Anambra, the homeland of Zik of Africa, was not a shark in the first place and could not survive among sharks in the Niger's heavily infested waters.

16

Mama Toko's Model Orphanage

Nomate Toko was not only a figure with national name recognition but also one highly connected to different kinds of powerful people. She knew political leaders at federal and state levels. She knew businessmen and women, she knew religious leaders and who was who in the entire country. She looked dignified and graceful in her early fifties. She had an affable personality that made her stand out in any circle in which she found herself. No one was therefore surprised when she was awarded the Grand Order of the Niger, the highest national award in the land. To many folks she deserved the award more than most of the others who were also conferred with the honour—politicians, party henchmen and women, contractors, businessmen, professor speech writers, and others that everybody knew were self-centred, sycophantic, and corrupt. The list of the recipients of the annual honours had till now become a national joke to the extent that disgraced politicians, robbers-turned-chiefs, and worse personalities had been conferred with the highest national award.

Comedians had poked fun at the recipients of recent national honours whom they described as pen robbers, chiefly thieves, and juvenile adults. The public always wondered how names of corrupt, indicted, and convicted governors and other politicians got to be slipped into the list and given such awards that should be sacred. They believed no Selection Committee worth its name would include convicts and other scandalous men and women as national role models. To them, honouring such dishonourable people was like honouring vultures and hyenas. Many other recipients literally bought the honours with campaign contributions or paid bribes to administrators of the award. Among those who got national recognition were unknown folks whose wealth's source nobody knew. Many cynics believed that dogs of the powerful and vultures would soon be on that list.

Nobody believed, with the name she had made, that Nomate Toko's award was tied to a payback or a kind of quid pro quo; unlike those of most other awardees. Nobody believed her award was lobbied for as was done for many others. In the country, the good people were rarely recognized or honoured; they were more often than not always passed over for mediocre ones. For a change a good woman, many people felt, a selfless woman, a sensitive person, and one who really cared for the disadvantaged had been nominated and given a great award. That was how things should be, people believed. Even before the presentation of the award, she received so many congratulatory messages from well-wishers on radio, television, and newspapers. The Concord and the Guard, in particular, had almost a whole week with pages bought to pay tribute to Nomate Toko.

In a country of so much hoopla with ethnicities, nobody ever cared where Mama Toko, as she was popularly called, came from. She had no marks to identify her. Nor did she have any accent that interfered with her English to betray her tribal origin. She wore what could be described as national dresses. She was a polyglot and spoke each of the nine languages she was fluent at as a native speaker. She was indeed a tribe-less person. Every ethnic group would have liked to claim her because of the good work she was believed to be doing. She was a new type of Mother Theresa, who was not a Catholic sister but a missionary at home. It was good that she did not emigrate to either the First World or some other part of the Third World as many missionaries in the country were then doing.

She was of average height and size. Her physique belied the now legendary fame that often preceded her before those who knew her in person. Did they expect an Amazon woman, muscular and gigantic who could throw any man down? Or did they expect Mrs. Fumilayo Ransom-Kuti spitting fire to threaten men to abandon their patriarchal privileges and cede human rights to women? Could she be one of those Aba women who rose against armed British colonialists and forced them to rescind obnoxious "head tax" impositions? Nobody preceded her name with any prefix. She might be married, divorced, widowed, or never married, but who cared about that when it came to Mama Toko? She was tender, feminine, but not one that men would call pretty. But she was enamoured to all the big men, and to big women too for that matter. She exuded a certain mystique and those mystified by her personality wondered how she came to be so beloved by everybody in a country of so many women-haters. No man or gossip columnist had used the p word to describe her in a country where so many, in their patriarchal arrogance and chauvinistic attitude, believed a woman could not be anything except by being a prostitute or a man's mistress. And beloved to so many she really was. She ran the best-known orphanage in the country.

Her orphanage was unique. Sanoma Children's Home had its sprawling but manicured compound in the Jabi area of Abuja. The compound was fenced round with a high wall painted white. It had an adamantine gate that glittered night and day with the bold name of the orphanage flashing as a disco club's inside lights. The gatemen were uniformed white and were always alert to those coming in or going out, saluting the drivers. They never accepted any tip, as other gatemen manning such impressive gates did.

Others ran ramshackle orphanages; Mama Toko's was a model home of neat boys and girls. The children looked well-fed and they always dressed in their starched uniforms of white at school and brown chequered in the hostels. They looked like children of the rich—their teeth shone white, their skin smooth from being fed with eggs, chicken, salmon, Irish potatoes, and other foods available at big men's tables. The gossip or rumour was that physicians, dentists, eye doctors, and other medical personnel volunteered their services free to visit the orphanage once in a while to examine the children. Every child there appeared to be enjoying supreme health. There were rumours too that only big people were allowed to adopt these children. No wonder children of the poor, who saw these children on television, were envious of these privileged orphans; they even wished their mothers and fathers dead to be orphans and be taken into Sanoma Children's Home.

Once the children's home gained national attention, newspapers, radio and television stations carried the events taking place there free. They had their Christmas Carols and Cultural Event Day to which selected members of the public were invited. You had to carry a special on Mama Toko's orphanage to show that you were supporting something good in the country. The orphanage ran kindergarten and elementary schools that paraded on television neatly uniformed boys and girls. A few were bussed to a private junior high school in town.

Mama Toko, according to her workers, only considered the applications of those who were really well-off for the adoption of any of the children in Sanoma Children's Home. To these workers, the orphanage was a revolving door that transferred and transformed derelict children to good health and then to homes of middle-class or high-class men and women. Grown-up boys and girls were placed by Mama Toko in homes of rich families but it was extremely rare to see any of them years later after they left the home. But this was not a school to have an alumni association to meet years after for a reunion. If anyone expected that sort of reunion, it might not happen.

Everything seemed normal and routine in Sanoma Children's Home until a female worker took a liking for one of the girls. The woman would follow the trail of this girl and discover what none of the workers had known about where they worked. She saw the visit of a Governor who came incognito and after which the girl disappeared. When she asked for who adopted her, she was told it was not her business.

"She's in good hands," was all Mama Toko could tell Mabel.

"We thank God," she replied.

What else could she ask Mama Toko? Could she drag the truth or any secrets from her mouth? Two days later, Mama Toko was driving a new Toyota Land Cruiser that was given to her by the same Governor. She had acknowledged the gift before her workers, speaking of the Governor as one of the most generous supporters of Sanoma Children's Home. Mabel soon realized that there was so much going on unseen by the workers and the rest of the country in the affairs of Sanoma Children's Home.

The way only Mama Toko ran the home was a classic example of micro management style. Only she knew who adopted the children. Only she signed the papers and yet there were no other records filed for future reference should there be either a complaint or any effort to track the source of any specific child. Only she knew the whereabouts of the adopted children. Only Mama Toko knew what was happening in the dark. Only she knew what was in the shadows of the orphanage. After all, she was the chief executive of Sanoma Children's Home. She was not the CEO of an organization with shareholders to whom she owed any annual report. The buck ended with her, as she saw her role as proprietor and executive officer of the orphanage she had single-handedly founded and was growing.

Mama Toko's three-story duplex bungalow was impressive. Her bedroom was on the third story. She received her dignitaries on the second floor, many of whom chose to visit at odd times, especially at late night. Nobody suspected her of being loose and flirting with a stream of men. After all, female dignitaries also visited her. Her workers had access only to the first floor of the house. A woman of so much standing had no permanent housekeepers, cooks, or servants. She lived alone but seemed to be comfortable with her style of living without a permanent help. The children's home's cleaners cleaned her house during the morning hours as they cleaned the hostels of the orphans. The workers believed Mama Toko prepared her own food.

Mabel had been intrigued by the adoption of Little Meg, as she called the now alumna of Sanoma Children's Home. She had brought her to Mama Toko in the late evening after a call from her boss to that effect. On their way to Madam Toko, Little Meg cried all the way. The young girl muttered amidst sobs that she did not want to leave the home; she did not want to die because she believed that she would certainly die when taken out for adoption. Mabel was shocked because she had thought that the expectation of adoption by a rich family would make the little girl excited and happy.

"Stop that nonsense!" Mabel had shouted at her.

"No, they will kill me," the little girl persisted with a stream of copious tears flowing down her cheeks.

Neither Mama Toko nor Mabel knew how haunted with thoughts of death Little Meg had been. She had first heard the lore passed down from bigger children to younger ones that went the round in the orphanage. Did she not hear about the boy—they never called him any specific name—who had returned from being placed with a very rich man who came back briefly before being taken away again? The boy, according to the story, had been placed with a very rich man who took him to a medicine man who refused to use him for whatever medicine the very rich man had wanted. According to the story, the medicine man said the spirit of the boy would not help the medicine to work and so he should be freed and taken back. The very rich man whom the boy could not identify beat him mercilessly for losing so much money on his account—the amount never told—and placed him at an intersection close to Sanoma Children's Home. Little Meg heard the boy later wandered into the orphanage and within a short time of being around and telling his experiences to a few who gathered round him was summoned by Mama Toko and taken away. Many children who had heard the story believed he must be dead. However, his story was passed from one year to another. Little Meg had nightmares in which she experienced what the boy was supposed to be used for. "What if my spirit does not refuse to be used as that boy's?" she had continued to ask herself.

In one of her nightmares, she was taken to the top of a rocky mountain and sacrificed like a goat before a big man who used her blood to bathe his body. After then the big man descended the mountain and as he descended the rock she shouted in her sleep and woke. Since then she had had the fear that she would soon be taken away ostensibly for adoption but really to be used as a sacrifice for the efficacy of a big man's money-doubling or political survival medicine.

Little Meg did not bring her things and was asked to go and bring them in another twenty minutes and return to Mama Toko's house. Mabel had chosen to give an excuse so as to have the opportunity to follow the little girl. The woman had a rare chance to ask Little Meg about what bothered her.

"How do you know the man adopting you will kill you?"

"We know that those taken out get killed," the girl said.

"How can those big men or women in cars kill the children they adopt?"

"No, they don't come to adopt. They come to buy us and use us for medicines," the little girl explained.

Mabel was shocked about the secret knowledge of children that they, adult workers in the orphanage, were not privileged to know about. She started to collect the girl's few clothes but within several minutes, Mama Toko came in as one who had come in a hurry. It appeared she had to come herself to ensure that Little Meg got back to her quickly without delay. Mama Toko barged into both Mabel and the little girl. There was no chance for Mabel to probe the girl with further questions. She knew Mama Toko expected her to leave, and she had to abandon the little girl to her fate.

Mabel who doubled as a messenger and teacher was intrigued but felt helpless. She had heard before and dismissed the rumour that the children were not really going to these so-called big men and women. All of a sudden she started to reel the film of history from the time she had spent there. Most workers did not stay more than a year or two in the orphanage; they were either dismissed or asked to go with a huge sum to start some profitable businesses. No single worker thus knew the history of the place beyond one or two years. This unusual high turnover of keepers and teachers mystified Mabel since there was a very high unemployment rate in the country.

As Mabel thought of the young girl crying hysterically, her mind flashed to things she had taken for normal. She now asked herself many questions. "Why was it that the strangest of the children or handicapped among them were the first to be adopted? The albinos, hunchbacks, blind, and cripples went faster for adoption than the rest of the orphan population. They were adopted at such speed that the more healthy and normal-looking children were at first jealous until they started to have a weird cold feeling towards the manner their physically challenged mates disappeared from their daily lives. To the outside world, Nomate Toko did not discriminate in her home—it was open to any type of orphaned children in the country that there was room for in her home. And the knowledge that she did not discriminate on whom to take in and later place in big or rich families endeared her so much to those who knew about the orphanage.

Despite the so many numbers of orphans coming in weekly and perhaps daily, adoptions were going on at the same high rate that left the place with a rather balanced population. Mabel now thought of rumours or gossips that she had heard and dismissed. Once an elderly big man came in a walking stick dressed in simple kaftan. The dress did not seem to fit him or he walked as he was not used to walking and the dress was not like what he was used to wearing. Gossip had had it from the children who had better instincts and keener eyes than their teachers that he was the President of the Federation—he walked with the same long and brushy gait as of the person they saw on television as the president. None of the teachers or children could talk publicly about the visit of the disguised big man that none could confirm with certainty.

Other instances of men and women in disguise visiting their compound came to Mabel's mind. Obas, governors, army commanders, and renowned pastors and bishops had come as ordinary big men but the children had contradicted their caregivers that these seemingly ordinary visitors were not what they were seen to be; they were very important people. When you had children from all over the country in a sort of national orphanage as Sanoma Children's Home was, now and then a child would know someone important from a place others did not know. The collective memory of the children was able to identify the different visitors no matter where they came from. However, the care-giving staff had thought the children were suffering from delusion or some other forms of mental retardation and dismissed their talks as nonsense.

* * *

Mabel had the hunch that soon she might be given a lump sum to retire to set up her own business or kicked out outright. She knew she had known too much for a worker in the orphanage and Mama Toko, with prescience for the littlest thing that happened around, might already know the weight of knowledge she was carrying. She continued to be haunted by the spirit of Little Meg she now believed, from her appearance to her in dreams, was not adopted by anybody but most likely used as a human sacrifice by the Governor asked by a medicine-man to produce a human, preferably a virgin girl, for a potent sacrifice that would facilitate, if not assure, his second term in office.

Awake at two in the morning, Mabel's mind opened up so many things that could be happening under her eyes without her seeing them. So much water was passing under the bridge, as she saw the situation. If she looked sharply, there was much to piece together in the seemingly efficient daily routine in the orphanage. There were things more than the prayers at dawn or before going to bed, the regular sumptuous meals, the classes, and playtime for the children. There was another narrative that was subsumed in the main daily lives of the children. Now she had amassed a memory-filled cache that all of a sudden was clear to her since her employment in Sanoma Children's Home.

Their orphanage was a breeding ground for children for all sorts of odd rituals that the big men and women of the society indulged in for political positions or money. The medicine men and women knew the big ones would not consider their medicines potent or efficacious enough without their demanding young ones, especially the most physically challenged and virgins, to prepare the medicines. And so they prescribed that their consultants bring them the ultimate animal for sacrifice that they knew was a human being. It was a delicate thing. No big man or woman, political, religious, or business, would entrust the procurement of a young boy or girl into even a confidant's hands. They wanted to keep everything to their chests. Not even their security details should be made aware of this deed because such could expose them when they fell out in future. And that was why they cultivated friendship with Nomate Toko to get the sacrificial humans from her own hands and taken directly to the attending medicine men.

Mabel in that deep night had a flash that exposed clearly why her "we-hail-thee" country was in such a mess. Even governors in difficult court cases and the President seeking masculine prowess were involved. Pastors and bishops who wanted bigger congregations and lavish offerings came for their human supplies. Wealthy folks, who wanted to more than double their already staggering amounts of money and be mentioned in Forbes among the richest in the continent, if not the entire world, also came.

The unionized medicine men and healers of the Federal Capital Territory had not only changed their sacrificial beasts from simple chickens, goats, sheep, and cows to humans but had also raised their charges a hundredfold. None of the big men would believe anything done for them would work if they were not charged hundreds of thousands or even millions of naira. Some medicine men had started to ask for their fees to be paid in dollars, pounds, or euros if their consultants wanted their medicines to work a hundred per cent well. They would not believe anything prepared for them would work if the sacrificial beast was a mere domestic animal. To the big men, it was easier to procure a young boy or girl from the "body shop" at Sanoma Children's Home than get a live lion or leopard as some medicine men had demanded. The stakes were high and demanded equally high sacrifices and charges. Now, instead of burying huge cows for powerful medicines, the marabous used humans who promised a higher efficacy rate of more potent medicines. Famed bishops and pastors building new national headquarters of their churches went to Sanoma Children's Home to pick their sacrificial lambs from Mama Toko. The rousing "Praise the Lord" became more tumultuous. The same folks who contributed money to the orphanage so as to be recognized went there for their human supplies. Boys and girls were buried alive under German concrete of churches and business premises that were promised prosperity. The pastor who vied for but failed to be elected CAN President gave thanksgiving a week after he opened a new mega church that used the skull of one of the alumni of Sanoma Children's Home. Governors sought human sacrifices of virgin girls bred in the orphanage to go through the Camel's Eye in airtight cases that would have either led to conviction to life jail or impeachment.

Mabel would use her haunted mind to undermine Mama Toko's reputation. As expected, she received the sack order within three days.

Mama Toko read her mind and knew that she had known too much for her comfort. It was an order and not a letter of dismissal. Mama Toko was a very smart woman and did not want to leave any paper trail in the event of a court case. She verbally dismissed Mabel and offered her seven hundred and fifty thousand naira. The director of the orphanage was surprised that the woman did not accept the money.

Mabel became "born again" in a church she was not sure did not have any link with Mama Toko's orphanage. She could not be sure because the pastors and bishops were like masquerades and you could not tell who they really were! In any case, once in the Garden of Eden Church of Christ she used her testimony to paint a gory tale of the orphanage. And that public confession was during the visit of an American evangelist in a public event televised all over the world by both CNN and Aljazeera and two Nigerian independent television stations. Mabel's testimony would lead to the collapse of the once famous Sanoma Children's Home.

The chorus was expected.

"Those who rise so high must fall," some said.

"How could these things stare us in the face without being seen?" others asked.

"She's a Nigerian after all," was the headline of the Guard. The Concord ran an editorial, "Too good to be true," which in part read: "From her friends and donors, she could only be a part of the national mafia. And it was the interest of foreign children's welfare organizations, even UNICEF, and others that led to the baring of this breeding ground of children for big men and women and their medicine men for human sacrifices. We did not know that young boys and girls were also slaughtered to harvest organs—kidneys and hearts—to meet the needs of racketeers of organ parts to keep families of big folks alive. Once the wind has blown open the fowl's anus, we can now see the sorry sight. From the many men and women who came to the tribunal and torn with grief, we now know that some parents, mainly poor ones, had given out their boys and girls for adoption after being seduced with staggering amounts of money and their kids publicly taken as orphans. That mighty fence with that indomitable glittering gate of Sanoma Children's Home really covered a lot from our wide-open eyes. Thank God we are free from this satanic network that many of us had praised as a God-blessed venture."

17

Re-named for the Other

Having no idea where Dwayne's ancestors came from in Africa and seeing his deep emotional attachment to the land made Ufuoma feel strongly that they might have been kidnapped from one Urhobo village or farmland and taken by boat by Itsekiri middle-men through the Warri River to Ughoton where the Bini made brisk business in trade by barter with Portuguese slave-buyers. She did not want to think about what a human being would have cost then but knew the Bini so valued mirrors to adorn shrines that she would not be surprised if a medium size framed mirror would have sent a young man into the land of no-return. Ufuoma could not call Dwayne "brother" when he called her "My sister." Brother and sister should not be in the relationship which was developing between them. In her mind, that was a taboo she did not want to contemplate. She should not have desire for any male she called brother because such a person belonged to her family however distant the cousinship.

If Dr. Dwayne Burton had done one of those genome tests she had heard were now available, where his African ancestry derived would have been established. Science had saved humankind from guesswork. You could guess that Kunta Kinte came from The Gambia. Now the test in a lab established with a degree of certainty where an African-American's African ancestors came from. However, Dwayne was not the sort of person going to the lab for his blood to be taken for that type of test. After all, he knew for sure that his ancestors came from Africa. To him, that was enough knowledge and he did not want to know more. As he told her, he did not even know where the Burton name he bore came from within the American South because he did not want to continue carrying that burden of slavery experience by pursuing such inquiries.

Dr. Dwayne Burton had gone to attend an international sociology conference on Comparative Perspectives on Families organized by her department at Delta State University, Abraka, and there and then he and Dr. Ufuoma Ubi struck a relationship that neither believed would bring them together again, not to talk of this close as two beans in a pod. They presented their papers in a four-person panel with almost contradictory themes; Dwayne spoke on "The Endangered Species of Manhood: The Female Carnivores in the African-American Society" and Ufuoma on "The Threat of the Phallus: Stripping Femininity from Niger Delta Women." Their papers were hotly debated after the presentation and in the remaining two days of the conference, the two exchanged papers and addresses.

Dwayne would invite her, Dr. Ubi, to a conference hosted by his University of North Carolina, which she would attend with trepidation because it was her first time of leaving Nigeria and she did not know what to expect outside, especially in the United States. After their exchange of mails, she could not contemplate not attending the conference Dwayne had invited her to; more so as he promised to facilitate things for her. If she could get the American visa with strong recommendations from the conference organizers and she would have free accommodation and feeding for the duration of the conference, she could take care of the air ticket to Chapel Hill, North Carolina. She would confess to him later how that conference trip was a life-changer for her; thanks to his hospitality which overwhelmed her and left her with the desire to reciprocate in kind. Now she wanted to be visiting Dwayne in the United States while he wanted to be visiting her in Nigeria.

To Dwayne, his time in Nigeria with Ufuoma was a heavenly spell that he wanted to make permanent. He was overwhelmed by the hospitality and vivacity of the people. Though a stranger, he was an adopted son and taken as one by every family he visited. Nobody was alone, cooped in an apartment, and susceptible to depression as was rampant in the United States. You needed no invitation to visit a friend or relative, and he enjoyed the spontaneity of human relationships. You met folks eating and you were instantly invited to share in the meal. That was a true communion that Americans had not learned despite their so-called development, he realized. Development, he was now learning from practical experience, did not reside in tall buildings and fanciful gadgets alone but more in the ethics of a society.

And to Ufuoma, the United States of America was the place to live a life of quality without the inconveniences and anxieties of her troubled nation. There was light all the time and she did not need to worry about ironing her clothes during the short spell it was available. Water flowed at all times and she could take her bath anytime she wanted mixing warm and cold water to her desire. She saw people dressing as they wished; nobody poke-nosing into your affairs as done back in Nigeria. America was really the land of freedom and the pursuit of happiness and she loved the place.

Dwayne had studied at Temple University, where he got all his degrees and was known for his Afrocentrism. At a point in his graduate studies, he could not make an academic statement or presentation without quoting Molefe Asante, his mentor. He had gone as far as calling him the prophet of Afrocentrism. Many believed he revered him as if he was a god because his faith in him was rock solid. His friends outside his alumni circle dismissed him as a dreamer who saw Africa as heaven and America as hell and neither, they believed, was what he thought because each place had aspects of heaven and hell together. They did not see the tug of war he fought internally, pitching his head against his heart.

When he announced to his friends that he had met a Nigerian woman from the Niger Delta, and an academic for that matter, they warned him against smart Nigerian ladies who faked love to get out of their depressing country. When he told them the love of his life had a grown child from a teenage pregnancy, they told him she was scheming to pass her burden of parenthood to him. Or, at worst, such people believed she wanted somebody to lighten her load of single parenthood through a partner. He felt he did not owe his friends any explanation that the boy now lived with his father who was a distinguished medical doctor in a popular clinic in Abuja, the nation's capital. He was not swayed by the persistent cynicism of friends and remained steadfast in a growing relationship with Ufuoma. Both had agreed to call each other by their first names after he rejected being called Dr. Burton even though Ufuoma did not care whether she was called Dr. Ubi or not.

Dwayne was tired of his fellow African-American ladies whom he found to be too fierce to be women. He feared being emasculated by any member of that female breed. He wanted to remain a man, a man whose manhood grew stronger in a relationship rather than the opposite. His idea of a lady was of a woman who was feminine, not domineering, but mindful of her rights. He wanted to be a man but not a patriarchal male and so did not want a matriarch for a partner. He would not have a warrior either for a partner because he feared being emasculated in such a relationship.

He liked Ufuoma's unique beauty: her large soft eyes, her midsize stature of being neither skinny nor weighty and her average height. Her rather pointed nose defied the stereotype of the African nose. Her lips were thin and her skin glistened in its chocolate shine. She walked vivaciously but gracefully with a regal demeanour. To him, she looked a perfect divine figure. He wondered why she had remained single with her high education and stunning beauty. But that had made her available to him, he reflected.

As for Ufuoma, after the initial misstep of a teenage pregnancy, she vowed not to go off course again but would wait patiently until she got the person she really loved. She had mistrusted her colleagues in the university who wanted fun with her but no serious relationship. Some of her friends had since her graduate school days been advising her not to be too choosy about men. "After all," they told her, "men are the same." She would not lower her standards just to get married. As she had heard some older women say, "A woman is never so starved of sex to make love with a goat!" She would wait and believed strongly that however long it took, she would have a male partner be a husband, friend, concubine, or whatever in a relationship that would be worth it after her long wait. Somehow, now, she knew Dwayne was going to be the man she had been waiting for all these years.

Dwayne, always active, wore a trimmed beard. He was rather mid-size in his five-six height. He wore size 33 pants but, when these were not available, picked size 34. His voice belied his size because it was sonorous like a bell and nobody failed to hear him when he was around and talking. Not in an intrusive way, but in a manner that exuded his passion. In fact, once he started talking about Africa or whatever else he loved, his voice rose to an alto that magnified his size to that of an incredible hulk that he was not physically.

"My darling, you don't know this wilderness called America; at least my space in it is unliveable," he once told Ufuoma.

"What will you call my country—wasteland? Which is worse, wilderness or wasteland? I will choose your wilderness," she responded.

"Left alone, I would rather live and die in that your wasteland than in the American wilderness," he said, thrusting his right fist into the air in a reverent manner, as if praying the gods of Africa to help him actualize his wishes.

Though young when the Black Panthers made news, he still revered them for their black activist roles. He unconsciously gave their salute when passionate about some political issues concerning his black brethren.

"You can't compare freedom of the Mother Continent to slavery of America," Dwayne told her.

"Slavery has been over for over a century. You think I don't know American history? As for me, it's an easy choice between the abolished slavery and the new slavery," she answered.

Dwayne was visiting for the second time after the international sociology conference. Ufuoma took him to a masquerade performance at Edjekota, near Ughelli. As the drumming intensified for the mother mask to come out, Dwayne was in a state he had never experienced before. It was as if the drumming was taking place in his heart, throbbing as if he was a part of the drum ensemble. He shook as if fever had seized him, and as soon as he saw the mother mask come out, he imitated every step by step, every gesture by gesture of the lead performer.

"That's what I have been telling you all along, dear. I am an Urhobo lost for three hundred years in the wilderness and have now found my way back home. It has taken the lost child more than three hundred years to come back home. I am home at last!"

"You are welcome home!" she said.

Still, Ufuoma was scared. Was Dwayne getting mad? He had talked to her about the epidemic of depression among blacks in America which manifested in multiple ways, depending upon the person. Had he been struck by a strain of malaria or dengue fever that affected his brain? She could not understand the change in the person she thought she now knew as Dwayne. He was no longer Dwayne. He had asked her several times in the past to give him a Nigerian name but she had resisted naming him. What was a Nigerian name? An Urhobo name, she thought. How would she name somebody she knew was in love with her? She could call him endearments and she had done that calling him "*Oshare re erhi me*," my soul mate, but not name him, she had thought before now. And he was three years her senior in age. How name a thirty-eight-year old man? She had asked herself several times.

As the performance continued, Dwayne danced as if delirious. He was no doubt seized by a spirit, perhaps the spirit of Uhaghwa, the god that performers sacrificed to and invoked for a flawless performance. As if being drawn into the spell, she knew the time had come for her to throw away her inhibitions and name him. She would name him Akpo, just Akpo, life. Life is a mystery and nobody knows its depth to fully explain it.

"Akpo, I call you!" she shouted above the drumming into Dwayne's ears.

"What?" he asked.

"Akpo! I call you from today Akpo. You are life; you give new life to both of us," she shouted to his hearing.

"I am Akpo. I accept my Urhobo name. Let Dwayne give way to Akpo!" he intoned, still possessed by the spirit of the drumming.

Ufuoma was surprised by the accuracy of his pronunciation of his new name, as if he knew the language well. From the way he called his new name, he was not a stranger at all to the name. It was something that he had all along without knowing it. Ufuoma felt she was just inspired by the possessing spirit to call him the name meant for him.

* * *

In the United States, he had problems with his new name among relatives and friends. To those who were cynical of his Afrocentric ideas and behaviour, this was it. He had gone to Africa, met a woman there, and screwed up. The person they knew as Dwayne was getting crazy. This was inevitable depression from his inability to come to terms with Africa as not home but just a distant, even forgotten, past!

"Akpo! What is Akpo?"

"That's a bag of baloney!"

"It's hogwash!"

When Ufuoma came to visit him, she asked to be taken to places of interest. She had come for a vacation and wanted to be treated to a great vacation and nothing less. Dwayne's mother and sister who lived in Brooklyn were as hospitable as polite relatives could be.

"Will you like to come to live in America?" they asked her.

"Sure! Akpo is a blessing to me," she told them.

"Who? Who is Ak-poo!?" his mother asked, as if halfway in saying "Acupuncture."

"I am no longer Dwayne, Mommy. I have my African name now, I am Akpo," he cut in, proudly.

"An Urhobo name," Ufuoma corrected.

"Whatever!" Dwayne's sister said.

Both Dwayne and Ufuoma knew they had a fierce and long battle to fight to win acceptance of his mother and sister. As for friends, he did not so much care. As he saw it, it was none of their business. But he really wanted his close relations to accept his love as their love too.

It was in the dog days of summer. The heat intensified in the high-rise apartments and defied what Dwayne was taught in high school that the higher you go the cooler it becomes. It might be there were too many people living in New York and the body heat combined with the raging sun and human excesses in pollution had exacerbated things. Tamika, his mother, took a hand-crafted flat piece to fan her face.

Though the house's cooling system was running full blast, she felt hot. She did not know what to make of her son. What was happening to Dwayne? Maybe she should discourage him from going again to Africa, where she heard women charmed men with all sorts of things ranging from food to sex. Africa, after all, was the home of voodoo, and she believed this African lady had already sought it to capture her son. What a mess! And Dwayne was her only son. She was struggling to make sense of her son and the heat she felt in her body. What she was experiencing was not her hot flashes but something else, though this was one of those summers when New York suffered from jungle fever. The discomfort also came from her son now being called a mumbo jumbo name by an African woman.

Dwayne was intent on returning home, going to the Mother Continent to live the rest of his life with Ufuoma, whom his relatives and friends simply called "Uuf." That Uuf had become her name in America. It appeared that, apart from Dwayne, nobody else in the company he kept, family or friends, wanted to take the pains to learn how to pronounce Ufuoma or Ubi. Tamika said Uuf sounded like an Egyptian goddess or princess. To Dwayne's sister, Uuf just sounded like the expression of delight, pleasure, relief, or just something sexy!

Resolving whether to live in the wasteland or the wilderness was not easy for two people who would ordinarily like to defer to each other. Neither Akpo nor Uuf had succeeded in persuading the other on where to settle when they eventually went further than just lovers and friends in their intensifying relationship. Each knew the other's preference but that favourite place to set up home was not acceptable to the other for now. They did not discuss this but they understood each other's feelings about having Nigeria or the United States as a permanent home for them as a couple. Somehow each felt time would come to their rescue by settling the dilemma they faced. They did not want this unacknowledged problem to destroy their ever-growing relationship. Akpo was happy he had met an authentic woman who loved him to the core. Uuf knew she was fortunate to have the best man any woman could get for herself—a lover, friend, confidant, and partner—and not a patriarch out there to give orders to her to obey or face reprimands and possible beating.

Uuf came on a late summer visit in August. The friends had become used to being called different names wherever they found themselves. Ufuoma was Uuf in the United States and called by her given name in Nigeria where Dwayne was simply Akpo even though he remained Dwayne in America. The crowded streets of New York were dwindling because the tourists from all over the world were returning home after a crazy summer, one of the hottest ever. It was even hotter than when jungle fever infected New Yorkers. Dwayne wanted Uuf to see as many interesting places as possible, so that she would feel at home in the US to understand the black person's condition.

One late evening, he took his friend to the Apollo Theater for a most exciting performance of music and dance that featured the Jubilee Singers from Fisk University and several black dance troupes from all over the country. Uuf did not see herself as an expert in the field but saw so many similarities between African and African-American music and dance. She could respond to the sounds and body movements as if she was at home in Nigeria. The percussion, call-and-response, and baseline make African-American music a direct extension of African traditional music, she felt. When it came to dance, she saw the same culture that nurtured the dances in Africa and their descendants in the Diaspora.

This outing for entertainment gladdened her heart. This was what she loved so much about Akpo—taking her out to experience life with him. She felt blessed as he held her hand and squeezed it affectionately. This physical contact made her always want him, inflamed her desire for him. Once in a while, as they strolled, he patted her back and kissed her at every opportunity. She enjoyed every bit of the relationship and prayed it grew stronger and an insurmountable bond should tie them into husband and wife at some stage in the future.

They had come to the theatre in Harlem by train. After the performance, Akpo wanted to take Uuf through blocks of streets before going back to the subway to return to his mother's apartment. Uuf had always told him that she liked walking. The further they went from the theatre, the more strangely interesting the streets became. Graffiti marked everywhere. No space was left unfilled with scrawls of black, white, red, green, or whatever paint to scribble gibberish, obscenities, or very witty phrases or sentences. The streets were neat but not as wide as in other parts of the Big Apple. So many fast food joints—MacDonald's, Burger King, Chinese take-away restaurants, and shops everywhere manned by Koreans and Jamaicans. Uuf had noticed joggers at any time of the day till very late at night in Tamika's part of Brooklyn but not here at this time, late evening.

"You care for ice cream?" Akpo asked.

"Yes," Uuf answered.

When only two of them were together, they called each other Akpo and Uuf and not Dwayne and Ufuoma for some reasons

"Let's have . . ." and the sound of a gunshot stopped Akpo midway in his utterance.

He grabbed Uuf firmly by the hand and pushed her down to take cover by lying flat on the ground to avoid bullets flying past them with fiery speed. There was a riot of movement as more gunshots filled the air with whew sounds. In the commotion of apparently two gangs shooting at each other, street walkers, and those running from the ice cream kiosk, some three teenagers—Uuf saw them clearly—snatched her Gucci handbag with her passport and money inside it. As this was happening to her, bullets were flying all over and many were hit and bleeding. She prayed Akpo who had been separated from her by the barrage of gunshots and stampede was safe. She did not know whether to run to where she did not know, remain lying on the ground as if hit, or stand and look for Akpo. In that split second of confusion, she moved forward. She stepped over some freshly dead bodies as she felt running towards the underground station would be a better option with the street battle not abating. The ground was painted red with blood.

To her pleasant surprise, Akpo was behind her. He had been held down by some rough boys who no doubt stripped him clean of whatever was in his pockets and purse. Just as soon as reunited, they saw a boy hit on the right foot. He seemed less than five years old. Uuf bent down to check him and before she could raise her head, gunshots from behind tore past her right foot. She fell, gasping for breath and life.

She did not know how she got to the emergency ward, where a bullet from an automatic rifle was removed from her right thigh. After regaining consciousness, she saw by her bed Akpo and Tamika who brought balloons to wish her speedy recovery. The police had found her Nigerian passport and traced her to the hospital to give it to her. As soon as her mind became lucid, after the pain killer had worn out, she asked herself, "This in America?" She felt asking Akpo this question would exacerbate her pain because he would use that as an argument later on why the place was an unliveable wilderness.

"We surely walked into a gang fight," he explained to her, as he held her hand.

"You have too many guns in America. How can a civilized people be carrying guns about and waging war in their streets?" she asked.

"That's the hell of America outsiders don't know," Dwayne answered, knowing that Ufuoma had made a strong case for him.

She did not heal totally before leaving for Nigeria. She had gone through hell and every night was a nightmare for her. She did not fall asleep on time and when she did, she was always being shot at from all directions. She shouted out loud to Akpo's hearing in the bed when she spent her entire sleep dodging flying bullets. She told Akpo she had to return to Nigeria to regain her sanity. He was happy that she wanted to leave America, not because he did not like her company but for the reasons which had been driving him crazy and for which he would prefer somewhere in the Mother Continent for home.

"I will go with you to Nigeria. You know how much I love your home country," he told her, caressing her shoulders gently.

"That will be great fun for me. I know I should be fully fine in a few weeks and your company will make me heal even faster."

"Thanks for cherishing my presence in your life."

"It's a two-way traffic and we are reinforcing each other in every practical way possible."

"Thanks for your love."

"And you too."

* * *

Ufuoma settled to her normal routine as soon as back home. Her university had been on strike and reopened about the time she returned. There were many ceremonies to attend, if one had the time, money, and energy. She took Akpo to as many as possible and introduced him as her friend. Some colleagues had started to ask her questions about him even before she introduced him to them.

"Is he your fiancé?"

"Is this your American husband?"

Akpo often did not wait for Ufuoma to respond but did the answering for her.

"Yes," he would say.

He had learned fast and had been working on his accent not to be noticed as a stranger's. He was tired of hearing Nigerians saying "Hi!" to him. Why not "*Mi guo*?" or "*Oma gare*" as they greeted among themselves? He wanted to be part of them while those greeting him with "Hi!" wanted to be part of the place he wanted to leave. He loved Ufuoma and also wanted to be at home in Nigeria. Young folks spoke black American slang to him. Don't they know that much as he loved Ebonics, he wanted to speak Urhobo or Nigerian languages and the English they spoke which had a uniquely interesting rhythm? He often asked himself. And he knew that these Nigerians spoke the worst kind of black American slang you could imagine; the affectation in their voice made them laughable and phony. Of course, you could easily tell it was phony, so artificial in tone that any street person in Harlem or Brooklyn or any major American city would know you were an infiltrator. He didn't care they saw him trying to do the same with Urhobo because they used to laugh whenever he greeted. He was becoming better because more and more nobody laughed before answering his greetings. He did not pretend to speak Urhobo well but was learning. That was the difference between those youths around in Warri and its environs who spoke Ebonics as if they were African-Americans, which they were definitely not. Maybe they had to go there and live with his people to really know as he was doing. But why go with open eyes to hell? He asked himself.

Burial ceremonies were a constant avenue for flaunting wealth in this part of the world, he had come to know. The father of one of Ufuoma's colleagues in Delta State University had died and was to be buried. Of course Akpo wanted to see as many of these ceremonies as possible, much as he wondered why reasonable people squandered so much money and resources on the dead they did not take as much care of while alive. Dr. Linus Iboje did not do things small and he wanted to create a record in the way he entertained his guests and he really did. From the huge tent that took over five hundred guests to the caterers that were busy with service of foods and drinks, every guest felt satisfied that Dr. Iboje could boast with the record until the next burial ceremony when somebody else who cared so much about his ego would shatter it for the competition to go on without end.

As they left Egbo, Ufuoma felt glad that Akpo's presence in her life was a great blessing. She knew that he also felt fulfilled. He had taken some red wine and refused to take Gulder or other types of Nigerian beer that he said were too strong for him. He was used to Budweiser that was mild and one had to drink a dozen or more small bottles before getting tipsy. He admired the women who drank many big bottles of those potent beers such as Gulder, Star, and Crown. He was happy though that Ufuoma drank only Smirnoff Ice, a mild alcoholic drink. As they drove home, Akpo was in very high spirit and started to sing blues, his favourite music. You gonna laugh even when what you carry is only light to lift but crushing to carry! Others envy you for smiling when you have dammed in enough water to fill the Mississippi! Nobody will envy nightmares for a deep sleep.

As they drove into Aladja, Ufuoma felt these songs were not as jovial as Akpo sang them. There was deep sorrow in the laughter of blues. She had noticed that among her own Urhobo people, folks laughed at funerals!

"Stop these songs! Let me sing you something for a change. I can sing and really make you laugh!"

Before she cleared her throat and opened her mouth for what she wanted to be a great performance, the first syllable of an *udje* song hung stiff on her lips. Ahead of them was a crowd. She wound down her window to ask what was going on. Soon there were more people adding to the already crowded place. She wanted to turn back but there was no way of moving forward or backward. Drivers were coming out of their cars for a spectacle, it appeared. Everybody was manoeuvring to a position to see what was happening. A young man of about twenty-five years had been stripped naked. He looked scared as he foresaw the harsh judgment of the mob surrounding him. Another man had accused him of tugging at his trousers from the back and he had instantly lost his manhood. He had exclaimed "See *gbomo gbomo*!" and the swift response was the spectacle, instant justice for one wielding diabolic magic to rid men of their penises.

Two boys brought two gallons of petrol to where the sacrificial victim stood immobile, by every means tied to a stake. A bulky young man had come forward with a motorcycle tire he pushed over the mob-condemned man and held by his neck like an oversized necklace. They carefully poured the fuel into the tire, doused his body with the fuel as if cleansing him for sacrifice, and threw a struck match at the neck-laced man as they stepped backwards.

Akpo was perplexed at what he was witnessing. Was this a dream or real life? It was real life. He broke away from Ufuoma who was holding him and ran as if he could stop the blaze. Some other men pushed him back. In close proximity he saw the young man cremated by the crowd. Ufuoma managed to get to him to pull him back. They watched a human being burnt to death with the clapping, laughter, and thunderous applause of a crowd as background music.

"Shit!" was all Akpo could tell Ufuoma.

"This is as bad as a lynching party in the South!" he shouted at her.

"It could be as bad as this here. Even worse sometimes," she told him.

"This is barbaric. Jungle justice!" he exclaimed.

"I told you about how bad this place is. I forewarned you about my people and what to expect in Nigeria," she said, as if defending herself.

As they wanted to leave, there was an attempt by some boys to seize Akpo.

"See the culprit's accomplice who wanted to rescue him from justice," one of the area boys shouted.

"Yes, he is," another shouted.

A crowd was building round them.

"No, he is my husband. He is not!" Ufuoma shouted.

"See the person there! See him running away," she said, pointing to a direction she knew would distract the mob and give her the chance to steal her man away from instant death.

As the area boys turned to chase the supposed accomplice, Ufuoma tugged Akpo away. She trembled as they entered the car and in the line of stranded cars just shook until there was movement. They got home very late.

"Is this Nigeria?" Akpo asked.

"I don't know. These things happen here once in a while," she replied.

For the next three days, Akpo suffered terribly from headaches and insomnia. The brief respite he had in a long night was filled with nightmares. Whenever he closed his eyes, fire started and continued to burn people till he woke. He sweated all night despite the air-conditioned bedroom.

A week after the incident, he had to cut his visit short. Ufuoma's thigh had healed after all. The partners realized that they had to either build a fresh planet to live in or brace themselves for the bitter and the sweet they were bound to experience in Nigeria or the United States.

18

Asabe Goes for the Third

Asabe suffered terribly for not heeding her mother's advice early enough. That affirms the proverbial saying that what the elder tells the child in the morning will surely come to pass sometime in the day however late. The day compares very well to a person's life. Many people only learn from practical experience and Asabe was one of such people. But heeding one's parent's advice aside, life is more complicated and has a force of its own that propels one towards a certain fate.

After graduating in English and Literary Studies from Dukawa University and completing the mandatory one-year national youth service, what was left for a young, beautiful twenty-four year old woman than think of marrying? In that way Asabe was not different from other young women in her community. She had to marry, as was expected of her not only by her parents, relatives, and friends, but also by everybody else who knew her. She was ripe for marriage at her age and she had gained enough education to get married and settle down in a family of her own. And so she convinced herself that she had to marry as everybody around expected of her.

Things went very fast once she had decided to marry, even though she did not know who her husband would be. A man of her choice would come to her, she believed, because she was beautiful and educated. There were many men who wanted such a woman in the community and she was sure that, once she made herself a prospective wife, suitors would come in great numbers.

She was right about the number of suitors. It did not take a long time to decide on one of them as her future man. It turned out that she became the second wife to a man who already had a young wife; only twenty-one. Within three months, the husband, Haruna, divorced his two wives. He did not go to any court, just divorced them without giving anybody any reasons. He was not obliged to give reasons for the simultaneous or double divorce. Asabe came home with her letter of divorce. As soon as they had the opportunity to be alone, her mother, Hajara, asked her: "Why were you not discreet in your marriage?" She was not surprised or shocked as Asabe's father was. Audu had thought he had raised a very well-behaved daughter who would, in her marriage, make him very proud, but the sudden divorce would make folks think otherwise. He felt he had failed in his duty as a parent because he took his daughter's divorce as a vote of no confidence on his parental ability.

Once she had experienced marriage, Asabe felt she could no longer stay unmarried. Much as it was not the bliss she had expected, still marriage had conditioned her to a new style of life that she had got used to and she felt like going back to it after leaving Haruna. It would be awkward too for her, a grown woman, living with her parents. Since it would be even more awkward for her to live alone in the same town, she was stuck with her parents. It had to be a temporary arrangement until she left to another marriage home. She knew she was beautiful enough to be courted by so many men and it would be a matter of months before she would be married again. She was mature enough to know the men who liked or loved her and so she would make her choice out of the serious ones. What would the men coming to visit her in her mother's home be looking for than a relationship with her?

The suitors kept coming once they knew she had become single again and the mandatory three months after her divorce had passed. Asabe's second marriage was to a man who had been at the university with her. Musa had observed then that she was not like the other girls who were going after so many men, frequenting parties, and looking for money. She had not shown interest in men. To Musa, she was the model on campus of the disciplined young woman who did not flirt or follow the bad ways of wayward girls and men. By the time he had wanted to marry, Asabe had already been engaged for her marriage to Haruna and so he had to marry someone else. He had blamed himself for not asking for Asabe's hand in marriage early enough. He had to marry what he considered his second best choice at the time, Ramatu. As soon as he heard that Asabe was divorced, he felt he had the chance now to marry his true love. He was confident he could take good care of two women and could cope with their demands in every way possible. He knew what it took to marry more than one wife and promised himself he would do his best to follow the religious customs required of him to love and treat them equally.

Asabe now saw it as her fate to always be second wife and she did not mind being second to Ramatu. So, she became the second wife to Musa whose first wife was also younger than her. At twenty-three Ramatu was in her prime; slim, tall, and divinely crafted. Musa was very pleased that both Ramatu and Asabe got on very well almost as soon as Asabe came in. They laughed together, giggled as they conversed, and did not behave like rivals as one would expect. Where was the jealousy that people and stories talked so much about co-wives? For sure there was no jealousy, envy, or hatred in his house. His two wives were always happy together and he was very happy that they were happy. A few times, when he came from outside, he saw one coming from the other's room and they behaved as the best of friends. He had barged on them talking as if gossiping or saying something confidential they did not want anybody else, including him, to hear. They even held hands and separated as soon as they saw him. He thus saw his wives as model co-wives.

But again, within three months, the new husband, Musa, divorced Asabe and she came home with a letter. And again, her mother asked in a rather quiet tone: "Why couldn't you be discreet enough a second time?" Asabe's mother's response to her daughter's second divorce in barely one year was quite unlike the father's since he was befuddled. To him, Asabe must have a bad character that men could not bear; hence they divorced her within only three months of marriage. He saw this as his destiny; the father of a young woman who was always divorced within a short time of marriage. He felt disappointed but knew there was little he could do about it. He could not take his daughter to the man who had divorced her. That was not done. The man must have reasons why he gave her the divorce letter. He prayed that if she married again she should marry someone who would overlook her failings till she grew into an experienced and good wife.

* * *

At home Asabe felt restless and bored. Three months had passed since she came back from Musa's home. She was now a free woman; yet men were not coming to her, as after the first divorce. She stayed at home with ragged clothes as if she did not have boxes of beautiful and expensive clothes to select from. Two marriages, however short, had stocked her with trunks of dresses that she could change daily without using a dress twice in several months or even more. However, unlike her usual self, she did not look at the mirror; nor did she make up before going out. As her boredom increased, she felt lifted into another planet in which she saw ogres pursuing her. A faint voice was telling her that she was an ugly woman that no man would ever marry again. When she came out of her lows, she knew that she was still beautiful.

At a point while so bored, she sent a fourteen-year old boy to buy her Benylin with Codeine, which she would pour into a cup of yoghurt and take. Though she was not coughing, she had discovered that taking this mixture made her feel fine. After taking it, she had no worries about being ugly or beautiful and cared less about herself. In that state it did not matter whether she was married or not. She just felt a certain type of contentment at least for hours. It was a state she could only compare with what she had experienced from her two co-wives that she was now separated from.

The boy returned much later than expected, looking ruffled and nervous. When Asabe asked him why he stayed so long and chastised him for going to play rather than do the errand he had been sent on, the poor boy had to confess to being forced by the man selling Benylin with Codeine to come in and, after being forcefully stripped, he held him down to assault him from behind. He cried out and others who came to buy medication caught them and beat the man. As soon as more people gathered to beat the man, he escaped and ran from the medicine store and back home.

Asabe recollected some events of the recent past and began to put things together. What did not make sense in the past started now to make a lot of sense to her. She had seen the chemist, whom they called the medicine-seller, with Alhaji Idris, a neighbour who was now widowed, but had not known what their relationship had been. Now she did not care about their relationship but knew what it was.

In one of her frequent her insomnia periods on a clear full moon, during an international football match between Nigeria and South Korea being televised nationwide, Asabe, through her window, had observed a man, the medicine seller, riding a bike. His profile was quite clear and she could not take him for any other person. The medicine-seller stood his bike by the wall and, after what appeared as a repeated knock on the door, the door opened and he went into Alhaji Idris's house. It was at about 3:00 a.m. Asabe wanted to see the end of this visit at the deepest part of night and glued her eyes to their neighbour's front door. She saw the medicine-seller coming out a little more than an hour later with his caftan half tucked in and its rope dangling and not in its proper place. Now Asabe thought she did not need to guess what had happened. She saw the signs of the medicine-seller having undressed and redressing hurriedly before attracting any attention and leaving before dawn.

Asabe's mother had observed her daughter's change from her sparkling nature to a rather gloomy young woman. She guessed why. Hajara sat her daughter down in her bedroom. Both sat at the edge of the bed as the daughter looked at her mother expecting her to tell her why she had called her.

"You should have sense by now. Only have a relationship with somebody you have power over rather than with somebody who has power over you! Love someone you can control, and you'll have peace."

Asabe listened attentively and only nodded her head and left.

By some chance, things would soon happen in Asabe's favour. Or things would happen that would make her to put her mother's advice into practice without strain or anybody imputing wrong motives. It would come so naturally. Asabe's father and Alhaji Idris met one morning on their way from morning prayers. After all, they were neighbours of sorts, their homes separated by one building. Alhaji Idris told Asabe's father that he would be coming to visit him soon.

"*Salaam alai kum*!"

"*Alai ka salaam*!"

"*Madallah*! You are always welcome in my house."

"I am coming to greet you in respect of Asabe."

Asabe's father knew what Alhaji Idris meant by coming to see him in respect of his daughter. He would not hesitate to grant his consent for the Alhaji to marry Asabe. He was very happy because his daughter was now going to marry a mature and experienced man who would be more caring and patient with her than the earlier young husbands and so there would be no possibility of another divorce. He would no longer be providing for an over-mature daughter in his house. That embarrassment would be gone in a short while. Though there were some rumours about him, because he lost his wife a long time ago and had not since then remarried, Alhaji Idris had only boys working for him—cooking, washing and ironing his clothes, and sending on errands. If he was not impotent, what else could be wrong with him? Audu had asked himself. But he dismissed the rumours. He assured himself, "If he were one of those men who don't like women, he wouldn't be interested in my daughter." He knew pious men who did not want to have women who were not their wives or relatives around them, and Alhaji Idris might just be one of such men. There were always maligning tongues in the community and he felt such rumours were not fair about his prospective son-in-law. To him, a man who had lost his wife so many years ago and did not mess around with women should be praised for his discipline. A disciplined man is always a blessing to his wife, he believed. He felt his daughter would be lucky to be the wife of someone like Alhaji Idris who should focus his love, care, and attention on her without succumbing to any distractions. Alhaji Idris was not the type to have multiple wives though he had the ability to do so, Audu thought. He felt happy for himself and his daughter should the arrangements work well and the marriage contracted.

The Alhaji came to see Audu who easily gave his consent to his neighbour marrying his daughter. Asabe and her mother were told immediately and they consented. Everybody in the house, father Audu, mother Hajara, and daughter Asabe, were pleased with the arrangement that they believed would solve whatever problem caused Asabe's divorces. Audu was pleased that his daughter showed interest in the elderly man who was many years older than her. She was a good daughter that obliged the father's wishes or rather whose wishes coincided with her parents' in the man she should marry. He was greatly relieved and felt a long-lasting marriage of his daughter would wipe away the blithe of two earlier divorces.

The marriage arrangements were done without delay. It appeared Alhaji Idris was an impatient would-be groom as Asabe was an impatient would-be bride. A date was set for the wedding. The three months went so fast that both man and woman were happy that at last the time had come.

Asabe was no longer gloomy. As she thought of her mother's advice, she became her old self again. She bristled with life and radiated with beauty again. She planned to look her best on the wedding day. She wanted to look even more attractive than she had ever been. She wanted to settle in this marriage for good and stop being an embarrassment to her parents. She could not contemplate a third divorce in her life. She was experienced enough now not to make silly mistakes she knew led to her two previous divorces. She did not blame any of her two previous husbands for the divorces. She had been careless in her actions. And she did not expect any husband of their type to condone what she did. She would now be in control of things and there should be no cause for her new husband to send her home with a divorce letter. She already knew what power to exercise over her prospective husband that would check her being given a divorce letter.

The wedding day arrived. May Allah be blessed, she intoned internally. She sat on a low stool surrounded by elderly women relatives who had come to beautify her before the wedding ceremony to which many people had been invited. These experienced women were traditional beauticians come to make her look the most attractive bride ever. They painted her with henna, had her manicured, perfumed and dressed as a most alluring bride. She did not feel like one who had gone through this ritual two times before. She felt as if this was really her first marriage. She believed no young woman went into marriage expecting a divorce so soon. She carried her dreams to the man's house. She would carry her dreams well so as not to shatter them this time. She now began to reflect on how she came to this point in her life.

* * *

When she was about ten years of age, the female house-help introduced her into what she could not withdraw from later in life and became an enjoyable lifestyle that she had to hide. She could recall the time the house help volunteered to scrub her well in the bath. It started first with her breasts—admiring and squeezing them, then later touching her most private parts. What started in the bathroom went into the help's room or her room. They lived in a big house and she had her room next to her mother's room. She was not just an only child but also an only daughter of her parents. The house help lived in the boy's quarter that was earshot beside the bungalow. They had plenty of time to be together, and the house help made sure she stayed with Asabe as much as possible. After all, she considered it as the most important part of her job description to take care of Asabe.

By the time she was twelve years old, Asabe had been much into it. The house-help had perfected her tactics. After arousing Asabe into a frenzied state of desire, she would walk away from her, knowing the delirious excitement she had led her into. She would not come to her for days so as to starve her. Asabe would then buy gifts and tuck into the house help's room for her to come back and give her the pleasurable experience she wanted all the time.

On one normal school day, she had felt so excited and possessed that she was getting out of her mind. At school, she suddenly became delirious for the sexual contact. She was so absent minded, she knew she could not wait till school closed to be home with the house help. She had to give the excuse that she was sick so as to leave school for home. The teacher wanted to call her parents but Asabe refused. She had to go home alone, passing through the house help's room, hoping to get her fulfilment from the fire burning inside her. However, she was not in her boy's quarter. She was also not in her room or the sitting room. She called her but there was no answer. Where could she have gone to at this time? She asked herself. However, she felt she must be in the house and was still bluffing her. She felt the house help would like to hide from her when she heard her voice to further starve her but she knew she must be somewhere in the house.

What else would she do to please her to come back to her? But as she went deeper into the house, she heard some loud moans from the mother's room and knew that the house help and her mother were having an affair. She peeped through the key hole to see them but could not see clearly but two women were there. She wanted to open the door but could not because it was locked and bolted from inside. Of course, her father had gone to work and would not be back till about 5 p.m. Her mother, a full housewife, knew when to exercise her freedom. After the mother and house help had satiated themselves, the house help opened the door and walked past her indifferently as if she was not there. Asabe went in and saw her mother lying naked in bed in the afterglow of sex, her legs spread-eagled and unabashed. Apparently, her mother did not care about the condition in which Asabe saw her. She might not even know the daughter knew what was happening that she had come to interrupt. As for Asabe, she knew what her mother had done. It was from the rather jealous look in Asabe's eyes that her mother intuitively realized that the house help was also having an affair with her daughter.

* * *

Asabe was now ready to marry and stay for good in a matrimonial home without fear of a divorce again. She was going for her third marriage more confident than ever. She had not only matured in the ways of the world but also had two reliable weapons she was taking to her marriage with Alhaji Idris. She had two powerful weapons at her disposal: knowledge of what she could do and the secret of the man she was going to marry. She would go with her own female house help while the man could retain his all-male servants.

19

The Healer's Favourite Son Dies

Aderha was born and raised in Kokori, Agbon's second largest town. Even his name had something that made who had not seen him believe he must be an extraordinary man. He left behind a strong impression on people wherever he had lived. His name conjured up the image of a superhuman being. The same reputation often preceded him to wherever he went or whatever he did. His name was given to him because his mother delivered him at a crossroads and he seemed to have imbibed the mystical, or rather spiritual, powers that crossroads held among Agbon people. Many old men and women wondered why his mother in labour could not endure whatever pain and walk or even crawl beyond a crossroads before delivering her baby where spirits gathered. But others felt it was his destiny to be a child of the crossroads where humans, under the watchful eyes of resident spirits, took directions to one way or the other. Who could tell what spirits, benevolent or malevolent, were there at the moment of his delivery? He had to be a lucky chap to survive being born at the crossroads and not being deformed or mad, the very old believed. If he were not so lucky, the spirits that kept the crossroads as their residence or refuge would have messed up his body or mind with their pranks.

Aderha grew up to be powerful in many ways—physically and mystically. He was not huge at all but rather built on the small side. His small size belied the general perception that strength and power belonged to huge figures. He was muscular and folks believed he had a singular muscle that was as strong as an iron string. He walked briskly as if he was being pursued or in a hurry to get somewhere so important that lateness would not be tolerated. At the same time he was a patient man who could outwait the crocodile stalking its victim. The spirits of the crossroads, to his townspeople, did not only give him energy but also restraint from precipitous action. As a child, he ran errands for his family and neighbours, who spoke well of one who did not hesitate to avail himself when needed.

His mother died during the delivery at home of Aderha's only sibling that survived the mother's massive blood loss. He lost his father soon afterwards at an early age. As a young man, he followed his uncles to harvest bunches of ripe palm nuts for eventual processing into palm oil. He did not climb any palm tree like his mates would be enthusiastic in trying to do or even did. However, he made a name that none of the climbers of palm trees would ever make. In one of such forays assisting his senior uncle, he was reported to have saved his uncle's wife from being hit by a palm nut bunch that would have killed or done irreparable damage to the woman who was sitting at the foot of the palm tree. Aderha was standing by the palm tree and he caught the falling palm bunch with his hands above the woman's head. A palm nut bunch had plenty of spikes that would pierce any palm or hand to bleed profusely and cause biting pain but not Aderha's. When people talked about his power, they referred to such attributes of doing what other ordinary folks could not do. He was a child of the crossroads because children born at home did not have the power that protected their hands from being pierced by spikes.

Later when he visited his cousin in Okitipupa in faraway Western Region, the belief in his being powerful spread to other lands. There he put an end to the notorious piracy of Adogun and his boys who so terrorized the area that nobody dared oppose their extortions. The story continued to be told in distant Okitipupa, his native Agbon, and elsewhere where his reputation of possessing extraordinary power of how his cousin, Umukoro, sent him on an errand to his wife, Ronke, in the market. Ronke was a trader. While Aderha was there to deliver his message, Adogun's boys came to seize whatever they fancied. When they came to Ronke, who sold cooking pots and plates, they piled pots and plates to take away as if they were buying wholesale what Ronke had in her stall. Aderha immediately seized the pots and plates they had forcibly taken and gave the items back to a grateful Ronke. The young pirates felt insulted and wanted to seize him but he shouted at them and they froze and withdrew from Ronke's stall. They felt he was too strong for them to confront alone and so went to report to their master who they expected would come and teach the brazen young man a hard lesson for defying him by preventing his boys from having their wishes in the market.

Aderha sat down and waited. It did not take too long before there was a commotion in the market. The master pirate himself had entered the market. Before a crowd of onlookers, Adogun in a swaggering manner went to Ronke's stall. He stared sternly at Aderha, as if his stare would make him run away. Aderha stood there and stared back at Adogun. The crowd watching from a distance knew a great confrontation was ahead for them. There was general silence. Then Adogun ordered his boys to take whatever they wanted from Ronke's stall, as he waited for anybody to challenge them. Aderha shouted "Don't touch any of Ronke's things!" The market crowd watched with dismay at this man who dared to speak against Adogun's orders.

Since he was not a huge man, Adogun felt he would be an easy challenger to defeat and humiliate and so lifted him from the ground and thrust him into the air. Aderha hung in mid-air with Adogun frozen in one place. The pirate leader could neither throw Aderha down nor do anything else to hurt him. His hands just hung in the air with Aderha glued to them. He had expected the young man to be light but he was a ponderous log once lifted. He had expected the small Aderha to cry or beg him for forgiveness but Aderha was mute. At first the master pirate's legs stood firm but soon he started to feel them being drained as if he was losing blood. Then numbness set into his hands. His legs started wobbling and soon sweat broke profusely all over his body. He knew he had met more than an equal. He put Aderha down rather gently because he was drained of any physical stamina. He expected relief from putting down the strange man stopping his boys from collecting articles they wanted. But really there was no relief as Aderha knocked him down and started to beat him. The market crowd cheered and nobody knew when and how the disgraced chief pirate slipped out of the market and out of public view. That singular action of Aderha put an end to the brazen manners of Adogun and his piratical activities in the Okitipupa creeks and environs.

Aderha came back home to his hometown of Kokori a celebrated powerful older man. So when he settled down and took to healing the mad, his people knew he had all the powers needed to do what he had chosen to do. Those who remembered that he was born at the crossroads and not only caught a palm nut bunch in the air with his hands but also defeated a notorious Yoruba pirate knew that if any Agbon person had the power to tame the spirit of insanity, it had to be Aderha. They brought the most violent and depressed of the mad to him and he was able to calm the violent and cheer up the depressed within a reasonable time and with time brought them back to normalcy and they returned to their homes.

For every mad person that came, he went to the forest to get the herbs, roots, or barks that he would use to prepare the medicine for the cure. He said he heard plants talk and understood their language. He asked the forest dwellers, as he called the trees, questions as to whether they had the properties he sought for his healing task. Was the plant capable of helping him to drive away the madness of the person brought to him? Did the plant need the combination of another plant or more for his task of healing a particular person to be accomplished? Before he went far into the forest, he would find a plant that told him that it could provide the cure and he collected either its bark or leaves or roots and returned. A few dangerous cases of madness made him spend hours in the forest, almost getting lost or getting disoriented as he inquired from plant to plant whether any had the power he looked for. The madness he could not cure in Agbon did not seek further treatment as that was dismissed as an impossible case for any other healer.

Aderha knew the plants needed for cures. But those who came to seek help from him knew that he had powers that extended beyond the right herbs, barks, or leaves. He also murmured incantations as he administered the medicines and those secret words assured the efficacy of the treatments. He did not charge much as he believed the gift he had from God should not be for sale alone even though he had to live on what he made from his healing profession.

Aderha's junior son, Edewor, was close to him. From a small boy, he started to be close to his father. It gladdened the healer's heart that he had a son interested in what he was doing and with time might take over from him. It is in the same line that certain gifts manifest among a people, he believed. It could be this son who would acquire his gifts and continue his practice after he had passed on to the ancestors. His two other sons had disappointed him in showing no interest in what he was doing. They baptized in the Catholic Church and seemed to even view their father with suspicion of being a wizard. They left the compound as soon as grown up and did not want to be associated with a father who healed mad people. But Edewor was different.

"Edewor, bring me those herbs in my bag," he would tell him.

"In your bedroom?" the boy would ask.

"Where else will they be other than where they should? You know where I keep the big bag."

Aderha had a voluminous hunting bag into which he gathered the herbs, barks, or leaves that promised him assistance in his healing practice. He kept it in a corner that was dark when the door opened, and only Edewor of his children knew well what he put at different parts of his bedroom. The young boy was growing as his father's reputation was also growing. Brilliant, Edewor topped his class from Primary One through his secondary school days.

"What do you expect of a strong man's son?" some asked.

Others asked: "How can you compete with Aderha's son and win when he is a strong man who is capable of fortifying his son in every possible way?"

"The boy has such a retentive brain that he forgets nothing he is taught in the class," a man whose son was Edewor's age-mate and in the same class said.

Like his father, the son, they believed. Edewor finished his secondary school with excellent grades. In the sciences, he was particularly good. He scored Excellent in Biology, Chemistry, Mathematics, and Physics. He scored the same in other courses but he had a passion for Chemistry which he wanted to study in the university. He was so good that he had double admission. He was admitted to the University of Ibadan to study Chemistry and also won a scholarship to study Chemistry at the University of London.

From the father's fame in restoring sanity to the insane, he built a big house and Edewor had a special room to himself. He still assisted his father despite his schooling. As he matured, he observed the mad ones. He had learned over the years the types of mad folks brought to his father to heal. Some were so withdrawn that they did not talk at all but just sat down in one place with expressionless faces. They looked bored by everything, including life. They ate little and only a minority consumed a huge portion of whatever food was given to them. Other mad men and women were violent and those had to be restrained physically. They were chained and Edewor had been asked by his father several times to take part in subduing and even beating the violent patients. Though slightly bigger than his father, Edewor was not huge. But he had physical strength too as he could hold down a big violent man without trouble. The experienced healer took beating the violent ones as part of their treatment. For such, the more they were beaten the more violent they became in their behaviour. Edewor saw the dilemma: should they be beaten or left to be violent? After all, such mad ones were restless and it was in that restlessness that they were able to obey the spirit possessing them. Was their violent behaviour not an expression of their type of insanity? He asked himself.

One of the memorable moments that father and son shared was when Edewor saw two of the mad, Birhe and Tekevwe, making love. Both man and woman did not seem to have had any close relationship in the compound in which every mad person was minding his or her own business. They did not seem to have the mind of making friends. In fact, Aderha had not observed friendship among the mad folks he had been treating for years. Tekevwe was in her late thirties and once in a long while took a bath in the open and she had a perfect body that folks spied on. She was rather slim and tall and stood out like a well-carved sculpture. Her breasts were firm and erect and her fairness gave lustre to her body. People did not talk of a neat mad woman but

Tekevwe was one. But beside that, no one noticed her in the compound. Birhe was moderate in size and height and did not talk to anybody but appeared to be talking to himself. He carried a certain dignity in his madness and Aderha felt that personalities were ingrained in humans whether mad or not. Birhe walked with an air of nobility that the madness did not make comprehensible.

Edewor, then eighteen, chanced upon them in a dark corner of the compound in the late evening, at the twilight hour. Their reflections exposed them before he noticed the two. The madman stood sticking his manhood into the woman from behind. It was a spectacle that captured his fancy. His father came in the process of going round the huge compound. They were surprised at the undiminishing energy of the man and the receptiveness of the woman to the man's frantic love-making. Both father and son knew that if this had happened in broad daylight and in a public place, men, women, and children would have congregated to share the free spectacle that would be the talk of town for so many years. When there was an ecstatic shout, it was not clear from whom but probably from both man and woman when they let out a mad scream at their simultaneous orgasm.

They noticed that the two mad lovers were the quiet ones but made love with such ferocity that one could not imagine what the violent ones would do. It did not take long after their lovemaking for both mad man and woman to recover their sanity and they would leave the compound and marry. Both Aderha and Edewor knew that there were things one saw and did not talk about. However, they had discovered that lovemaking helped speed the recovery of some mad ones.

Each year Aderha had what had become known as his festival. It was really more of a big party celebrating what he had achieved the preceding year. During the festival, there was a parade of those he had healed who were asked to return for this ceremony. That year too was the year that Edewor was to leave for London. They expected a special festival. The father felt so; his son felt so. Many healed patients and their relations volunteered to bring animals to be sacrificed in gratitude for being restored to good health. A bull would be slaughtered at a shrine Aderha had set up at a corner of his compound for the god of healers.

Father and son had been having a longstanding debate as to the necessity for Western education and what help it had in healing the insane. Edewor saw his education as making easier his father's work and he would study Chemistry to know the chemical components of the barks, roots, and leaves that his father used to cure those brought to him.

"And what of the incantations?" he asked his son.

"It is the components of the plants first before the incantations," the son told his father.

"You have followed me long enough to know these things well. The two aspects go together," Aderha said.

"I agree with you but the incantations alone will not work without the plants."

"You get it, my son. But how do you replace the role of the incantations?"

"That's what science or my studies will look out for. How do I use the chemicals without the arcane incantations to reinforce the efficacy of these medicines?"

"That will be a good inquiry in your science if you can get that replacement," Aderha told his son.

It was an on-going conversation that father and son undertook and knew there was some common ground they were yet to achieve.

The highlight of the festival was the music and dance in which the healed mad men and women and outsiders participated. Both Birhe and Tekevwe caught the attention of onlookers not just because of their dance but because of the infectious love they showed for each other. A year ago they left the healer's compound; now they were a newlywed couple. Only Aderha and Edewor who had seen them making love in the compound knew the depth of their love for each other. Tekevwe at a point sat on Birhe's laps and looked at him with intense longing that everybody knew was natural and not made up. They danced with such passion because of their love for each other that they brought the crowd to their feet in admiration. Many "sprayed" them currency notes to show admiration for their dancing skills and being an exemplary social couple.

"Theirs is dangerous love," one old man commented. "One cannot live without the other. If one does or dies, the other will run mad again or die."

"We have not seen this type of deep affection between man and woman in Agbon before," another old man said.

"Love like this is rare. I wish we can all love like this," a gaunt man said.

"Then we will be mad. Only mad folks can love in this extraordinary way," the old man said.

"But they are no longer mad," the other old man interjected.

"Can the mad really be cured? Once mad, always mad! We are all mad in varying degrees," the same old man concluded.

Aderha overheard the conversations and wondered how these people without the benefit of knowledge of their lovemaking as mad man and woman could read this from their romantic behaviour to each other. Love itself heals and cheers one up, he learned from their example of partnership. Was this the other ingredient that Edewor said could replace his incantations after preparing the medications to heal? There was always something not known that needed to be learned.

The festival lived up to its expectations. Aderha was elated that he had brought his profession to a fulfilling point. Even if he did not cure more mad men and women, he reflected, he had already done enough work to be a legendary healer of the mad. The rest he expected his son to do. Edewor was happy for his father. He knew he was pleased with the turnout of not only those already healed but also the public come to witness a celebration of his success. Edewor hoped someday he would through modern science and medicine have a similar impact on the sick, especially the mad that he would study to treat with the same chemicals that his father was using so successfully. He did not doubt that he would be a worthy son, picking up from where his father stopped no matter when that would happen.

Edewor had been moody as the time for his going overseas drew closer. The father was not happy about his going abroad but felt should he want to continue with his education, he could attend a university within Nigeria. Aderha remembered clearly their conversation the previous day.

"What will you gain by going abroad?" he had asked his son.

"People go to study abroad for various reasons. I wouldn't have contemplated going abroad without this scholarship. Now I want to learn something there and use the knowledge to transform our medicines into modern ones," Edewor explained.

"What if the white man's spirit kills your African spirit? Will there be anything left in you to do anything good for your people other than get a good salary for yourself?"

"If it were just for a salary after graduating, I would not go."

"May the gods of our people open the right course for you to follow! It's not too late for you to rethink about going overseas or changing our medicines into modern ones, whatever you mean by that," the father concluded.

"Father, don't confuse me! I already know what I want to do and that's why I am going overseas. More talk on whether I should go or not is not good for me. I am not going for myself; rather I am going for you and all our people who need the medicines that you use to heal them," the son said.

Aderha was moved by his son's passion for what he wanted to do. He promised himself that he would not discuss the matter with his son again. It was true he, as father, was not happy with the idea of his son going abroad. He feared he might get lost. Could the leaves of the forest not tell him how to change his son's mind? That was what he felt was possible.

The euphoria of the festival hung thick in the air. But the third day after the festival and three weeks to Edewor's departure for London, the seemingly unexpected happened. Edewor went into the forest in the morning and had not come back by evening. All the years of following his father, he had never gone into the heart of the forest alone. Aderha knew the spirits that lived in the plants and was strong enough not to be distracted from his mission of extracting from them the promise to help him heal particular cases.

Aderha entered the forest and thought his son would not go farther than they had gone inside together. He knew the forest as one a familiar place and he knew the names of every plant possible. He would look around and if he did not get him, he would speak to the plants to tell him where his son was among them. But he did not need to ask the plants because he did not go far into the forest before he found the subject of his search. Edewor was sitting by an *akpobrisi* tree, the most feared tree in the forest. The few times the *akpobrisi* spoke to him, he had to go back, strip himself naked to get the bark and leaves of the powerful tree and run back to dress up. Nakedness had always been his armour against the strong spirit of the *akpobrisi*. There was the belief that the spirit of the *akpobrisi* would hunt down whoever extracted something from it. And to protect himself, Aderha, like others who healed with a part of the tree, stripped to go and get what he wanted and ran away to dress before passing the same spot again. In so doing, the *akpobrisi* would not recognize him as the one who had earlier come to rob it of its limb. He normally would keep Edewor far from the powerful tree. He saw his son there and knew something was amiss because his son knew that he should not be there at all. He dragged his son away, realizing soon after that he forgot to strip before approaching the tree.

Aderha brought Edewor home already mad. His was the quiet type and he would not talk to anybody, including his father, who saw a challenge in his hands. He was famous for curing the most vicious types of madness and now had to cure his son's sudden attack. He would go into the forest and do everything possible by engaging every plant to assist him. If by chance his son had taken what he prepared to make him change his mind or mellow down from not going abroad, he believed the same forest plants would show him an antidote.

"This treatment is for my own favourite son who has lost his sanity!" he prayed to all the spirits in the bush. No nearby or distant plant spoke when he asked for help. All of a sudden the plants had become deaf and dumb! He walked through the forest so many times for seven days but no plant volunteered to assist him to cure his son. He suspected the other trees were afraid of the *akpobrisi* and offered sacrifices to many of them but he could not serve all the trees in the forest that refused to speak to him. If he were to do that, he would become mad himself.

Aderha thought deep about his son. Had he, in trying to discourage him from travelling abroad, brought the madness into his own house? Was the rat blowing the same spot of the sole it had bitten and infected? Had the spirit of madness that he had been so adept at driving away from other folks come to seek refuge or lodge in Edewor? He asked himself so many questions that he could not answer.

By the day Edewor was supposed to leave for London, he had become more subdued, quiet, and in no position to travel. The powerful Aderha took it as a challenge and since the trees had ganged up against him by not talking to him who had a special ear to hear them, he realized he would not be able to cure his own son. The son died from a self-inflicted stab to his side. The day he was buried, Aderha let out an unending cry that frightened the sane and the mad who could not now tell the difference between the healer and the mad under his care.

20

Can't Wait!

The motorcycle was always the culprit. For the inordinate greed that led to speeding on a narrow rugged road. It was guilty of robbery; it was equally guilty of violence. Whatever dastardly act done, the motorcycle always came out condemned. The verdict had always been the same: Guilty! It farted along the way. It coughed without stop and did not cover its mouth exhaling stale breath. It smoked furiously. Its fumes did not bother its rider. People used to smoking cigarettes and inhaling fumes of Bell Oil Company's gas flares beside their farms and homes took the acrid smoke as another flavour in their now acquired voluntary and involuntary smoking habits.

The motorcycle, a neglected assistant, was not adequately maintained. Beauty has to be maintained to remain beautiful, the saying goes. The rider stretched the motorcycle's patience hour to hour, day to day, week to week, and month to month. It was a rare feat for one to live beyond a year with all the hazards that it had to go through. The indefatigable rider believed the iron mule would always trot along when whipped with a starter. Once there was fuel in the stomach, it would move. It was a living miracle that would continue to run with or without rest as long as it was filled with fuel.

"Tomorrow, when I make three thousand naira, I'll take it to the mechanic."

The following day, like one that could be exploited without protest, its driver broke the promise without qualms.

"Machine no be man! E fit work every day without rest. Not me dey ride am? If I no tire, how e go tire?"

That day the rider made four thousand naira, and that made him daydream about buying another motorbike to give out for rent. Good business is a soap that foams and foams when used in washing. The motorbike business was a good one. Of course, if the motorcycle increased his earnings that day, it could go on for one more day or a few more days before the weekend.

"Man dey wait for weeks and months to get what e want, why can't *okada* wait a few more days before mechanic fix am well well?" the rider asked.

It was not clear whether he was asking himself or the *okada*, who must have fallen deaf for all the revving that went on in the name of speed. Of course, the motorcycle had to wait till the iron mule driver was ready to part with a fraction of the money it made for him. Exploitation has always been there for the helpless, and the *okada* bore its aches but still cranked on when started. It did not have the voice to say "God dey!" as humans in its position would have done. It did not have the capacity for peaceful or non-violent protests until it broke down.

The motorcycle was found guilty of impatience that led to the death of a pedestrian at a boldly marked zebra crossing. Really it was manslaughter. Only the motorcycle was found guilty. Neither the rider who sped along as if pursued nor the passenger standing where he should not was culpable. It spent time in the police station until the rider paid for its release. Twenty minutes before another accident, a passenger had coaxed the driver on to the disaster.

"I am already late. I want to be there in no time."

"Don't worry," the driver had assured, as the passenger placed the crispy one hundred naira note on his right palm.

He had started the engine with a flourish. Even a stunt man would not have done better. With one leg stretched backwards, his behind in the air, his right hand revved the engine with a stuttering staccato that belched out smoke that heralded the mad race to his destination. The motorcycle, not the driver, flew through the snail-paced snaking traffic. It veered north, east, between cars, almost knocking down whatever was on its path. And then *gbaaam*! Bystanders and passers-by gasped at the extent of the devastation. So much speed through a walking zone. The motorcycle had claimed another victim. It knocked down a pedestrian, who haemorrhaged to death before any assistance could come. It would take one hour to reach the hospital for an ambulance and there would be no fuel to drive it. Of course, the person knocked down bled and bled before onlookers, and gave up life.

Even a cat of seven lives would not have escaped the impact of the flying heavy metal of a motorcycle upon the man walking. The police had arrived soon to start the investigation that would lead to prosecution. Things usually went one way—the culprit rider would bribe the police with his year's salary and the case would go nowhere. "After all, the deceased was closing his eyes and stood on the road where cars and motorcycles pass," the barely readable police report concluded. Case closed! The motorcycle rider breathed a sigh of relief and the following day, the rider got his motorbike back from police custody and gave it a bath that rid it of human blood stains. Immediately the bath was over, the rider put his clean iron mule to service again.

* * *

Another day there was another memorable but unpleasant experience. The motorcycle was rude, crude, and obscene.

"You dey crase?" the rider shouted.

"Na your mama dey crase!" was the swift response.

"You be *ashewo*!"

"Na your wife be *ashewo*!"

At the destination, another harangue began.

"No be hundred naira we talk?"

"I no go take only one hundred naira. Di distance pass dis money. Bring another thirty naira."

"Na only the hundred naira I don give you I get."

"You go pay me today or you no dey go anywhere."

"Make I see how you go hold me for here."

The scuffle that ensued went on till both realized the wasted effort and went their separate ways. It was the motorcycle that caused the argument and not the attitudes of the driver and the passenger.

* * *

One regular day as the driver scrambled on the busy street, the motorcycle screeched to a noisy halt. It howled a dying groan before it fell silent. The driver tried to re-start the engine but it would not start. Checking the engine, there was no oil. The motorcycle's heart had failed. The rider did not weep for the *okada*; he wept for the loss of naira he would have made the rest of that day and the following days. He needed the iron mule to come back to life to complete his own life. Tomorrow it would go to the mechanic and stay in the workshop for a week. There the mechanic would perform his miracle. The mechanic performed surgery on the failed heart of iron that would make the *okada* be on its feet and racing again. Wonder of wonders! Only the motorcycle died and resurrected in the land. The mechanic was the miracle worker whose touch and attention would bring the dead back to life.

* * *

Only an *okada* man would lose his leg and not know and still go on as if nothing had happened to him. The leg tore off his body after the collision with a car, but the motorcyclist rode on. Onlookers, who had screamed in shock at the ghastly accident, stared at him as he rode away. They wondered how one could go on that way—legless and still riding a motorcycle, without any indication of the torn-off ligaments and leg and the bleeding that followed. Fortunately, there was no passenger. The *okada* rider was racing to pick a teacher from Ekpan Elementary School, a few kilometres away. He wanted to get that done as soon as possible so as to go to his favourite street to make more money that afternoon. The car owner had, on his part, sustained severe injuries too and came down to inspect his car and stretch his neck. He had jerked forward to knock his head against the dashboard; he was not wearing his seat belt.

At Jakpa Junction, the crowd of cyclists, motorists, pedestrians, and hawkers of articles brought movement to a halt. There was no way the stunt rider would fly over them because he would still land on people! Then Tefe was compelled to slow down and, as he mentally used his leg to press the gear, he physically felt the wound and bleeding. He had no right foot to press down the lever of the gear. The pain stung him instantly and he fell clumsily from the roaring but disabled machine.

Fellow motorcyclists noticed the emergency at hand. They belonged to an association and took each other as a brother. In fact, others saw them as if they were members of a cult or a fraternity in the way they took the other's problem as theirs and communicated with secret signs. Those who saw the extent of the wound were aghast at the savagery of the crude amputation. They took him up and set him on another motorcycle's passenger seat and took off for the nearest clinic around. Tefe sat behind the motorcyclist, while somebody else sat behind him so as to steady him on the seat.

The rider revved the engine, which exhaled thick dark fumes and acrid breath. Belonging to the same secret society, the riders had mastered the same craft. In a matter of seconds, this rescue iron mule was meandering swiftly through heavy traffic as the amputee wailed sharply from intensifying pain and bleeding. It was as if he had been sleeping before now or the leg had been numbed and the alleviating medicine had worn out. The pain was sharp and biting—needles were piercing the raw flesh with vengeance.

Miraculously, another motorcyclist arrived at the same time at Castle Clinic with the severed leg. He must have come by air through the crammed streets. Ovie Palace Road, where the clinic stood, was swarmed with onlookers amazed at what they were seeing. In Effurun, people gathered where there was a free spectacle, and this severed leg was one such treat. Children, women, and men swarmed to the gate of the clinic to see what was happening. Many would not see anything but hear bits of news that they would embellish and relay to others who could not see things first-hand.

Tefe did not see his other leg that had been cut off before the doctor and his team of nurses knocked him out with anaesthesia. He did not know how for hours his leg was sewed back to his hip. Yes, sewed back to his hip, as if he had lost nothing. His first response to what had happened after he regained consciousness and the pain kept at bay with strong morphine injection was asking the nurse, "My *okada* well?" like one asking of a darling partner after an accident. And that was despite treating it like a slave before now, the same way a patriarchal man treated his hardworking wife until she was not around.

"You go ask your brothers who brought you here."

"Make them no thief my machine-o!"

"You bring am here?" the nurse asked.

"No be him bring me here?" he asked.

The nurse could only shake her head. Now she realized what she had heard was true—the motorcycle and its rider had the same personality. In addition to the morpheme, the doctor prescribed Codeine to ease the pain.

* * *

After staying in the clinic for three weeks, Tefe was discharged to return home. He would stay at home for a year, longer than the average lifespan of an *okada*, and spend all the money he had gained in five years of killing different *okadas* in paying his medical bills. At least one iron mule had taken its revenge. As Tefe recovered, he did not want anything to do with the motorcycle again. He preferred to walk with a limp than take *okada* to anywhere. And he would not ride any!

21

Foolish Professor!

Daniel Akpojevwe celebrated his promotion to full professorship with a memorable party. That had been his dream since he started waiting to achieve the academic pinnacle. When the opportunity came for him to live his dream, he was ready to borrow money to celebrate it. After all, he told himself, his Agbon people have the saying that one borrows to make a grand impression during the gunpowder festival. He was ready to work hard later to pay back the debt he incurred to throw an unforgettable party. What intrigued those he invited to the party was that it was not going to be held in his house in the university campus as other newly promoted professors did but at his pastor's house. To him, the pastor's home or the church compound was the logical place. "You pay back in kind or cash for the good turn done to you," he reflected, before telling his wife about the venue he had chosen for the party. It was the tone she was used to—whenever he talked in that churchy tone he did not want to be contradicted. It was as if he had received a command from God and nobody dared contradict the divine order. She knew that her husband so revered his pastor that he took whatever advice he got from him as something from God. She was not going to ask questions concerning this as she had done without changing his mind in the past. After all, it was his party and not hers and there was little she could do about the venue.

After waiting for the promotion for over twelve years when he had been supposed to be due for it, he had asked the pastor to intervene on his behalf. To the "man of God", that meant he should advise him and also pray for him to be promoted. He was used to being an intercessor for others and this request was not strange. Among the pastor's recommendations were dry fasting for one week in the month, the professor's participation in the all-night vigil the last Friday of the month, and constant prayers for God to set Holy Ghost fire to exterminate those blocking his progress. Those blocking his progress were a powerful force and extreme sacrifices should be made to overcome them, the then Associate Professor was told. He should not shake hands with people from his village nor should he sleep with any of his female students as many of his fellow academics were doing. He should pay his tithe from his monthly pay slip pre-tax amount and as at when due. He should continue following the prescriptions until the evil forces working against him were totally destroyed. The pastor said he could not tell how soon the hard battle was going to be fought before they, meaning he and the academic, would win. But victory was certain, he confidently predicted to the relief of the spiritually distraught academic.

Dr. Akpojevwe followed his pastor's recommendations to the letter. He embarrassed his fellow villagers when they visited or he visited and they stretched out their hands and he shook his fist at them as his new way of greeting. Strange as it was, he kept to that command. Whereas there are Ten Commandments of God, the pastor gave him only seven! The most difficult commandment was not sleeping with his students which he, like many of his colleagues, had been doing and they called "bush allowance." Many times, he was tempted by female students he desired or who tried to seduce him for favours of grades they did not deserve. He resigned himself to the sacrifices he had to make to become a professor someday. If the goal was eventual professorship, he was ready to go through hell to get there. After all, he had begun to feel ashamed of himself because the colleagues he had obtained the doctoral degree with and entered River Niger University at its inception were now all full professors. He was moving at a good commensurate pace with his colleagues till the roadblock had been thrown on his way to hold him down in one place since he became Associate Professor almost fifteen years ago. The task he had contracted his pastor was to remove the roadblock so that he could zoom past and arrive at the professorial post.

Then, the young graduate of Mass Communication that would become his pastor had come to congratulate him as a newly promoted

Associate Professor. The young man was doing his National Youth Service in the University and was posted to his Department of Mass Communication at River Niger University, Abraka. After the national service there was no job for him in the newspapers, radio and television stations, and the state civil service. After doing odds and ends as a private advertiser making programs for weddings and burial ceremonies, he felt he had to marry. Life suddenly became worse after he married the secondary school teacher, two years his junior but at least had a regular job. He saw many unemployed graduates building ramshackle schools from crèche through elementary to junior and senior secondary classes. Others he had graduated with but without government and company jobs were flourishing by opening new churches in any street with vacant plots. He chose to be a pastor and try his luck where others were thriving. His church started with four white plastic chairs in a rented room. It did not take a month to have the rented room filled with worshipers and he had to move church to a temporary structure before the now imposing church with thousands of members.

The Associate Professor took as a challenge what his pastor, as "a man of God," had prescribed for him to do. The prescriptions also tested his manhood, as he now saw it. A man who could not do whatever difficult assignment to rise to the pedestal of his career was a weakling, and he was confident that he was not a weakling. As professor, every door not only in the academy but also in society would open to him. He would fight the obstacles placed on his way by evil and malicious folks to cross over to the promised land of professorship. If he were told to drink his own or someone else's urine or eat animal or human shit, he would to get what he wanted. If the pastor had prescribed for him to leave his wife to become professor, he would not have hesitated to do so. Any suffering, wounds, or sacrifices he experienced would be temporary and he knew he would not only recover but live his longstanding dream.

He was a rather thin man and the more he carried out the sacrifices, the more gauntly he looked. His cheeks had sunk and his eye sockets deepened into twin hollow pockets on his face. It was evident to those who knew him closely that he was losing weight and did not know what to make of him. Had he contracted HIV/AIDS? Or was it cancer slowly eating him up? In the society sick people hid their problems and nobody expected Dr. Akpojevwe to tell what was afflicting him to lose so much weight and look far older than his fifty-six years of age. Whenever he attended a social ceremony, burial or wedding, he did not drink or eat, and people noticed it. Something must be happening to his stomach that it could not accept anything, they thought, because he used to be cheerful and ate and drank at such ceremonies.

He had become frugal, preferring to not only just pay his tithes and become a strong pillar of the Garden of Eden Church of Christ but also "sowing the seed" monthly with much of his salary. He saw this as a way of demonstrating to his warrior pastor his faith in the church. It was also an encouragement for the "man of God" to intensify the war against his personal enemies. He did not fail to play a major role in the church's projects and the pastor praised him as an academic who had not lost his mind in books but was mindful of God in whatever he did. When his wife grumbled that she needed money for the upkeep of the house and the two girls they had, he always called her a devil under his roof for trying to subvert the wishes of the "man of God" and able warrior.

"Do you know what he is doing for me?" he would ask her.

"How will I know?" she would shoot back.

"Do you know that he is placing his life at risk fighting demons to make me live and overcome obstacles?"

"But we need to live rather than die from starvation and not taking care of ourselves because of the battle he is fighting but which we do not see."

"Oh woman of little faith!" he would exclaim.

"Look at it. The other day Ufuoma was sick and I could not find money to buy medication for her fever. You asked me to wait till the end of the month. When the month ends, you'll get your pay and then the money disappears in one week. You pay more tithe than the governor of our state or our local government chairman. Upon the lavish tithes, you give him money and call it 'sowing seeds.' Is there sense in what you are doing?" she asked.

"The pastor prays for me and my family so that no evil will befall us. We have been enjoying good health since he has been fighting my enemies," he would explain.

"How long will we go on like this?" she would ask.

"I am sowing seeds for the family and you will be happy in the long run. Help me bear the pains for the time being. We are going to smile at the end of all these pains," he would say.

"I believe that is what Pastor tells you," she said.

"Woman, speak no ill of the man of God!" he shouted at her.

Najite, his wife of eighteen years, had given up on him. She even believed that if the pastor asked her husband to bring her head or of any of the two daughters to do anything diabolical, he would not hesitate in carrying it out in order to become a professor. "Professor! Foolish Professor!" she would call silently and hiss while alone and thinking of the stressful life they were going through in order for her husband to become a professor.

Within two years of the prayer-warrior pastor's take-over of his case, the letter came. Najite was not at home and before calling his wife to tell her the good news, the elated professor ran to the pastor's house to proclaim his victory at long last over the evil forces that had prevented him from being promoted. The roadblock had at last been removed and he has arrived at the professorial station! He felt this was not a message to be delivered through a cell phone; it was more important than a phone message. It would surely be dignifying and pleasing to the pastor for him to be his own messenger and bearer of good tidings.

"Praise the Lord!" he proclaimed, as he threw the letter at the pastor who was reclining in his settee and sipping cold Coke as he read the Psalms to acquaint himself the more with the arms with which to fight Satanic forces attacking so many members of his congregation. He fought many battles and he had to prepare as an experienced warrior. He did not need to wait for the battle to even break out before he sharpened his weapons. He must remain a prepared intercessor at all times. He believed that once he put his energy into the right verses, his prayers would work for the person or people he prayed for. After all, God created the world with the word from His mouth. "In the beginning was the Word and the Word was God," he intoned. Through the word, the pastor believed, his prayers on behalf of anybody would be fulfilled. If he, in a certain state of spirituality, invoked the Lord with certain verses from the Holy Book, his prayers would be answered.

"Praise the Lord!" Pastor Dennis Ojakovo shouted, as he raised his head up to size up the university teacher of chemistry who rarely smiled but was now beaming with smiles. The academic appeared to him to be full of life rather than the sluggish man he knew he had been praying for.

Pastor Ojakovo put aside his Bible and took the letter before him to read. "Congratulations. On behalf of the Senate and Governing Council of River Niger State University, I wish to inform you that you have been promoted to the rank of Full Professor with the salary and benefits the rank bestows on the position..." The pastor did not need to read what followed. It was signed by the University Registrar. He held up the letter, as if showing it to God, but really in gratitude to the Almighty who made all things to happen.

"We defeated the forces of darkness!" he shouted joyously, as he stood up and offered his hands for a handshake to the new professor, one of the pillars of his Garden of Eden Bible Church.

A tall and ebullient man, the pastor towered over the professor. His voice boomed with authority; the way he talked or prayed. He motioned the professor to sit on a chair to his right and Professor Akpojevwe obliged. He always envied the comfort of the pastor's house. Now that he was a professor, he hoped he could furnish his own house to the standard of the pastor's and yet the man of God had barely made it through the university with a Third Class degree in Mass Communication.

"We defeated the forces of darkness," Professor Akpojevwe repeated after his pastor.

"He who has faith shall be saved!" the pastor proclaimed.

"Amen!" answered the professor.

As a pastor he had practiced how to give thanks for prayers answered. He had to strengthen the faith of members of his congregation. Another prayer answered was a promotional tool for his church to recruit members from the university and business communities. After all, everyone who found himself into the University teaching staff wanted to be a professor someday irrespective of performance. Prayers moved stones and so could catapult a weak lecturer to become a professor. Now more academics and politicians who wanted success would come to him. However, this was not the time to think about the growth of this church but to attend to his happy professor.

The pastor knew this member of his congregation had come with good tidings. Good tidings that would turn a mournful face to a shining face! Happy tidings that would give a spritely demeanour to one who normally lumbered. He knew the professor must have cut from his age because he looked older than fifty-six years but must have shaved many years off his real age to avert retirement which brought an end to an enviable career.

"We shall give thanks to God appropriately," the pastor told the new professor.

"Of course, I must thank God for his blessing," Professor Akpojevwe replied.

The professor, who had not told his wife about the good news, immediately requested for a thanksgiving service the following Sunday. In his mind nothing would be too big to spend to thank the pastor and treat the entire congregation with a big party.

Najite rejoiced with her husband when later that day her husband came home from the pastor's house to break the good news to her. She knew the entire family had gone through a lot to achieve what her husband had battled for: the professorship.

"You should have waited to tell me for us to agree on the date for the thanksgiving," she told him.

"Why wait longer than this coming Sunday?" he asked her.

"It is all right. We can start preparing immediately because Sunday is only four days away," she said.

"I don't have enough money now but will get an overdraft from my bank tomorrow to make this thanksgiving impressive," he told her.

"Everything will be fine," she said, concurring with her husband's wishes.

Najite knew her husband very well. He was like someone under a spell when in the presence of Pastor Ojakovo and the pastor must have charmed him into taking a date for thanksgiving that the man had not discussed with his spouse. However, now was not the time to argue about dates for the thanksgiving but to give the maximum support to ensure a successful party! What is thanksgiving other than another avenue to please the pastor and his church with so much money spent in cash or kind? She reflected.

Professor Akpojevwe put two hundred and fifty thousand naira in a big envelope together with a bag of imported long-grain Carolinian rice, a Sokoto ram, and a big thank-you card for the pastor. The service was short since the pastor had so many other thanksgiving services to perform that day. He preached on the theme of "Ask and thou shall be given!" taken from Matthew, Chapter Seven, Verse Seven. The newly promoted professor had asked to be elevated from Associate Professor to Full Professor and had been granted his prayers. As long as members had faith in God and followed the Almighty's path, their wishes would be fulfilled. At the end of the service, the members of the congregation were feasted with fried rice with chicken and soft drinks in gratitude to God for the professor's promotion. The new Professor went out of his way to impress those at the party by distributing gifts of handkerchiefs and plastic plates, as done in wedding and burial ceremonies. One could tell from his spritely gait and cheerfulness that the professor was immensely grateful to God for the blessing of his promotion and he was doing his very best to give thanks to God and the "man of God".

So, when he received his arrears six months later of five million naira, he realized that the many years the evil forces had held down his promotion had been a form of savings for him; a blessing in disguise. Now the salary he would have earned the past so many years was being paid to him in bulk sum and he was elated. After paying back the overdraft, he still had a hefty sum left to spend. His mind quickly went to an eight-cylinder Toyota jeep—a Sequoia. That was the car he had fancied for years and now he had enough arrears paid to him to buy one. That was a car that befitted his new status of a Professor.

The day he bought the car, he went with the pastor to the dealer's shop. He drove his old car, picked the pastor at his home, and went to the car company where he paid a ponderous sum for the brand-new Toyota Sequoia. After he got all the papers he needed, he drove with the pastor to license the car and then drove to the pastor's house. All along, he drove his old car and the pastor drove the new car. He parked the car in the pastor's compound to be blessed and test-driven by the "man of God" to make it safe for him to drive. He drove home his old car and expected to be back in a few days after his new car would have been adequately sanctified by the "man of God," his victorious prayer-warrior. He wanted to be sure that the evil forces that had held him down for a long time would not plot new evil when they saw him with a new car. He had to be careful because those witches were quick at discovering new ways of hurting the person they were envious of. Evil ones would want everyone to be poor like them but now he had become a professor and bought a car of his dreams, he wanted to drive safely all the time. His prayer-warrior pastor would make him very safe in his new car. He would pray for three days over the car and sprinkle anointed water all over it to make it safe for him to drive. On the fourth day he would take possession of his car and drive anywhere with utmost confidence.

* * *

The news of the fatal accident involving a brand-new and newly licensed Toyota Sequoia with a pastor driver and a beautiful lady running into a stationary truck some minutes past midnight caught everybody who knew the pastor in Abraka and the River Niger University community by surprise. They did not wear their seat belts and were facing each other at the moment of the crash. The pastor was wearing a designer suit and a pair of shoes that a member of his congregation who had travelled to Dubai had bought for him. His Gucci watch was ticking fine and stylishly after the crash. The woman, an attractive divorcee of thirty five years, was a caterer whom the pastor had engaged many times whenever a celebration took place in the church. She had been recommended by the pastor to Professor Akpojevwe to provide the food and drinks for the thanksgiving which had cost a hefty amount. Not just surprised but shocked to paralysis was the new professor who had committed all the arrears of his back-dated promotion to buying a car befitting his new status as a professor.

Once it was established that the car belonged to the professor, the police visited him for questioning and took him to their station for further investigation into the accident that took the lives of a pastor and a female companion. The professor's car that was a total wreck was not important enough to talk about when two lives had been lost. The professor had opted to insure the car through the third party option only, which meant that nothing would be paid to him for the total wreck of his less than one-week old Toyota Sequoia.

The following Sunday, Professor Daniel Akpojevwe missed service for the first time in over fifteen years. He who would go to Sunday service even when malaria could hardly allow him move his legs was physically fine but made up his mind not to go to church. Not going to church was no longer a mortal sin to him. In fact, he did not feel it mattered to him. He did so not just because Pastor Ojakovo had died and arrangements for his burial would take place that very Sunday but because he did not want to see any pastor, including the Assistant Pastor Amos Jovwo, who would now appropriate the fire in his late pastor's mouth and brand his congregation with the delirium emanating from his tongue. He could not reconcile the loss of his brand-new jeep through his pastor's late night dalliance with his woman friend to following teachings that made him look very much like a fool. In fact, he gave two hundred and fifty thousand naira from a quickly arranged overdraft with his bank manager to the police to avoid being further harassed and embarrassed as the cause of the pastor's death with a woman who was not his wife, and the untrustworthy police had called him "Foolish professor!" upon that. What a cheek but what could he do? The police could mess him up and he did not want that. He did not want to die a fool at his age which he had officially tampered with. He had done that because he knew that around one could get anything by arrangement! He had arranged with some office boys with the collusion of the Registrar to shave off ten years from his actual age of sixty-six years. He would now go into retirement with his old car which in fact broke down as he left the police station. And another overdraft on top of the disaster!